Beyond Broken

Beyond Broken

by **Karen Silberman**

I AM Publications

I AM Publications

(617) 564-1060

contact@iampubs.com

www.iampubs.com

Printed in the United States of America

First Edition, 2017

ISBN: 978-1-943382-01-9

DEDICATION

To Don and Brian every single day.

And to Scott, forever in my heart.

ACKNOWLEDGEMENTS

Sometimes a story writes itself. But, even then, turning it into a novel is the product of human effort. And a lot of it.

Thank you BJ for being my friend [without qualifier], and the first reader of my first draft over 12 years ago, and for encouraging me to get it published.

Arielle, your editorial comments contributed in no small measure to this completed work. You asked exactly the right questions. You edited with honesty and insight, and I am profoundly grateful. And to Loretta, your comments and suggestions assured me I was on the right track, fueling my commitment to get it finished.

Mary, thank you for giving me the tools I needed to finish this book. For the tiny binoculars, the silver three-legged pig, the necklace with a large, plastic match hanging from it, for the brass shovel, and the delicate clay figure of the little girl who only has to stand and see. Each of these gifts delivered with love and meaning into my hands, they are my treasures. For the books you shared, for Morita, Lindburgh, Mann and Pema, they will be in my heart and mind as I continue to write, paint and photograph my little corner of the world.

To all my surrogate mothers and sisters who love unconditionally: Shay and Julie Pulie, Melissa and Karen, thank you for being there, holding the unholdable. To Rhonda and the girls for honesty and laughter. To Sandy, a second mother to my boys, and a dear, dear friend who helped me think through many aspects of the narrative. And to Judy & Beth: writing, 'arting' and laughing me through some dark days. I hope someday you'll meet.

To Ngozi, for making being Mom2.0 a continuing source of unconditional love and support, trust and respect. For reading and editing, for unparalleled tech help, and for helping me get this manuscript published.

To my Rabbinical School cohort, who lived through the loss of my son with me, who held me in the most gentle of containers. Particularly, Brian, Tamar, Eliana, David and Dude: I don't think I would have made it without you. And Ebn, who showed several hundred mourners at Scott's shiva what many of us believe: that when you pray, God is present.

To Illan, Gail, Matt and Allie, for the many visits and long phone calls where you held me close, laughed, cried, and helped me come back to life.

And to my husband Don and son Brian for everything you are. I love you to infinity and back.

ABOUT THE COVER

I found this stone while walking on the beach in Wellfleet on
Cape Cod, Massachusetts. It had what I thought was an
interesting dark stripe that seemed to run all the way around it.
It turned out to be a fissure, dividing the delicate rock into two
separate pieces. Yet, it was sitting there top seated on the
bottom, as if whole. What caught my eye was the shadow the
pieces cast: seamless, appearing solid. People *are like that rock,* I
thought, Some of us have been broken, shattered, to our core.
But we pull ourselves back together, and allow the light to
shine on us, casting a whole shadow. This rock is *broken, but it
tells of existing beyond broken. In the fissure lies its fragile, beautiful truth.*

CHAPTER ONE

2:30 P.M.

It was no surprise this year Maddy came home alone, empty. She had expected it. Remembering why, and realizing for what felt like the millionth time what would never be, made the room spin. Her chest tightened. She breathed in hard, forcing the elastic bands twisted tightly around her lungs to snap, providing a now-familiar, and too-temporary, relief. Steadied for the moment, one thing was certain: it would never stop.

Earlier that day, the patchwork of prayer shawls and head coverings blanketing the sanctuary was dotted with the sparkling of exquisite finery taken from safe deposit boxes on "special occasions." What a pointless show of economic success. Maddy wanted to yell, "God doesn't care what you wear! Stop pretending this matters! God isn't even real!"

How disgusting she had actually once believed. Now, it was practically impossible to sit through the show: the parade of rich congregants, taking turns ascending the podium to recite the ancient blessings, as if by doing so, their success might rub off on everyone else. Did it matter that under his Armani suit and silk socks, Arnie Goldstein wore an electronic ankle bracelet? Or that even as Erika Klein proclaimed her love and fidelity to God, she also proclaimed her undying love to to her next-door neighbor on the three nights a week the successful consultant sitting beside her worked out of state? Maddy watched people catching the eye of friends and waving, mouthing superficial conversations, pantomiming compliments. She saw others avoiding the eyes of friends-no-more, folks down on their luck, or God forbid, ill. She was not sure which she was. Looking around, she noticed that no one was looking at her. Actively not looking at her. Sitting in a room full of people, she felt completely alone.

1

Coming into the synagogue earlier, the traditional New Year's greetings of "Shana Tova!!" and "Gut Yuntif!!" were an assault on her ears. And, though the words printed in the book on her lap were familiar, she could not get herself to utter a single prayer. Because, she thought, God is a lie.

As Jews around the world vowed on this most holy day to perform good deeds to help repair the broken world, Maddy cursed a God that let the world break in the first place. She couldn't help but feel sorry for everyone who was diligently reciting the Hebrew prayers—as if they were an incantation against evil—as if asking God to be inscribed and sealed in the Book of Life, as Jews had for millennia, actually did anything at all.

Not long ago, Maddy would revel in the Jewish High Holy Days. But today, sitting through the service was practically impossible. An insult to everything she knew about a God who isn't there. She remembered countless luncheons following services where everyone—herself included— could talk only about the rabbi's sermon and how he made life make sense and somehow made each person listening feel important and good. This year, his words missed the mark for her completely. They rang hollow— how could they not? And twice during the sermon, she had to press her lips tightly together to keep an involuntary hiss from escaping, press her eyes shut tight so no one could see them rolling in disagreement. She left after he finished speaking.

Home again, she removed her hat as she headed down the hall. She wasn't even sure why she'd worn a hat at all. Maybe she thought it would make things like they used to be. It hadn't. Maddy hung up her suit and put her heels back in their box. She thought about keeping the hat handy for the next holiday, just ten days away, but knew she would not wear it again. She put it back in its box and headed for the cedar closet.

Dim and musty, the space was a sartorial scrapbook: college sweatshirts, T-shirts from family vacations, ski sweaters and long-outgrown baby clothes. She went to the place where her hat box had been. She jammed the box onto the shelf beside a pile of plaid wool camping blankets that still carried in them a hint of pine. The box bounced back a bit, lessening the intended finality of her action. She reached behind the box, grabbed whatever it was that prevented the box from sitting in place on the shelf and, as she pulled it into view, realized what it was. She clutched it in both hands and drew it to her face. In spite of more than a year in the cedar closet, her smell was still clinging to the fabric. Memories rushed in, and at that moment, she could only feel the depth of her loss, knotted into colorful crosses, the eternal emptiness, and the everlasting, futile search for peace.

Once things started to crumble she could not keep them from disintegrating completely, and ultimately, they slipped from her grasp, taking with them any and all hope of a return to normal. For a while, she had wanted to know why—and why her!—but now, even if she could know why such things happen, she knew it was too late.

Slowly, she walked up the stairs, looking at the house as if it would be gone tomorrow. The baby grand piano. The fieldstone fireplace. The bookshelves filled—stuffed—with information and a literary documentary of their various interests. And so many memories.

It was as if the family in the long line of photographs led to her bedroom, knew what she was doing.

"Don't!" her father seemed to scream through his squinty, permanent smile. Sitting in the cab of a forklift, he was raising his children, piled on a pallet, high above the neatly stacked cartons in the warehouse of his small supply company. Looking at her nine-year-old self, Maddy remembered that day. Her face still looked like her, but the thrill in her eyes was gone now. The thick lashes that once lined her eyes had morphed to heavy circles. She looked at her younger brother, Kevin, unsuccessfully trying to hide his nervousness, his brow knit in clear distress, and Robin, still a toddler, trying to decide if she wanted to be like Maddy or Kevin. Standing off to the side was Katherine, clearly unaware she was being photographed, hands on her hips, lips pursed, looking away from her

children, immortalized in the act of checking to be sure no one was witness to this spectacle.

"Oh, Daddy, how could you possibly understand?" Maddy whispered back to the man in the forklift.

"Please Maddy, no! We can make it better!" Maddy could imagine Ben whispering urgently into her ear as they danced their first dance as husband and wife.

"Ben," Maddy thought, "you were fine then, you are fine now, and, as always, you will be fine." Maddy shook her head, wondering how he could be fine anymore; relieved, and maybe a little jealous, that he could weather what she could not.

"Momma! We need you here!" A portrait of her children, waving from the top of a bell tower, reminded her of the days when life was whole. They looked so happy! They _were_ happy, she thought. Staring at her daughter's bright, laughing eyes, her wispy pigtails, and her baby toothed smile, Maddy could only wonder why.

How could she explain to her children that she knew they needed her, but that she was not really here anymore anyway. The person she was—the mother she wanted to be—was already dead. She hoped they would be okay, maybe someday even forgive her. She wanted to hope, but she had lost the ability to hope.

She straightened up around the house, never allowing to leave her grasp the tangible reminder of why it had to be this way. She brushed her hair and teeth. She turned to the medicine cabinet. Vial after vial spilled onto the counter by the sink: Xanax, Valium, Halcion, Percocet, oxycodone. She scooped the colorful pile into her hand. She thought about putting them down, but she held the blanket to her face, breathing the pain enmeshed in the fabric deep into the hole that would never be filled. That would never go away. She downed the pills in two swallows, washed down with a cherry-flavored codeine cough syrup, prescribed years before when one of the children had croup.

She lay down on the bed in what was now the guest room. There were no tears left. She clutched the memory of what was never to be close to her face, the smell was paralyzing. She watched the sunlight attempt in vain to brush away the leaf shadows on the ceiling, and she knew she was right: life is a random, cruel test of survival, and we are incapable of escaping the chaos that follows us from the day we are born. And she knew she was done with it all.

As the pills made her drowsy, her body grew heavy. As she drifted off, her mind started to wander...

Fall, 1968

When she heard the storm door slam, Maddy jumped up, dropping her half-dressed Barbie unto her cardboard "yard," barely missing the cat's tail as she ran to the front hall to see him.

"Daddy!"

Seven years earlier, her father had bought a half-acre lot in a new subdivision being carved out of granite and limestone in Newfield, Connecticut. Maddy knew that even though he didn't finish college, he was smart. She had heard him tell neighbors that he had drafted the plans to the modern three-bedroom ranch himself. What she couldn't see then was that he'd also drafted the plan to include many large windows of opportunity for himself, his new wife Katherine and their yet-to-be-born children. In his mind's eye, he pictured they would become a model American family in a tidy, suburban community just like the ones on TV. Or as close as a melting pot of first-generation Americans could be like the white, Christian towns where the fathers wore suits and ties to their engaging office jobs and the mothers wore pretty dresses every day, while gleefully tending their delightfully impish children, serving them warm cookies and milk when they came home from a fun-filled day at school. In Newfield, the fathers were more likely to be welders and truck drivers than doctors and attorneys, and most of the Newfield mothers also worked, if only part time. Another big difference: on TV, the dogs didn't roam freely around the neighborhood, leaving "presents" for kids who didn't watch where they stepped.

Though he drew the house himself, it looked a lot like all the other homes in the neighborhood: a sea of small ranches and multi-levels, distinguishable only by shade of pastel clapboards. One-car garage, and carports were luxuries. Many homes had nothing at all to protect a family' four-door Chevy or wood-paneled Ford station wagon from the heavy snows that were typical of winter in New England. Jack took particular pride in his light blue ranch and carport: the shrubs were neatly trimmed, the concrete walkway was always swept clean, and the kids' toys were stored out of sight in the back yard.

Maddy threw her arms around her father's legs, even as Jack was flipping through the mail piled on the front hall table. Kevin and Robin barely glanced up from the couch, lost in *Mr. Roger's Neighborhood*. Trying to ensure her siblings wouldn't come along, she whispered the magic words, whereby— *abracadabra*—she could turn the tired working man standing in front of her into her laughing, playful father.

"Gimme a ride!"

"Hi Pumpkin!" The nickname was even more fitting, now that she'd lost several teeth. She reached up, ready to climb onto his back for a bouncy ride back to her bedroom— where he'd dump her on her bed—but instead of bending low enough for her to climb on his back, he surprised her with, "No ride today, Pumpkin. I think I pulled something in my shoulder at work today. It still hurts, so I can't pick you up."

She stepped back to look at him. *Was he okay?* A pat on her shoulder and a tug at one of her braids only left her wondering what to do next. She followed him down the hall, hoping he'd at least go into her room, even if not to play.

Hurt at work? Maddy thought, *what happened?* Maddy knew that her dad was the senior vice president of Margate Materials International, it said so under the "Jack Berger" name plate on his desk. Maddy heard him describe what Margate Materials did so often she could recite it by heart. They "warehouse and distribute textiles for use in industry." What Maddy would see when she visited was that it involved bringing truckloads of fabric into the warehouse where they were washed, hand-cut into smaller pieces and boxed for shipment by a dozen plump, Polish women, dressed alike in aprons and kerchiefs, speaking to each other in Polish, like they were sitting around a table in Warsaw having coffee and kolachkes.

What wasn't written on his desk, or something he ever repeated, but rather something she figured out over time, was that her father worked for an unglamorous company he hoped eventually to buy from its owner, who happened to be his father-in-law.

Maddy knew it was not easy. She'd heard her father complain to her mother that the manufacturing centers of New England were moving south to places like Alabama and Tennessee or overseas to places like China and Japan. He was working hard to stay competitive and would present his new ideas at the dinner table. *None of this would make him hurt*, thought Maddy.

Jack rubbed his shoulder as he sat on Maddy's bed, trying to remember what he might have done to cause this much pain. It was rare he would strain himself, let alone to the point of injury—even when he spent the day working in the warehouse. Sure, once in a while he'd be out in the uninsulated metal building on a frigid winter's day and his fingertips would split open and bleed, but it didn't happen often that Maddy remembered.

"How's Grampa?" Maddy knew they worked together. Sam's nameplate, which sat next to another small sign that said "The Buck Stops Here" said, "President." Jack curled up on his side and rubbed his shoulder.

As second-in-command, Jack had a lot to prove, as Sam—he could never call him "dad"—was a tough man to please. Some would call him a perfectionist. Also, because Jack's job came with a wife attached, he had no choice but to do his very best all day, every day, just to keep people from thinking he was taking advantage of his situation. So, fueled daily by pots of "hi-test" coffee with three sugars and cream, packs of non-filter cigarettes, and food that was exceedingly high in fat or sugar (or ideally both), he'd work with an intensity that he knew even Sam couldn't fault.

Maddy looked at her father and saw it had been a hard day: the sleeves of his white button-down shirt were rolled to over his elbows and there was dirt under his fingernails. Granted, even on a good day he didn't look like any of her friends' fathers who had modern professions and offices. He didn't wear three-piece suits and a gold watch to his high-rise law office like her backyard neighbor Robert Davidoff's dad. And his job wasn't nearly as cool as Mary Pelligrino's papa: he was a dentist and he had chairs that went up and down and he gave kids toys as they left! Nor was Maddy's father an engineer in the firm that was building the city's newest and tallest buildings—that was Lloyd Levinson's father. Nope, her father was a '"*shmata man*'"; a rag man. The Yiddish word fit; in spite of Jack's best attempts to bring the business into this century, the business felt, looked and smelled like the old country.

A long, rusty sigh would always announce her arrival as she swung open the gate to the office, meant to keep truck drivers and their muddy feet in the entryway. First she would run to give Ruth—who always bought her the birthday or holiday gift, wrapped and ribboned beautifully—a hug. She would sink into the secretary's plump and perfumed lap, typing 'letters'—D…e…a…r…weoiflkasjdf rotdf sakjf;orijt ;ld—sacrificing accuracy for speed so she could type as fast as Ruth. Maddy loved Ruth because Ruth always smiled when she looked at her. After she finished typing, Maddy would go to her father's office, where she would climb onto the heavy black vinyl chair, swiveling back and forth and spinning until she made herself dizzy.

Pretzel's fur tickled Maddy's leg, as the orange and white cat stretched out across Maddy's lap. Maddy mindlessly pet her soft belly as she thought some more about her dad's hurt shoulder, hoping he didn't rip it up inside. He'd done that to his heel playing tennis last summer, and it took weeks to get better. She looked again at her dad. *I hope he's okay.*

It wasn't until she returned home the next afternoon that she knew for sure what had happened, but it started on the way in to school when Patrick O'Brien—skin and bones with sparkling blue eyes and a flat, freckled face—which somebody once said had the map of Ireland in it, though Maddy couldn't see it—half-chanted: "Hey Mad-a-line, I saw the am-bu-lance at your house last night." Fists on his hips, his head cocked at an angle; it was easy to see why no one in her class liked him. It wasn't that he was a bad kid, nor was he a bully, exactly. But no one liked a busybody know-it-all who used information like currency, and they all came to dislike Patrick, who was practically gleeful as he traded in the losses and privately-held secrets of his classmates. Squinting, head tipped to one side and smiling but really sneering—he tried to look like it was all in good fun, but he was mean. Everyone tried to keep him in the dark, knowing that once he got hold of something, it would be broadcast widely, like it was on the evening news. His singsong tone immediately set Maddy's teeth on edge.

In Maddy's neighborhood everyone knew what everyone else was doing. Maddy had heard her mother refer to it as a fishbowl, but Maddy didn't think so; fishbowls were filled with water, and except for their blow-up pool in the back yard, there was no water in their neighborhood at all. Furthermore, most houses were filled with young families, so anything that wasn't immediately apparent through windows was magnified and quickly spread through Newfield's small elementary school. Especially by Patrick.

If there *had* been an ambulance at her house, she would have known it. *I would've heard the siren, right? How would I not know if someone in my house was rushed to the hospital?*

"There was *not* anyone at my house last night except my family, and if you don't stop..." She heard her own voice waver. She pressed her fists into her hips, trying to look serious. She hoped he did not detect her worry or things would get worse, although she wasn't sure how..

She was interrupted by the first bell and by her best friends Lloyd and Stuart, tossing a dodge ball back and forth as they approached the school's front door. They stopped when they saw Maddy. In unison they said, "Hey Maddy—what happened at your house last night?"

Patrick looked at her with an 'I-told-you-so' grin, which made Maddy want to punch him. Instead, she turned to Stuart. While he was known as the class clown, he was also her oldest friend. She'd known him since he was born, less than two months after she was. Their parents had been friends since they themselves were in elementary school, and the two children spent many hours in the same playpen, stroller, playroom, neighborhood, and now classroom. Whatever else he was, Stuart was reliable. She could count on him to be the distraction from drudgery of math or spelling but she knew she could also count on him, *period.*

Stuart's humor was not mean, and never directed at anyone, especially her. He wasn't one to play practical jokes, and she was uneasy thinking maybe something *did* happen.

Lloyd confirmed Stuart's story. "Yeah, Maddy, there was an ambulance in your driveway and the red and white lights were flashing into our living room!" He pushed his glasses up higher on his nose,as if seeing better would help him envision the best way to handle Maddy's obvious confusion. Deemed 'genius' at age four, he'd always led the class. Maddy and he often matched wits, and Lloyd usually won—except at word games and puzzles, where Maddy was his match, and often beat him.

Leaning closer to Maddy as if it were only a matter of privacy he whispered, "What happened?" While he could do hard multiplication in his head, unlike Stuart, one thing he could not do was joke around. Unless she was the latest victim of some ill-conceived first-grade prank that included her two best friends, something happened at her house last night and she was apparently the very last to know.

"Stop it you guys! It...it isn't nice!" She wanted to believe they were teasing, but something gnawed at her: the feeling they were telling the truth. As they walked to room four, she forced herself to replay the events of the previous night.

After her dad had come home, she had followed him to her room where she put the finishing touches on the living room of her new Barbie dollhouse. Jack lay on his side on one of her twin beds, one arm crossed in front, holding his opposite shoulder, as he watched her tape material from his warehouse onto Barbie's living room window.

While he rested, Maddy continued to decorate the house Jack had helped her create out of a large cardboard carton that originally held three dozen rolls of toilet paper. It was really a terrific dollhouse because it was big enough for Barbie and Ken to walk around in standing up. She'd used bits of wood, fabric, and carpet that she'd scavenged on one of her trips to her dad's warehouse to create furniture, draperies and flooring. She'd painted and colored tons of brown and white paper with crayons and glued it to the inside as wallpaper. Many times over the last few weeks her father would come home from work, give her a 'ride' to her room, dump her on the bed, then sit with her on the floor, helping her with her Barbie house.

After a while, she'd grown tired of playing with the Barbie house, so she turned her attention to the puzzle that was spread over her floor. She sat humming quietly to herself so as not to wake her father, who had dozed off. She was careful not to go too fast. She didn't want to finish it yet, knowing it would be a while before she could get another. Instead she satisfied herself with a lazy rhythm of pieces clapping into place. It had five hundred pieces, which Maddy made a little more challenging by taking the box and putting it in her closet so she wouldn't be able to look at the picture of the completed puzzle on the cover. When she finished it, she'd have nothing to do until she would get another, which was on rare occasion, like when her siblings had birthdays and her grandma didn't want her to feel too jealous of their gifts and attention.

As she had sat at her front-row desk, she put her notebook on the shelf under the attached chair. No ambulance had come to the house, at least not up to then. She remembered that she'd left her dad snoring loudly on the bed as she went to the kitchen to help her mother with dinner.

"I'll set the table, Mommy."

Maddy took the napkins from the ceramic holder she'd made in kindergarten and set them at five spaces around the table. She then got out the right combination of silverware, forks, knives and spoons and laid them in their proper places. Her mother, meanwhile, was cutting up potatoes into a pot of water. Maddy's mouth watered as she thought of them mashed, mixed with butter, sour cream and salt.

"Madeleine? Would you please tear up the lettuce and keep an eye on the potatoes? I'll be right back."

Her mother turned the heat down under the pot, pulled a large wooden bowl from the cabinet, and set it by Maddy. She tore the lettuce and stirred the potatoes pretending she was the mother making dinner for her family.

When Katherine returned, she opened the cabinet under the sink, took out a large black garbage bag and said, with the kind of encouragement that never failed to spur Maddy to do her very best, "Thanks for being such a good helper, Madeleine. Now, Big Sister, go get Kevin and Robin, and I'll give you each a *quarter* if you can make the playroom spotless!"

Maddy grabbed the bag, found her siblings splayed out in front of the TV and, feeling like a good big sister but sounding more like a general addressing her troops, said, "We're getting a quarter apiece! Do a good job and let's see if we can fill this bag!" She herded them to the basement where her charges scattered and started cleaning and collecting.

As the oldest, Maddy was the highest-ranking organizer, the final word on whether something was trash or not. Robin, the youngest, brought her a dried and cracked, multi-colored Play-Doh creature that was missing one of its legs.

"This?"

Maddy held out the bag, "Trash."

Kevin had an overflowing armful of newspapers folded into dozens of hats and boats and the *Curious George* book from which the directions for both creations came. "Trash?" he'd asked.

"Everything but the book. That goes back to the library." She helped him stuff all the paper into the bag and put the book on the steps so they wouldn't forget it when they went back upstairs.

They spent the next half-hour sorting Legos, blocks, Tinker Toys and checkers from a pile on the shag rug in front of the TV and soon the playroom was tidy and the back bag was full. Maddy tried to think of a way she could straighten out her secret room without Kevin or Robin knowing. But she knew she couldn't and she didn't want to risk it. She'd come back to it later.

She remembered how the space under the stairs was an unintentional gift from her father. When he finished making half the basement into a rec room with a bar, he put a small door behind the bar, leading into the space under the stairs where he imagined he would store extra liquor and mixers. He envisioned hosting parties, laughing grandly as he shook martinis for a small gathering of friends. As best Maddy could remember, her parents had never had such a party. In fact, she'd never even seen them drink. Maddy would spend hours there, away from the noisy, confusing life upstairs. Most times, she would read there, but sometimes she'd write in her very first (locking!) diary, which she hid inside a cloth-covered carton-cum-lamp table. The space was hers alone and there she could be hidden from the world.

A black trash bag brimming with refuse was its own reward to Maddy, who loved feeling of things organized and in their proper place. They dragged and pushed the bulging bag upstairs, proud of their accomplishment.

"Mo-oom!" Two notes. They heard no response, so they added, "Were doo-oone!"

Their mother came down the hall, "Oooh! Isn't this terrific! What good cleaners I have!" Each grew a bit taller, nourished by the praise. Katherine turned to Maddy, "Madeleine, please put the library book on the front hall table." Then, to the others, "And you two, go wash your hands for dinner. When you come back, I'll give you all your *reward!*" They scattered again and returned clean, eager for their quarters and hungry for dinner.

Later, Katherine fed them, bathed them, read them bedtime stories, and heard their prayers, as she did every night. She did this all in reverse age order, one of the few instances where Maddy, who could stay up the latest, went last.

Maddy's still-damp head was buried; face down in her pillow where the herbal essence of her shampoo reminded her of spring and freshly mown grass. She relaxed, the pleasant fragrance and soft sheets suggesting the end of the day. As her mother scratched her back, Maddy whispered her prayer, which had been the same since she'd learned it.

"Now I lay me down to sleep, I pray the Lord my soul to keep. Thy love stay with me through the night and wake me with the morning light. God bless my mother, my father, Kevin, Robin, Grandma and Grandpa Berkowitz, Grandma Berger, Aunt Vicki, Uncle Daniel, and Pretzel." Maddy's immediate family was small. Her parents each had only one sibling and neither her mother's sister nor her father's brother was married. Maddy insisted on including the family cat, because she feared excluding her would leave her little orange kitten unprotected.

The only change to her prayer came when Grandpa Berger died. It had taken her almost a month to remember to say the prayer, which she recited by heart, without his name.

The words flowed easily from her mouth. She felt that God knew that she meant every word even if she didn't understand what all the words meant.

"How can you see with these?" Her mother ran Maddy's glasses under the hot water in the bathroom sink. Rubbing them dry with a soft cloth as she shook her head, she finished the morning ritual by pinching them in her fingers like they smelled bad and handing them to Maddy.

Maddy thought, *How can I see without them?* Placing the warm and very clean frames in place, the world zoomed into focus. And it was true. Without her glasses, Maddy couldn't see her night table or the lit-up numbers of the alarm clock that sat upon it.

Since it was a sunny and warm fall day, her mother laid out one of the two dresses she had just finished sewing, and a pair of not-too-heavy tights. Maddy loved the fabric of the smock dress: a velvety, cherry red background, dotted with maroon crabapples and bright green leaves. She'd been allowed to select the material and the pattern herself, from the few choices her mother offered her. She loved the ruffles on the bottom and on the sleeves and it fanned out as she twirled around. Maddy put on her brown and white saddle shoes—which she could tie herself—and went to the kitchen for breakfast.

The smell of burnt toast hit her as she came close to the kitchen. Maddy hated breakfast: the slimy textures of eggs, the sickening sweetness of instant cold cereal, the sour taste of orange juice—especially when it mixed with cereal-milk. *At least this morning I'm not gagging.* Anxious to be done trying to make it look like she'd eaten more than she had, she pushed the eggs to the edges of her plate, and started towards the sink. She laughed to herself when she realized she must be the only kid in the world who'd rather be in school already.

Seeing Maddy had eaten little, and clearly having no interest in having another conversation about it, her mother prepared an English muffin for the school bus. As she often did, Maddy gave the toasted, buttered, paper towel-wrapped package to the bus driver, who was all too happy to relieve her of her morning fare.

After thoroughly retracing her steps of the previous evening, and even the morning, Maddy couldn't think of anything else, unusual or otherwise, that could have caused there to be an ambulance at her house. Her dad hurt his shoulder, but that wasn't an emergency that would have needed an ambulance. *So what happened?*

She looked at Stuart and Lloyd for some clue, still not sure what to think. Her throat tightened and she could hear her pulse in her ears. She took a deep breath to try to loosen the bands that were squeezing her lungs as the hurt sunk in.

It wasn't the first time she felt this way. Last year, her mother had knit her a soft, gray angora wool hat that fit snug around her head with small pearl buttons that closed down her neck in the front. It was as warm and soft as a bunny. Maddy loved it and couldn't wait to wear it.

She remembered her excitement the frosty morning it was finally cold enough to wear it to school. Before she could sit down, someone behind her—Patrick?—announced that Maddy had an octopus head. He said it again. And again. Soon, everyone on the bus was chanting, banging to the beat on the back of the seat in front of them with their winter boots: "Oc-to-pus head! Oc-to-pus head!"

Maddy tried not to cry as she unbuttoned each silky pearl, and, without looking at anyone, balled it up, soft as a baby kitten, on her lap, then slid it into her coat pocket. She knew that she'd never wear it again.

Maddy would be okay with the teasing. This time, the alternative was far worse. And she was beginning to think they weren't teasing. The feeling wouldn't go away, not during long division, not during chicken patty and tater tots, not even during Four Square.

At the end of what felt like a longer than usual day, Maddy came home to find her mother in the living room watching "Dinah Shore," folding a load of laundry. Katherine did not look up. Maddy entered the room and stood between her mother and the TV.

"Mom?" Katherine looked startled.

Maddy could feel the blood pulsing in her neck, she was clammy and she realized she was nervous to ask—and more nervous to know—the answer to the question she had wanted to ask since Patrick had told her about the am-bu-lance.

"Some kids at school said that there was an ambulance here last night…"

Katherine tried to laugh it off, but the sound got caught in her throat and she coughed instead. Again, Maddy was struck by the thought she'd be happier if she *was* the victim of a school prank. It was better than whatever she was now sure she was going to learn about what really happened last night. She turned away so she wouldn't have to see the truth. So the truth wouldn't see her.

"There wasn't….right?"

Her mother stopped folding. Maddy watched as her mother sat up perfectly straight on the couch. It reminded Maddy of the statue of an Egyptian Goddess she'd seen in school. Except this statue had wide-open eyes darting around the room. Maddy thought, *I'm right here! Answer me!* Finally she spoke. "There was an ambulance."

Maddy watched Katherine's jaw muscles jump in her cheeks. When she clenched, Maddy thought she looked shrink-wrapped. Almost in a whisper, she continued, "Your father is in the hospital."

A television commercial broke into the silence that had practically swallowed Maddy whole: "Mmm-mmm-good! Mmm-mmm-good! That's what Campbell's Soups are mmm-mmmm-good!" Like a fish on the deck of a boat, Maddy opened and closed her mouth several times. She sat down on the floor, hoping that it wouldn't fall out from beneath her.

"Maddy, I didn't want to upset you. And besides, there was nothing you could do."

What!? That's not true! She would have made one of her deals with God, who would hear her and help. And now it was too late for that. And even if it wasn't true, *it was true, but not being able to help is not the same as not mattering enough to tell!*

She was struck numb with the thought that her father might have died, *might be dying right now,* even as her mother folded his white V-neck T-shirt. How could her mother say for sure that he was okay if he was at the hospital all alone? How could anyone know anything for sure when nothing was for sure? She needed her father, and so did her mother. And what about her grandmother? Her son wasn't supposed to die before her, right?

She had experienced exclusion from the grown-up world before, but it hadn't hurt like this. There was a particular afternoon about a year ago when there were a lot of adults in the house. They spoke in whispers which Maddy knew were reserved for those things that if you didn't say them aloud, would be like they weren't real. Maddy knew some whispered words: *cancer, divorce,* and *mentally retarded,* and it was only by coincidence that Maddy's eyes fell on her mother at the moment Katherine mouthed the words *heart attack* to Mrs. Davidoff.

"Who had a heart attack?" Maddy regretted blurting it out, in a too-loud voice almost immediately.

Without saying a word, Katherine pointed to Maddy's bedroom. Maddy thought she looked like the picture of the Queen of Hearts in *Alice in Wonderland* when she says, "Off with her head!" Maddy sat on her bed and waited for she didn't know what.

A few minutes later, her father had come in, closing the door behind him. He sat down next to her, and very quietly explained that his father, Grampa Berger, had died of a heart attack.

"When?!" she asked.

"Yesterday morning." He held Maddy on his lap as she cried, her tears darkening the shoulder of his best charcoal suit. He got up and returned with a commercial box of Kleenex. She cried long after they all left her, Kevin, and Robin with a babysitter. She cried mostly for the loss of her grandfather and a little for the insult of not being told about it until everyone else already knew.

She was going to miss him. Maddy was the oldest grandchild—the first on both sides—and while she was the center of attention of the family in general, she was Grampa Berger's favorite. He delighted in her; he'd called it "payback" for a sad and difficult childhood.

Maddy could practically recite his oft-told story by heart: his poor Russian family shipped him to live with distant cousins in the United States when he was just six years' old. He never saw his parents or seven siblings again. He was sent to work at the Colt Firearms factory in Hartford, where, over the years, he had gone from being naturally good with his hands to a skilled metalworker.

Maddy remembered how he would put out his cigarette in the red bean bag ashtray and get down on all fours to play 'horsey' with her. Maddy would hold on tight to his collar as his short, thick, body gently bucked, trotted and 'neighed' around the living room of his small apartment. Best of all, he wouldn't stop until she'd had enough. Maddy couldn't remember much more than that about him anymore, but she would never forget his horsey game, and the way his wheezy laugh and her cries of delight would bring her grandmother from the kitchen to quiet them down.

Though she was only five when he died, she understood that she'd never play with him again. And that never was a very long time, marked every single night in the space in her prayer where his name used to be.

"Madeleine, Daddy's had a heart attack, and he's going to be in the hospital for a while—we don't know yet how long." Katherine's comment cut into the spicy, smoky smell, the hoarse laugh, the bucking bronco rides—and brought Maddy squarely back into her living room and what she feared was her new, uninvited and unwelcome reality.

"When did the ambulance come? Why didn't I hear it? What is a heart attack? Isn't that what made Grampa Berger die? Can I see him?"

With the last question, Katherine put the T-shirt she'd been rolling in her hands down on her lap, and looked up at— no, right through—Maddy.

"No. He can't have any visitors right now."

Her tone made Maddy feel like she'd just dare to ask for ice cream right before dinner. Softer, but no more comforting, her mother continued,

"A heart attack is when your heart stops beating properly. You won't be able to see him until he's out of the ICU, the Intensive Care Unit. It's a special place where the doctors can watch daddy's heart beating every minute of the day and night."

Maddy knew that her mother was trying to make it sound like everything would be all right. She tried to picture this 'ICU.' All she could imagine was a hospital room like she'd seen on *Marcus Welby, MD*: beeping and blinking equipment on the wall and a steady rotation of doctors, nurses, and staff, all pressing stethoscopes to her father's chest, recording their findings in a metal flip chart that hung from the foot of his bed. Maddy also knew the answer to most of her questions, though she still knew too little to quiet the gnawing fear that something terrible had gone wrong with the Big Plan, and that no medicine was going to make it right. The ambulance must have come when her mother sent them downstairs to clean. Maddy was disgusted with herself for being manipulated into missing out by her mother and the promise of a lousy quarter.

The days and months that followed were a collage of snapshots. Casserole dinners dropped off at her house by family friends: disposable pans, wrapped in tin foil with neatly printed heating instructions and well wishes taped to the top. Phone calls from friends and relatives more distant socially or geographically. Long play dates at the homes of friends while her mother stayed in Hartford Hospital. There were piles of cards being delivered by the mailman every day, which her mother would place like good china on the buffet chest in the front hall, the same spot her father used to stand and flip through the mail when he came home from work. While Maddy would have given anything to get him home, she also didn't mind all the attention she and her siblings were getting.

Once he'd been moved out of intensive care, Maddy would make a weekly trip to Hartford Hospital with her mother. She would sit with a book on a couch in the lobby for an hour, while Katherine sat with Jack in his room on the third floor Cardiac Care ward. There, Maddy would watch the people as they came and went. She wondered whom they were visiting and whether it was as sad and scary for them as it was for her.

When her mother finished her visit, they would bundle up in preparation for the brisk walk back to the car. Once outside, they'd turn back to face the long, three-story building, which, except for the row of ambulances parked out front, could have been an apartment complex. After an hour or more of waiting, Maddy would finally get to wave to her father who, after almost two months of recuperation, was allowed to stand at the window of his room and wave back to her. For that brief moment, Maddy would strain to take in every detail of her father and try not to lose heart at what she saw: a man she hardly recognized, an older, thinner man with loose, grayish skin, in a looser grayer bathrobe. His unkempt hair, unshaved face stubble-specked with gray. Even his hand wasn't the same: bright white bandages held tubes that ran out of sight.

They'd blow kisses to each other. Not one or two, but ten. Twenty. Until her mother would take her by her mitten and pull her toward the parking lot across the street. They'd drive home in silence.

There was one thing she remembered whole, not as a snapshot at all, but as a full-length feature film. Maddy remembered she was spending the afternoon with Grampa Sam, telling him about her weekly visits to her father. She must have mentioned how much she wished she could just hold her father's hand. He stood suddenly and put on his long tweed coat, tucked his cashmere Burberry scarf around his neck, ran his forefinger and thumb along the brim of his Fedora and tapped it into place. Maddy thought he looked distinguished. He looked *important*, thought Maddy. *And that's why he usually got what he wanted,* and now he wanted Maddy to see her father who was on a "no children allowed" floor of the hospital. Without saying anything, she followed him to the Caddy and they were on their way.

Sam Berkowitz hadn't made his fortune at such a young age and in as difficult a business as selling rags by letting other people tell him what to do. He was fastidious, almost neurotic; he reminded Maddy of Felix Unger from *The Odd Couple*. He was known to whip out his pocket comb to tame the stray hairs of his grandchildren, even as they played outside. And everything he owned was kept in perfect condition. He was always neatly groomed and dressed, never complete without his hat and cigar.

They arrived at the hospital and, as he brought her through the lobby, he delivered one instruction, lovingly with a wink: "Don't say a word."

Maddy knew what that meant and she wouldn't disappoint him again. Once, in Florida, he and Bess wanted her to go downstairs and wait for them in the lobby. He'd told her not to talk to anyone. She didn't know why she couldn't wait for them in the living room, but he'd insisted and she obeyed, even if she didn't understand. She knew she'd done something wrong: when he asked if she'd spoken to anyone, she said that she hadn't, explaining that she'd told them all, "My grandparents told me not to tell you anything!" Maddy hated seeing the look of disappointment darken his eyes, even though it almost immediately disappeared into a smile and a hug.

In the hospital elevator, Sam unbuttoned his coat and told her to stand close to him. He then re-buttoned the coat, with Maddy inside, in front of him and facing forward, and as the elevator door opened, a man with four legs—two in trousers, two in tights—got off. Maddy could detect the acrid and antiseptic smells of the hospital even over her grandfather's

Bay Rhum cologne. He stopped at the nurse's station, where, though muffled, Maddy could hear Sam announce himself, check on Jack's status, and thank the nurses for their good work. Then, Maddy heard them tell him he could go to Jack's room. She almost forgot to wait for him.

When they got to the room, Sam unbuttoned his coat. Maddy took a half-step forward and stopped. Before she could brush static-filled hair from her eyes, Sam had tamed her strays with a comb that appeared as if out of thin air. Then, for the first time in many, many weeks, Maddy was so close to her father she could touch him. But, she could not bring herself to continue toward him; while he resembled her father, the man propped up by white pillows on either side of him was so much thinner. His body, his hair, and even his skin seemed thinner. She could see the veins in his forehead and his eyelids were so dark. Maddy swallowed hard, trying not to look as if she was the only one in the room who knew this man was very, very sick. Complicated-looking machines, beeping and blinking, sat at the head of his bed. Maddy noticed how the wires connecting them to her father's arms and chest were taped onto his skin, her stomach turning at the bruised, scabbed areas surrounding the tape, places they'd stuck and taped before. There was hardly any good skin left. Maddy forced her eyes away, trying to find some part of him that looked like the father she remembered. All she had wanted to do for the last many weeks was hug him. Now here he was, right in front of her, and not only was she afraid to touch him, she didn't even know what to say.

There were so many things she wanted to say, how she loved him and missed him. How scary it was to almost be that family that has no father. How scary it was to think that they really were that family with *this* father, a man she hardly recognized. He reached up and wiped a tear that had started to roll down her cheek.

"Oh Pumpkin, don't cry." His voice was gravelly, like it hadn't been used much. Hearing her nickname, she began to sob. He pressed a button attached to a wire that was not attached to him, and the bed started to hum. It sat him up a little, and, with the arm that had fewer wires attached, he reached for her hand, and pulled her a little closer to him. She let him. He cleared his throat. Then again, a little harder. Then, in a voice that sounded a little more like the one Maddy knew, he said, "It's okay, Maddy. I'll be okay. I promise." She leaned closer to him and her head came to rest on his shoulder. He brushed her hair in familiar, reassuring strokes. "Shhhh."

Then, she was crying for all the days she missed him, for almost losing him, for everything that had changed, and for everything that was never going to be the same. Her sharp, deep breaths slowly became sporadic, spastic sighs. He sat her back against the bed rail and smiled at her. She noticed his eyes now creased at the corners when he smiled, but she focused on his smile instead. Gentle. Sad. "That's my girl. Tell me what you've been doing with yourself."

She told him about her diorama of an autobiography book project and how she'd picked Eleanor Roosevelt, and how she was going to dress her Barbie in a suit and hat and put her inside a box that she was going to decorate to look like the White House, just like they'd decorated her doll house, only smaller. She talked about the musical program they were preparing in Hebrew School to honor the early Zionists and first pioneers of Israel. It seemed like she'd just come when her grandfather, who had gone to smoke a cigar in the lobby, returned and told her that it was time to go. She hugged the man who was looking and sounding more and more like her daddy, promised him she'd be good to her brother and sister, and that she'd help her mother with the chores when she got home.

Sam put his coat back on, but he didn't button Maddy in. He took her hand and they left. As they passed the nurse's station, he turned toward them, nodded, winked, and kept walking. Maddy tried not to look, but worried they might be coming after her, she gave a quick glance over her shoulder. They were smiling at her. She looked up at her grandfather. He winked and smiled at her.

"Rules are rules, Maddy, but you needed to see your father. I hope you feel better now."

Maddy wasn't sure, so she just smiled back. He buttoned Maddy's jacket, then his own. He put on his hat and took her hand. Before they crossed the street, she stopped. Sam let her. She could see her dad waving to her. She blew him a kiss. They each turned away, Jack to his bed, Maddy to the car. She knew that things would be all right—someday. But, at the same time, she knew that "alright" and "all right" were two very different things.

When Jack finally did come home, things were very different. He didn't smoke cigarettes anymore. He was calm. Medication saw to it that nothing would get him too excited. But the biggest difference, the one that affected everyone in the family, was that he was thinner—and he needed to stay that way.

Jack complained bitterly. He claimed the only reason his heart attack didn't kill him instantly was so he could starve to death instead; a small-portioned, bland, flavorless, death. Fresh fruits and vegetables, low fat foods, no caffeine, lots of water, no salt, and little meat; this dramatic change meant that the entire Berger family, even the ones who didn't have a heart condition, ate only healthy foods. Pretzel was the only one ever to eat liver again.

Where Maddy had once carried peanut butter and jelly on Wonder bread in her lunchbox, she now had lean turkey on whole-grain bread. She used to bring potato chips, her mother now packed her a container of carrot sticks. Baggies of Chips Ahoy or Oreos were replaced with a Tupperware filled with sugar-free Jell-O. In the school cafeteria, she was left to eat what her mother packed for her, as no one wanted to trade.

Not everyone was miserable. Katherine continued to eat her petite-portioned, almost ascetic, meals off saucer-sized plates and seemed to enjoy the ease of putting out fruit instead of baking a dessert she wasn't going to eat anyway. Also, probably because they were younger, Maddy's siblings didn't pine for the forbidden Yodels, Ring Dings, Snowballs and Twinkies the way Maddy did. Like anything else, over time everyone got used to the new diet.

And they grew used to the new man that used to be their father. While he certainly looked like a different person, it was the fact that nothing seemed to faze him anymore that made Maddy certain that he was, deep down, not the same person he used to be. The man who'd accelerate hard at yellow lights and speed up so cars couldn't get in front of him was now the guy who waved cars in and let people go even when it wasn't their turn. He was leaner and didn't smoke anymore, but he wasn't *happier*. He took pills morning, noon, and night. He was smaller. He missed the foods he used to eat. He missed smoking. Maddy would hear him take a deep breath like he had when he used to smoke but when she looked, he was looking far away at nothing, rolling a pencil between his finger and thumb. He'd see her looking and look away. It seemed to Maddy that nothing mattered anymore—not even her.

The woman who used to be her mother had become a different person as well. Maddy believed the reason Katherine now laughed less and cared more was that, though Jack had survived his heart attack—the 'event,' as her mother called it— killed the happy girl who once lived inside her. Maddy had heard her describe how almost becoming a widow as a twenty-seven year-old mother of three kids under the age of seven had made her 'sober up' to the harsh realities of life. She stopped watching *As the World Turns*, claiming that watching other people's misery was pointless. She stopped playing in her weekly Mah-Jongg game, she cut her hair very short, and she developed a sense of urgency in the things she did. Maddy felt that she, Kevin and Robin were reminders that there were other things she wanted to do. Her mother returned to school to earn a master's degree in education. Maddy didn't understand why Katherine wanted to be away from the family for so many hours a day, especially since it seemed like things would be easier if there were a mother at home taking care of everything.

This frightened Maddy. Not so much because the new reality was scary, but because she realized that anything could happen at any time and they would have no choice but to face another new reality. Things she couldn't yet imagine would shape her life, and for the first time, she knew that everything *wasn't* under control. Even though her parents obeyed all the tax and traffic laws and she was faithful in saying her prayers every night, things could turn upside down at any time, and she would have to adjust. The only thing she could count on was change.

She started having a recurring dream. In it, she'd be reading a book or playing quietly in her bedroom, when she would hear someone coming down the hall. Sometimes she knew it was her father and he was angry. Sometimes, from the heavy and unfamiliar footsteps, it had to be a stranger. Sometimes it was a burglar who had broken into the house. Most of the time, it was an evil and ugly monster with long black robes and yellow eyes, nails and teeth. Whoever—or whatever—it was, she knew it was coming for her. She'd hear footsteps coming down the hall, and, sensing she was in danger, she would hide in her closet, or sometimes she'd scramble under her bed. The monster would claw through her room, pausing only to sniff the air in an attempt to catch her scent. When it was clear she was going to be found, either because she'd coughed or sneezed, or because he had checked everywhere else, she would jump out of her hiding place—her heart thumping so loud she was sure he could hear it—and she would race him to the door. Each time, she would just barely manage to get by him. Sometimes she would use force, like poking him in the eye, and sometimes it would be by her wits. She would look behind him and scream, and in the split-second he'd look away, she would escape down the hall, out the front door, and into the yard.

Sometimes the front door wouldn't open right away. She'd twist the handle and pull with all her might, her hands trembling as her pursuer closed the gap separating them. She'd manage to get out the door just in the nick of time. He would get within grasp of her, but just as he was so close she could feel his stale breath on her neck or his bony fingers clutching at her clothes, she'd be willing herself to escape with such force she'd actually start to lift from the ground. Sometimes she'd have to flap her arms to keep aloft, other times she would effortlessly float in the air. She'd escape by the thinnest margin, almost always having to push him away as she floated just out of reach.

Up and up she would rise, until she could see her house, her yard and her neighborhood from over the trees. Far from her pursuer, she was free to fly. She would slip between the power lines, careful not to touch them, and turn somersaults in midair, alighting on a rooftop or a treetop to watch the world unobserved. There, high above it all, she would catch her breath, taking in the sweet smell of leaves and the distant sounds of life below. At some point, she'd realize her precarious position and get dizzy. More than once she'd come falling back to earth, waking as she landed in her bed, feeling safe but not secure. Even though the idea that intruders were trying to get her was terrifying, there was something about the flying that made the dream less than a nightmare. She loved the freedom to go where she wanted, and there was something almost other worldly about being liberated from the earth, where people couldn't escape monsters. She would wake up in the morning, feeling sad, no longer able to fly, but also special—like she had been flying with angels.

CHAPTER TWO

2:35 P.M.

Maddy felt now as she had in her childhood dreams, relieved and a little scared, escaping the monsters that pursued her on the ground. Like flying in her dream, she felt only freedom, as she willed herself higher. Unlike flying in her dream, though, she would not alight in the trees and rest. Nor would she startle awake—if she was lucky she would not wake again.

She was anxious to find rest far from the hurt and humiliation of being the last to know about her father, far from the disbelief and disappointment in a mother who could not reveal the simple truth, as if holding it in would keep it from being so, and far, far away from the reality that nothing was ever going to be certain again.

Winter 1970

"Why does Maddy get to go to Florida again?"

Robin was only four, and it seemed to Maddy that her little sister was forever measuring her portion against others and coming up short.

"Why does Kevin get more cereal in his bowl than me?", "Why doesn't Maddy have to go to bed yet?", "Why does my friend have a dog but I only have a cat?" She was upset when she heard Kevin had chicken pox and she didn't, until Maddy, secretly wishing Robin would get them—*it would serve her right*—explained what it was. Maddy didn't want anyone to ruin her plans to spend time with her grandparents all by herself. She glared at Robin, maybe even nudged her slightly with her elbow. Robin retaliated, "Mo-omm! It's not fair!!!"

Maddy didn't understand why this chubby little girl with cow-brown eyes and two curly brown, tightly-pulled pigtails felt she was getting the short end of the stick. She was usually the center of attention when they went out as a family. When she wasn't, Maddy thought, that was when she complained.

In this case, Maddy understood: a week-long visit to Grandma Bess and Grampa Sam was without a doubt the best vacation a Berger child could have. They had retired early, the cold Connecticut winters coupled with the promise of rapid real estate appreciation in south Florida was all the lure necessary to hook Sam and reel him in on Fort Lauderdale's "Gold Coast." While the young retirees enjoyed the warmth in the winter, they sorely missed their daughters and grandchildren. They compromised, spending winters in Florida and the rest of the year in Connecticut. As the grandchildren grew old enough to travel on a plane, they would take turns visiting during school vacations.

Maddy loved Florida. There, she was free from the chores and responsibilities required by her parents and from the noise and nuisance of siblings. But it was more than that: when she was with Bess and Sam, she felt like they cared what she thought, and that they genuinely enjoyed hearing about her life. They weren't the kind of grandparents some of her friends had, the kind she thought were embarrassing to be seen with: old people who dressed weird and made grunts and sighs standing up, sitting down, and sometimes for no reason whatsoever. Quite to the contrary, her grandparents were fun. And she felt they loved her. They would spend all day on adventures with her, and at night, Maddy and Bess would play card games and do puzzles while Sam watched the business news.

Maddy loved sitting in his late model Cadillac, which, like everything he owned, was spotless, and, even after so many years, still smelled and looked like a new car. He'd drive around singing all his favorite songs from the days when he was himself a young man in a voice that sounded just like the scratchy records he'd play for her on the giant console in their living room. Cigar clenched between his teeth, one arm out the window, "Yessir, she's my baby/ no sir don't mean maybe/ yes sir, she's my baby nooooooowwww" or "Jee—pers, cree—pers/ where'd you get those pee—pers." Some had funny words that meant nothing to Maddy: "Mares eat oats/ and does eat oats/ and little lambs eat ivy." Others came from the time of the Depression and described a hardship Maddy could sense upset her grandparents—they'd both get just a little bit quiet.

A man of leisure, Sam would spend time at the track, watching, then playing, the horses. Maddy would sit with him while he reviewed the list of which horses were running in which race, then follow him to the window while he placed his bets. Though he'd watch the horses carefully before the race, he would place his bets with as much consideration for their names as their form. Then they'd go to the bar, where Sam would have a top shelf scotch, "neat," and Maddy would have a Rob Roy—Coke and cherry juice—served with a cherry in a tall glass with ice, just like a grown-up drink.

As the two sat there, men in bright pants, golf shirts, white shoes and plaid caps would come by to chat with Sam about the horses, the weather, and where to get a good deal on an Early Bird meal. They'd always ask her about home and school. She felt smart and important. She especially loved when he'd let her use the sharp silver clipper that was on his key chain to snip the ends off his big cigars. She would carefully slip off the paper band, careful not to tear it, and wear it on her finger like a ring. Even when she was quite a bit older, she could never smell a cigar without remembering her grandfather and the track.

Maddy loved all her grandparents, but she loved her grandmother Bess the best. Bess was not four-foot-ten on a deep breath; she wore little jewelry and less makeup. She was easy to overlook—unless you tried to overlook her. She'd grown up in Brooklyn during the Depression, and while a hard life can have a very different effect on different personalities; on Bess, a childhood filled with want seemed to make her street-smart, the kind of person who could get what she needed.

Her hungry roots had not made her bitter. Instead, they made her laugh. Bess treated life like it was a grand show being staged solely for her personal entertainment and enjoyment.

Maddy remembered the time her grandmother had taken her into Manhattan. They were walking down a busy street when they saw a paper taped to the door of a Chinese restaurant: "CLOSED-PLEASE COME BACK!" was printed in block letters across the top. The bottom was filled with Chinese characters. Most people would assume that it said the same thing in Chinese as it did in English, but not Bess. She looked in the window, and, seeing only Chinese diners seated at the tables, she traced her finger up and down the bottom half of the sign, pretending to read the Chinese characters, "Look Madeleine, it says, *if you can read this, come on in!*" They ate in a Kosher deli.

Bess' complete lack of self-consciousness was tantamount to screaming "look at me!" which was the exact opposite of what Maddy wanted to say. Uncomfortable in her oily, blemished, adolescent body, the shape and smell of which changed daily, she only wanted to be invisible. Last winter when Bess and Maddy were walking on the beach, Bess decided they should practice good posture and exercise abdominal muscle control, just like she'd seen on a TV fitness program.

"Let's walk all the way to the jetty. Stand straight, Madeleine, and we have to pretend we have a penny squeezed between our tushie cheeks, okay?"

"But, Grandma, I don't think we…"

With that, Bess was off, shoulders back, waddling down the beach in a bright floral bathing suit, checkered sun hat, and oversized white sunglasses. Maddy did likewise, but she was feeling very conspicuous just walking with her shoulders back, never mind the penny. As she waddled toward her grandmother, she realized that unlike when Katherine told her to stand up straight, as uncomfortable as she felt, she felt taller.

"Mo-oom! I said, It is. Not. Fair."

Four years of accompanying her brother and sister to the airport for a trip that wasn't about her in any way was too much for her.

"Tell me!" She was whining now, "Why?"

"Well, Robin," Katherine assumed a soothing tone, speaking just loud enough to reach back to her youngest, who was stretched across the way-back of the station wagon, "We go in age order. Madeleine is ten, so she goes first. Then Kevin is seven, and he goes next. You, Robin, are four, so you'll go after Kevin. I promise." Quiet moments followed, as Robin processed. Then Robin yelled, "Mo-oom, I want another number!"

Maddy saw it first. The car directly in front of them slammed on his brakes and came to an immediate and complete stop. Their old wood-paneled station wagon skidded and crashed into the car in front of them, sending Kevin and Robin from the way-back into the middle seats. Maddy, who was sitting in the front, went smashing into the dashboard.

Like a cartoon when a fox goes into the henhouse, noise started all at once. Robin was wailing. Kevin was calling everyone's name to see if they were all right. Maddy was shrieking. The noise she was making was muffled, though, by her hands, which were covering her face. A single word stopped the cacophony cold.

"SHIT!"

Katherine shouted it as she slammed her palms on the steering wheel. The silence that followed was palpable. Her three children stared at her, eyes and mouths wide open. Recovering her composure, she straightened in her seat, turned to Maddy, and through a clenched jaw said, "…and don't go running to tell your father I said that! You hear me?"

She didn't. But she had never heard Katherine swear, due to the fact that Katherine prided herself on her ability to find another way of expressing herself in those situations; she would tell her children swearing was the sign of a weak and unimaginative mind, ending the oft-heard lecture with, "you are better than that, anyway." Maddy understood what Katherine was saying, but sometimes, it seemed, nothing had quite as much punch as a well-placed swear.

Maddy was looking at her mother through her fingers as she tried unsuccessfully to stem the flow of blood that was dripping from her nose like a faucet with a broken washer. Her hands in front of her mouth, which was filled with blood,

Maddy could only manage to say "Bell, bob, your bad bouth isn't by biggest probleb right dow." With this, Katherine realized her daughter was injured, and she sprang into action. She reached behind the seat and produced a large white terry cloth towel—something the daughter and wife and daughter of a 'shmata man' wouldn't be without. She handed it to Maddy, who wiped her face, tipped her head back and felt the skin tighten as she watched her nose swell up right under her eyes. Warm, salty blood filled her throat.

After deciding no police were needed, given the minimal damage to the car, and that they'd left home extra early, their plans were delayed but not derailed. The whole quiet brood continued on to the airport. By the time she boarded the plane, her nose had stopped bleeding and was only a little red and swollen. The stewardesses gave her wings and a special drink like the kind she'd had with Grampa Berkowitz, which made her feel a little better.

Being the focus of Sam and Bess' attention made it easier for Maddy to overlook the bump in her nose. Maddy knew that even after her nose healed, it would be a sore point when she'd remember that just after a car crash, her mother was more concerned that she cursed than she was about her own daughter's injury. At least while she was with her grandparents, she felt cared for in a way she never did at home. It wasn't all about her, but it wasn't all about anyone else either. She felt seen, heard and understood without trying. Their full acceptance of her, just the way she was, made her feel quiet inside. She did not have to try to be anything 'more' around them than she already was, something that was harder to enjoy that it seemed, because sometimes she didn't know what she wanted to eat, to do, to see; just that it was up to her to decide.

Most days they would go somewhere special: to the racetrack, the movies, the beach, the open-air fruit market, the zoo. They'd eat in restaurants for dinner almost every night, and sometimes they'd eat breakfast out too. Her grandparents would take her shopping at one of the large department stores, and buy her whatever she wanted. It was in Florida that Maddy got her favorite sandals, with crisscrossing leather straps that laced up to her knees like a gladiator, and a white sweater with a fake fur trim that was the envy of her classmates back north. She loved Florida, and she felt like a young celebrity when she sat on a velvet chair in the lobby of Sam and Bess' new, exclusive high-rise on the ocean.

The Reina de la Playa sat majestically between the Atlantic and a palm tree-lined private street in a newly developed part of the beach in Fort Lauderdale. The residents had to be fairly well-off to afford the amenities. Sam and Bess were some of the youngest residents. There was a lot to attract young retirees from the north. The elegant lobby was elaborately decorated for each holiday. The pool and Ping-Pong room, men's and women's card rooms, library, locker rooms and gym—complete with a gyrating belt machine that was, Maddy assumed, supposed to jiggle fat off—didn't come cheap. Without question, the bingo game was the biggest event of the week. A large crowd would gather in the social hall, people would buy their cards—no one bought just one—and then sit in one of the long rows of tables with each card displayed in rows in front of them. As the caller would shout out numbers, normally genteel elderly folks would become fierce competitors, managing six and seven cards at a time, competing for a nominal cash prize and priceless bragging rights. Maddy thought it was funny that these old women, smoking cigarettes and wearing housecoats, were the same slow-moving but well-heeled people who, when behind the wheel of their cars, couldn't focus on one stoplight long enough to recognize that it had changed from red to green. But she understood their enthusiasm. Though the stakes were low, winning was clearly a blast at any age.

Like Maddy, Bess liked games and puzzles. She liked card games, especially gin. When Maddy was with her grandma, they played games. Lots of games. A quick hand before breakfast, a game of Scrabble after dinner: Bess taught Maddy every variation of Gin that she knew, and was always telling Maddy how smart she was to pick up the new game so quickly. Bess taught her how to score and how to knock: tapping out different rhythms on the table when they'd throw the knocking card. They would tap out the five beats of "Shave-and-a-haircut" and, in lieu of the words "two bits," they would sing "I— win!"

CHAPTER THREE

2:37 P.M.

Maddy heard a knocking, though she couldn't quite make it connect to anything. The knocking persisted, and then she thought she heard the doorbell, but, leaden and liquid, she was not certain, and, in any event, she was powerless to respond. The rapping sounded like it was coming from a great distance away. Even if she'd known it was her best friend stopping by to give her a quick hug and say, "Happy New Year," she still would not have wanted to answer the door. Go away! This was not a game she was going to lose: she wanted out, and no one was going to keep her from folding her proverbial hand and walking away from the table.

Finally the knocking subsided.

Winter 1970 (continued)

Since coming home from visiting her grandparents in Florida, vacation was over, and she'd returned to school, waking in the dark and going to bed long after it got dark, not sure why anyone would choose to live in New England. She was sitting on the floor of her bedroom, trying to lose herself in a book of word puzzles, part of a set of puzzle books her father's secretary Ruth had given her for Hanukkah a few weeks before. She had finished a word search and was starting a crossword when her mother poked her head into her room.

"What are you doing?"

Maddy shrugged, holding the book and pencil out for Katherine to see.

"Well," she warned, "if you don't go outside and play until dinner, I'm going to find something for you to do in here!"

Maddy knew what that meant: Katherine viewed idle children as a personal failure of their parents to properly manage them. None of the Berger kids were allowed to be doing nothing. Ever. The words "I'm bored" would prompt Katherine to give them a chore—usually something that made them wish they had not said anything at all.

The storm door slammed as Maddy emerged from the house, zipping her coat as she hurried to avoid giving Katherine the chance to make good on her threat. The door slammed again as Kevin followed right behind. They sat on the driveway, as the last sliver of sun hit their bodies and cast elongated shadows across the yard. It was getting chilly, but neither Kevin nor Maddy wanted to go back inside for more clothes. Instead, Kevin fussed with his sneaker laces. Although he could tie, he couldn't seem to get these laces knotted right. Twisting them, wrapping them around each other, trying to get them to at least look tied, Kevin was working hard.

"Want help?" Maddy offered, but without looking up from his feet, he shook his head and asked, "Where's Robin?"

"Mom said that Robin, the big baby, can stay inside and watch *Sesame Street.*"

Kevin shrugged, oblivious to Robin's protected status or Maddy's resentment about it. "What do you wanna do?"

She shrugged back. As she ran through the possibilities, she dismissed the swings, two-square and hopscotch. "How 'bout we roller skate?" Without waiting for an answer, she jumped up and headed for the shed. She turned to see Kevin still sitting there.

"Maddy, I don't even have roller skates!"

While Kevin was a good sport, always willing to play along, roller-skating without skates was beyond even him.

"Oh, right. Sorry, Kev. How about I roller skate and you ride your bike?"

Kevin emerged from the shed first, carefully guiding the bike he'd gotten for his birthday past the car. It was a low-rider with an aqua blue metallic paint job. It had a banana seat, long curvy handlebars, and a really high, chrome sissy bar. It was the exact bike he had wanted, and he loved to ride it. Maddy followed right after her brother, skates in one hand, putting the red ribbon holding her metal skate key around her neck with the other. She sat down on the driveway to put her skates on.

"Hey Maddy! How about if I pull you with this?"

He had gone back into the shed and had come out like King Arthur holding Excalibur. He held the water-skiing towrope, which was neatly coiled and cinched tightly in the middle, in one hand over his head. Kevin must have gotten it from their father's "high-up shelf," the home for things specifically *not* for them.

They carefully tied the line to the big metal sissy bar. Like a knight on his steed, Kevin mounted his bike and started down the street. Maddy held the end of the rope—a two-foot-long tube with the rope snaked through it—in her hands. When Kevin got far enough away, the rope drew taut. Then, a sudden jerk left her arms stretched tight in their sockets.

They got to the end of the street, which was one of the quietest streets in the neighborhood. It ran along the top of the hill and was intersected at each end by roads that saddled the hill. Her father had told her that from the air, the streets looked like a giant "H"; Maddy's house was the exact center and geographical high point of the cross piece. At the bottom of both ends of the saddle roads were busy roads that led out of the neighborhood onto one of Newfield's two main roads.

Kevin turned left at the end of their street, and started heading down the hill. He'd passed two houses when he turned to check on his sister, and, in doing so, managed to catch one of his loopy shoelaces in the gears. The bike seized up and fell to the pavement, pulling Kevin down with it.

Picking up speed as she headed down the hill, and certain she could not stop, Maddy started to panic as she rushed past her brother. She was out of control and still tethered to the bike by the well-knotted tow-rope. She frantically pulled at the rope around her wrists, even as the small steel wheels gathered speed under her. She was panicked by the fear that there was no way to avoid falling, *or crashing!* Certainly no way to stop. She stared at the knot, twisted the bar under two loops, one over another, then through the middle of a jumble of the quickly tightening rope. It slipped from her arms and, while she didn't look back to be sure, she heard it hit the ground behind her. She filled with a rush of relief. And gratitude. It wasn't a fully-formed thought, but more of a sense that one of her dream angels had somehow helped save her.

The feeling was short-lived. Opening her eyes, she was horrified to see she was already entering the intersection. She closed her eyes again, certain only that she did not know what was going to happen next. What did happen next was that she sped straight across the street, her skates slammed into the curb, and, for a brief moment, she was airborne.

Like in her flying dreams, it was exhilarating. Again, the feeling was short-lived. She landed—chin first—on the sidewalk and everything stopped. She didn't move. She couldn't breathe. She heard her brand new wire frame glasses hit the sidewalk. She didn't know what being dead felt like, but she was certain she was dead. It would be confirmed only when she opened her eyes, if she were to see herself lying on the sidewalk, like in one of those out-of-body experiences she'd once read about in a magazine at the dentist's office. It would mean that she was dead. If she looked up and saw the sky, then she was still alive. Either way, she was convinced it would only become a final, irreversible reality when she opened her eyes. So, if she just stayed there, eyes shut tight, she wouldn't be dead.

She tried to cheat a tiny peek—a peek so small no one (*not even God?*) would see—but she was afraid to open them too much, just in case. She heard her brother panting and calling her name. She opened her eyes.

He was looking down at her. Down at her! Her body rushed with pins and needles, as, for the second time in as many minutes, she felt intense gratitude toward something she could not understand, but just sensed *was*.

She stood up slowly, scanning her body for damage, and was upset to see she had skinned her knees. Her elbows were dirty, her chin was bleeding and starting to ache, and, even though she was okay, she was worried it wasn't going to look good. Kevin picked up her glasses and cleaned them off with his shirt and they headed home.

There, Katherine cleaned them up. She washed their scrapes and threw their torn clothing right in the trash. Maddy looked at Kevin, with Band-Aids on his chin, both elbows, both knees and his right shin, and tried not to feel sorry for herself—she'd only needed Band-Aids on one knee and her chin.

Even if Kevin had it worse, now that her mother let her occasionally wear taupe tights with dresses, the bandage, or eventually, the red scab would certainly show through. Her mother told her so.

At dinner, Maddy only picked at her food. It wasn't until after midnight that Maddy found herself at her parent's bedside listening to Jack snore. His rhythmic sawing was as comforting as soft music. Maddy would wake up when, very occasionally, he wouldn't be snoring at all. The quiet would be deafening.

Tonight, however, it wasn't Jack's snoring, but rather a sharp, stabbing pain in her jaw that woke her and wouldn't let her go back to sleep. Maddy knew that there were some people who were pleasant and calm when woken from sleep. She also knew that Jack wasn't one of those people. Since his heart attack, he'd been heavily medicated, especially at night. Maddy used to be scared of him because of his snoring. Now, she was scared for him when he wasn't. She missed her old daddy, and wished one day he would wake up and be back to normal.

"Mom," Maddy whispered, "my jaw hurts."

Her mother opened one eye, leaned up on an elbow and mumbled, "Madeleine? What's wrong?"

Maddy tried to pull her own jaw back into place, so she could say "never mind," but as she did, she was jolted by pain that made her heart race and her eyes fill up with tears.

"My bottom teeth are crossed over in front of my top teeth, and I can't push them behind. And my whole face hurts."

Katherine sat up completely. Jack snorted deeply and rolled into his side. After a brief pause, the rhythmic snoring began again. Katherine took Maddy's face in her hands and gently tried to push her lower jaw back. Maddy saw a spark explode into a thousand flecks of light in the space behind her eyes. Fourth of July. She shrieked and Jack jumped out of bed like he'd been bitten by a snake. Spinning around, lost in the dark and confused, he fumbled for his glasses on his night table. He switched on his bedside lamp and as he got his bearings, he sat back down and turned to Maddy.

"Madeleine's mouth hurts, and her bottom teeth are crossed over the top—they're supposed to be the other way around. She must have done something to it when she fell."

He took her head in one hand and, with the delicacy of the man who smacks the TV to improve reception, tried to jiggle her jaw back with the other. Maddy screamed. Unlike the time she'd awoken from a dream in the middle of the night and her eyes were crossed and wouldn't go straight, or the time her arm had fallen dead asleep and could only hang there like a piece of overcooked spaghetti, this time her parents didn't send her back to bed with the assurance that it would be better in the morning.

"Jack, you get dressed and I'll get Madeleine ready."

Ready for what? she wondered. Katherine brought Maddy back to her own room where she pulled clothes from the closet.

"Here Madeleine, put this on. It buttons down the front so you won't have to put it over your head."

Maddy wondered where she was going that required such a shirt; it made her a little nervous. As they left the room, Katherine pulled the word search book and a pen from off Maddy's desk.

"You can do these while you wait."

Wait for what? Maddy still had no idea, but when they got to the kitchen, she saw her father tying the laces of his Docksiders. His down vest was unzipped, revealing a red and black flannel shirt underneath. He was dressed to go fishing, which Maddy knew could not be where they were going.

"Ready Pumpkin?"

"I guess so."

The car ride in to the city was quiet. Finally, Maddy got up the courage to ask where they were going. When Jack told her "Hartford Hospital," she started to cry. She remembered visiting him there and knew it was a place for really sick people. She'd only fallen, but maybe it was in worse than she'd thought.

"Well hello!" The admitting nurse was clearly surprised to look up and see a young girl in the inner city emergency room in the middle of the night, a time usually reserved for the victims of gunshot wounds and violent accidents.

"My daughter fell this afternoon and now her jaw is crooked and it won't go back." Jack looked concerned as he glanced around at the motley crew scattered in chairs around the waiting room.

"Oh my. Well, fill this out, and we'll see her as soon as we can."

The plump and pleasant woman, who smelled fresh and clean like flowers, was handing Jack a clipboard with the pen attached, holding several pages for him to complete. As if apologizing for the midnight exam, she added "standard hospital procedure."

What happened next was, indeed, "standard hospital procedure": Jack and Maddy sat for a very long time. Maddy watched an old man who smelled like alcohol, dressed in layers of dirty clothes, telling an equally grimy woman sitting next to him about how he'd fallen down a flight of stairs. There were two Asian teens—one with a bloody towel wrapped around his hand—and there was a black man who was arguing with his girlfriend, claiming his foot was fine—even though Maddy saw it was the size, shape and color of an eggplant.

Maddy was tired and would have fallen asleep had she not been in so much pain. She didn't want to stare, so she tried to distract herself from all the dramas going on around her with her puzzle book, staring instead at the grid of letters, searching for words, horizontally, vertically, and diagonally. Even though she was only half concentrating, she finished the word search in just a few minutes.

Her dad rubbed her back, "How ya doin' Pumpkin?"

Whenever she was down, he would become so affectionate; he'd use that soothing "dad voice," he'd rub her back, or twirl her thin, silky hair in his large, rough fingers. She knew it was wrong, but sometimes, she found herself wishing she were injured more often. She wasn't sure whether he meant "how ya doin" with the word search or with the waiting, answering both, "Okay, I guess, daddy."

He looked over her shoulder and tried to help her with the search.

"Gosh Mad, you find the words too fast—I can't help you one bit!"

It was true. Maddy could see patterns and solve these kinds of puzzles quickly and easily. It was almost like she wasn't in control, the answers just seemed to jump out at her. At home, she was working on a circular jigsaw puzzle with one thousand pieces, all red. She would finish it in a few days. Though the pieces were all the same color, one after another, the exact right shaped piece would catch her eye, and sure enough, she would snap it into place.

When they finally did bring her in to the examination room, Jack told Maddy they would probably have to wait some more, but the doctor came in right after them. He was holding a clipboard, and when he looked up he was surprised to see a pale and sleepy twelve-year-old girl with a protruding jaw. He bent down to her level, and with a slight smile on his face, he said, "Hi there. I'm Dr. Birnbaum. You are..." He checked the clipboard, "...Miss Berger?"

She nodded and he responded, "Well young lady, what brings you out at this hour?"

Through her twisted jaw, Maddy tried to explain, "Well, I was roller skating and I fell on my chin. It didn't hurt too much at first, but now it really, really hurts."

Maddy wasn't nervous, exactly, but the closer she got to finding out what was wrong, the closer she got to bursting into tears. The doctor tried to slide her jaw slowly side to side, like the Tin Man did when Dorothy oiled him.

"Owwwwww!! That really hurts!"

He picked up a tongue depressor and told her to bite it and hold it while he tried to move it. She couldn't get it to stay between her teeth. The doctor turned to the opening in the curtain that was pulled around them and announced loudly,

"Juan, I need two films of her right maxilla, mandible and condyle. Front and side."

A square, dark man with a thick, black mustache appeared from behind the curtain. The doctor explained to Maddy, "Juan is an X-ray technician. You need to go with him to the radiology room so he can take some pictures of your jaw, okay?"

Maddy nodded and looked at Juan.

"Dees way pleeze." His voice was high for his largeness, and she hoped that it was a sign that he'd be delicate—or at least more delicate than everyone who had touched her jaw so far. He led her to a colder, darker room and in a heavy accent he said, "Jew need to put jour head ober here."

Did he just say "Jew?" When she looked at him, he was smiling at her sympathetically. She looked to her father, who seemed, at least in this regard, unconcerned; he didn't even look up from the article in the fishing magazine he'd been carrying around since the waiting room.

Juan was patting one end of the metal table that was centered under a large metal octopus suspended from the ceiling. He put the X-ray film on the table and adjusted the machine overhead. She lay down on the table and turned her head to try to get into a comfortable position, but she could only turn her head so far until she felt a sharp pain.

"Eef jew can't turn too much eet is no problemo. I will help jew, okay?"

Maddy was relieved when she realized he wasn't saying "Jew"; he had a Spanish accent. He gently placed her head on the film plate and twisted her face around trying to lay her face flat on the table. Even though he was careful, it still hurt. A lot. *If my jaw wasn't broken before, for sure it is broken now.*

When Juan finished taking the X-rays, Maddy finally got up the courage to ask him, "De donde eres?"; –"Where are you from?"

She loved Spanish class—the yackita-tackita of conversation was musical and the grammar was like putting together a puzzle.

"Yo soy colombiano."

She understood: "I am Colombian."

"Mucho gusto."

Nice to meet you too Juan, she thought. *Under the circumstances.*

He smiled at her, took the film plates under his arm and left. She and her father went back to their space inside the giant shower curtain that delineated their portion of the room and waited for a few minutes. They couldn't help overhearing the commotion next to them. The man with a bloody hand was relating to the doctor, between blood-curdling screams, how it was nearly sliced off in a fight that involved a machete and the honor of somebody's sister.

When Dr. Birnbaum returned to Maddy, his arms were loaded with stuff. He had her films in one hand and what turned out to be metal instruments all wrapped in paper in the other. While he laid instruments on a smaller table that he had rolled over from the corner, he cleared his throat and turned to Jack.

"The X-rays were conclusive. Maddy here fractured her condyle—the small bony protrusion that connects the lower jaw to the rest of her skull. It will have to be immobilized and, like most bones in kids, should heal completely in about six to eight weeks." The doctor then turned to Maddy and softened his tone, "Now, young lady, you broke your jaw, and in order to set it back in its proper place, I'm going to have to push it around a bit."

Maddy's eyes filled with tears as she tried to process what he had just told her and what was about to happen.

Dr. Birnbaum handed her a tissue, "I won't lie to you Madeleine. This will probably hurt some. But, in order to make it hurt as little as possible, I'm going to give you something for the pain."

She tried to smile. Then as she caught sight of the needle he was taking from the drawer, she froze. She stared at him, sure she looked like an animal caught in the headlight—and tracks—of an oncoming train.

"We also need to give you an antibiotic. And, since your father can't recall when you last had a tetanus shot, we need to give you that injection as well."

He pulled two more syringes from the drawer. When he told her that they had to be injected in her gluteus, she didn't object—until she realized where her gluteus was. Maddy was mortified at the embarrassment of showing her bottom to this man, even though she knew it was his job and that he was there to help her.

"Mr. Berger, I'm going to ask you to step outside."

The doctor snapped his rubber glove and turned toward Maddy. Jack picked up his jacket, cap, and four-month-old copy of *Field & Stream* and glanced back helplessly over his shoulder at Maddy before he disappeared beyond the curtain.

After a series of sticks and stabs that made Maddy think of her mother's red tomato pincushion, the doctor and a nurse sat down: the nurse in Jack's now-vacant chair and the doctor on a swivel-stool he pulled from under the counter. They seemed to be waiting. Maddy did not know what they were waiting for, but she waited too. They made small talk and while Maddy responded, she never looked at him. She was watching the tools he'd fanned out on the metal tray, trying to figure out what they did and what they were going to do to her. The conversation continued until her answers to their questions sounded like they were coming from Otis Campbell, the town drunk on *The Andy Griffith Show*. Shpanish. Schwim team. Schkating. Tennish.

Dr. Birnbaum nodded to the nurse. They both stood up and positioned themselves between Maddy and the tray.

"Now lie down, Madeleine. You're going to feel some pressure, but just try to relax." Dr. Birnbaum continued to talk to her as he was pushing her jaw back into place, using the metal table for resistance.

"You know it's a good thing you had braces on your teeth, young lady! The four top front teeth are very loose, and I'd be willing to bet that you'd have lost them had your teeth not been wired to each other."

As he pushed and pulled on Maddy's face, she felt nothing but pressure.

"You'll need to be careful, though, because your teeth are going to be loose for another few months."

While she tried to consider herself lucky, he wired her top braces to the bottoms like he was lacing a pair of ice skates, pulling the two flaps tightly together, then pulling some more. When he finished, he sat her up.

"Now, the shots I gave you for the pain and for infection may make you queasy. The shot for tetanus may make the area around the injection swell and feel warm. This is completely normal."

Maddy didn't hear him. The blood was slowly swirling from her head the way water drains from a bathtub. Through clenched teeth, her tongue numbed by medication, she tried to tell the doctor that she didn't feel right. The room began to spin like she was on a ride at Riverside Amusement Park.

"I...I...uh...feel...pretty...weird..."

Maddy's eyes rolled back in her head and her face went cold. In an instant, the doctor pushed her head down between her knees. He held her there, and after a minute, the lightheadedness passed. He let go and slowly she sat up again. But the queasy feeling came back again, and this time she started to wretch. She tried to open her mouth but it was wired shut. In a series of awkward gulps, she tried to swallow the sourness that was rising from her stomach, but there was no way to stop it. Vomit squeezed out of the sides of her mouth. Most of it fell onto the paper of the exam table, but she also hit her sweatpants, the floor, and Dr. Birnbaum's shoes.

The surreal sense of it all—midnight, fear, pain, anesthesia, nausea, humiliation and injury—overwhelmed her. She began to sob. Dr. Birnbaum put down the wire cutters he'd grabbed in case she started to choke and handed her another tissue. Hearing the commotion, Jack came anxiously back into the cubicle.

"Is everything all right?" He surveyed the room and understood what had happened.

"She's okay, Mr. Berger." The doctor was wiping his shoes with a paper towel as he explained to them both what

Maddy would be able to eat over the next eight weeks. An orderly appeared out of nowhere with a towel, mop and bucket to clean up the mess.

As they rose to leave, Dr. Birnbaum added, "You should sit here for a few more minutes to be sure the nausea has passed. Then, if she feels okay, you can take her home."

He went out of the cubicle and came back with a few plastic bags.

"She's probably okay now, but you should take a few of these with you for the ride home—just in case."

Like bringing coals to Newcastle, Maddy thought. She took the bags and held them close; after everything she'd put her father through that night, she didn't want to ruin his car.

Jack took the bags from her and jammed them into one of his vest pockets. He thanked the doctor and the admitting nurse, then gently took his daughter's hand as they left for home. When she got outside, she looked back at the window where he used to stand, but the venetian blinds were closed.

As they drove back to Newfield, dawn was slowly illuminating a city that was coming back to life. The delivery trucks were strewn across the main street—flashers on— picking up and dropping off their cargo. Jack's occasional heavy sighs would break into the drone of the AM station, bringing them the news in a subdued monotone that filled the car with sound but added nothing at all.

Maddy was surprised that there were no reproaches for playing a stupid game—with his off-limits boat equipment no less. Both she and Kevin could have been killed! Maybe, she thought, he knew that, and didn't care so much about the rope—or her tights. If it had been her mother's stuff that she'd used without permission, there would have been some serious consequences. She could just hear it now. Angry: "You shouldn't have touched what doesn't belong to you in the first place!" Victim: "As the mother of three wild children I can't have anything nice!" or, "Madeleine, you could have been killed! How would that have made me feel?" She would end with the rhetorical question that meant the conversation was over:" Do I have to go and lock up every little thing that you're not supposed to touch?" Maddy could hear it all in her mind, as if it had been said for real.

While Maddy imagined that Katherine would have had a lot to say about what she'd done, her dad said nothing, which made her feel worse. She knew that she shouldn't have bothered his stuff, that she could have been killed. She also knew that he was hurting for her, but she didn't say anything. Besides, her whole head was pounding, and what was there to say?

In the morning, her whole face was dry and crusty and her body felt the after- effects of the fall and of all the injections, but it was her mouth that felt the worst—it was furry and had a terrible, sour taste in it. She could only brush the outsides of her teeth, and even that hurt.

"Good morning Sunshine! I have something for you to try."

Maddy couldn't understand why her mother seemed so happy. Holding up a glass of pinkish, pasty liquid: "Since you can't eat, I thought you would like a milk shake. Strawberry Instant Breakfast…"

Maddy looked behind her mother where the blender and an assortment of ingredients lined the kitchen counter. Maddy had never liked breakfast, and this was going to stretch her tolerance for morning food to its limit. Her mother told her that in order not to starve, she'd need to drink high calorie shakes. Her mother told her she would blend at least one egg into everything Maddy drank. She was going to start with Carnation Strawberry Instant Breakfast and ice cream (with an egg) which Maddy tried to swallow. It tasted like strawberry-flavored medicine and chalk.

Unlike Jack's post-heart attack diet where everyone participated, in the days and weeks that followed Maddy's accident it was clear she was on her own. Disgusting creations: orange juice (with an egg) blended till foamy, Campbell's Chicken Noodle Soup (with an egg) blended at least until the little chunks didn't get stuck in the straw, and Carnation Instant Breakfast in chocolate or strawberry (with an egg), all left Maddy craving something of substance, something she could sink her teeth into. And it wasn't just the smell of food cooking that made her mouth water so much she had to spit; watching her family chew and chew was torture, especially since all she could do was sip.

The one thing she missed more than anything else was gum. Over the past month, the wires binding her teeth together had loosened, and she could almost slip her tongue between her back teeth. *It is possible*, she thought, as she snuck into the top drawer of her father's bureau and quickly took out a pack of Wrigley's spearmint. It was at least worth a try. And it wasn't like anyone would miss a few sticks of gum.

Since his "episode," as her mother sometimes called it, her father had quit smoking. He still had a three-pack a day habit, but now it was packs of gum. He'd chew a piece of gum long enough to get the sugar off the outside, maybe a few more chews, then he'd spit it out and wrap it in the paper from the new piece. Given that he was and always would be a man of habits, the family had to accept that he was a chain-chewer. A cache of at least ten packs of gum lined the top drawer of his bureau, and, though her mouth was wired shut, Maddy was determined to chew a piece. She went back to her room, where she hid it, a pirate with her ill-gotten booty.

As she sat on the floor of her closet, Maddy slowly opened the outer wrapper, and smelled the pack long ways, like her grandpa would smell his cigars. She couldn't get anything near the size of a whole piece in her mouth; she had to satisfy herself with breaking off the tiniest piece, pulling her mouth open as far apart as the wires would let her and squeezing it in between her molars. The gum only lasted a minute, then it dissolved in her mouth, leaving her with only the mint taste.

CHAPTER FOUR

2:40 P.M.

Though she could still smell, almost taste, the gum she'd so desperately wanted, she couldn't help feeling like she was missing something about the whole event. Something that made her feel bad about getting hurt, that made her mother practically gleeful. Whatever it was, it made her feel queasy.

Winter 1972

Maddy looked at the clock as the bell rang. Ten thirty already! The fastest forty-five minutes in the entire school day were those spent in Myrna Kaplan's class. Why couldn't all her classes be with Ms. K? Being around this eccentric woman with a heavy New York accent made Maddy feel free from the real world of fitting in, teasing and being teased, self-consciousness at every movement or sound. Ms. Kaplan would have none of it in her room. She called it "Shangri La" and, while Maddy had no idea where that was, based on the way the room looked, she imagined it to be a lush and exotic island. Ms. Kaplan's room was the only one in the school with macramé plant holders cradling clay pots of long, healthy plants hanging in front of each window; psychedelic posters of peace signs and symbols thumbtacked to the walls; vocabulary words written in thick magic marker on colorful construction paper stuck to desks, doors, walls, and even the ceiling, which was arrayed with a random display of colorful planets and stars hanging from clear threads.

It seemed to Maddy the room was a reflection of Ms. Kaplan herself. Long black wavy hair, streaked with a few silver strands, ran wild over her shoulders; flowing, tie-dyed skirts that brushed the floor, and pointy-toed, high-heeled, lace-up shoes that looked like witch's boots. A profusion of glass, wood and plastic necklaces clacked and clattered, while long earrings dangled and jangled as she moved. The best days were when she would read aloud. Whispering so quietly everyone had to lean forward just to hear her, or screaming so loudly, new teachers would come running from other classes to see if everything was all right. Maddy loved that she would use squeaky, guttural, or sweet voices and accents from England, Ireland, Russia and Germany. She made the characters feel real.

"Okay everyone, that bell means…it's time to go to choooo-ruuuuus!" Ms. K sang the last word in a high falsetto, making chorus with Mrs. Fink—"Mrs. Stink" when she wasn't listening—sound like fun.

Music class was broken into two of the four vocal groups—tenors and basses still non-existent in fifth grade. Most of the kids were sopranos—, including the boys. Maddy was an alto. Mrs. Fink snapped her fingers and chirped, "Listen up children! We're preparing for the Winter Holiday Concert, and there is still a lot of work to be done! We must practice several songs today to make sure that you are all ready for the Big Night." She sang the last two words.

Except for Maddy, it seemed like the class rolled their eyes. The Big Night was only two weeks away. All parents, grandparents and extended family of the entire fifth grade class were invited to the school auditorium to enjoy this year's rendition of, among other holiday favorites, *Jingle Bell Rock*, *White Christmas*, and *Silent Night*. Though the songs weren't part of Maddy's world—Jews didn't learn *The Little Drummer Boy* in Hebrew School and no one had any of Perry Como's Christmas albums at home—the songs were very much a part of what made the holiday time of year feel extra special to her. When she sang these tunes, she felt like she was a part of something beautiful, powerful and universal. As an assimilated Jew, affiliating with people filled with Christmas cheer was something that made her feel a twinge of guilt—even though she wasn't religious, singing songs about Jesus didn't seem right—but she couldn't help loving the music. She was even hoping there would finally be some snow. It would be a miracle though, since the whole season had been unbelievably warm and snow wasn't in the forecast.

The Christmas music affected Maddy so deeply that, unlike most kids who truly hated preparing for the concert, she was compelled to sing her heart out. The somber and holy words made her feel like what she was saying mattered. As the class was leaving, Mrs. Fink asked Maddy to stay behind for a minute.

"Madeleine," tucking her chin so she could look at her over a pair of reading glasses that were attached to a gold chain that hung around her neck. Maddy bristled at her tone—even an eleven-year-old knew it was patronizing.

"Dear, you are a very enthusiastic little singer, and you've worked very hard to prepare for the performance."

Maddy nodded, wondering if maybe she was getting something extra for her added efforts. *A solo?*

Mrs. Fink paused, pulled her glasses off her nose, and let them fall to her chest. She shook her head.

"But, Madeleine, I think it would be better if, for the performance, you just move your mouth to the words and don't sing out loud." Mrs. Fink sat down in her chair, put her glasses back on, and started to fiddle with her songbook and some loose papers. When she looked up, she seemed almost surprised to still see Maddy hadn't moved. "You're dismissed, Madeleine."

Yes. Yes I am. As humiliation burned at her cheeks and tears were stinging behind her eyes, she wanted to run from the woman who with a few words had just crushed her like an ant under the heel of her shoe but she couldn't move.

Maddy blinked several times, trying to process what had just happened. Before that moment, she had never considered whether she could or couldn't sing. She just sang. People just sang. And now her voice had been taken from her. In a few cruel sentences she'd been singled out, and worse, she'd been judged inferior to everyone else. Worst of all, shouldn't the feelings that moved her to sing so passionately in the first place *count for something?* She vowed to herself that, no matter what, she would never sing out loud again. Ever. From that moment on, she was, and would always be, a person apart.

She struggled to drag herself to her next class, where Mrs. Kaplan was already reading the *The Gift of the Magi* aloud to them. While they were studying O. Henry and his use of irony as a literary tool, Maddy felt she was equal to any of his characters: a girl whose heart was stirred by the message of the season, moving her to sing so loud that she is heard over the others. As a result, she is directed not to sing the very songs that made her feel part of something bigger, making her smaller than she'd ever been. The watch fob and hair comb story paled in comparison.

Maddy made it through school, but when she got home, she couldn't even bury herself in her room. She had to go to Hebrew school. Their synagogue, Beth Tikvah—she learned that it meant House of Hope—was brand new. Her parents and about forty other families who had been meeting in the basement rented from the church had finally grown large enough and saved enough money to put cash and promises of cash into a beautiful new building with a modern offices, a paneled rabbi's study, state-of-the-art kitchen, designer reception hall, a beautiful sanctuary with a large stained glass window over the carved, wooden ark, and a long wing of classrooms for a growing religious school. All Maddy's friends were allowed to skip the late afternoon classes, but, personally, financially invested, her mother would not allow Maddy to skip.

"How would it look if my daughter didn't go to the school we helped build?"

It was pointless to argue. She gathered her book and a pencil and, wishing she didn't have to go, she headed out the door toward the car, where Katherine was already waiting.

Today all the students were assembled in the sanctuary to sing two prayers they'd recently learned. As they started, Maddy looked around: she counted thirty-seven people, but it sounded like hundreds of people were singing! She almost joined in, but she remembered her promise, so she was silent, mouthing the words so she wouldn't get in trouble for not participating. The voices swirling around her lifted her up, even as the horror of the day, and her decision not to sing again, weighed heavily on her. The power of the voices chanting in unison made her feel rich inside. It wasn't the Hebrew words, which she didn't understand. She could almost see the voices blending together into one giant prayer. She could feel there was less power in the prayers as her voice wasn't a part of it. She also felt that she was the only one who noticed or cared.

CHAPTER FIVE

2:42 P.M.

A solitary telephone was ringing somewhere in the distance, eventually bringing her back from the many voices in the sanctuary. Even if someone who cared enough to try to save her was calling, she had no intention of being saved. Saved from what, she wondered. Shards of memory stabbed at her, but she was not going to fight them off. Instead, she let them stab her, piercing her numbing, slowing heart.

The phone rang again, and she realized that if someone was calling her who knew she was supposed to be home, they could decide to come by to check that everything was okay. No. No one is coming. It was probably a telemarketer or a wrong number anyway. She'd never know it was her husband calling from next door, and by the time the phone stopped ringing, it didn't matter to her one bit.

Winter 1973

"We're moving to Westham!"

Katherine had assembled the whole family around the kitchen table so she could deliver the big news. They'd been in their house more than a decade and Katherine believed that her children would be better off growing up in the less industrial, more suburban town which bordered Newfield to the north. Her father didn't disagree. His business was doing well enough that they were able to buy a larger home on a side street right near the new high school, farther from traffic. By Newfield standards, the house was tremendous. While Jack had moved *around* as a child, sometimes to smaller apartments in strange cities as his father chased down various jobs and opportunities, now he was moving *up*.

The next afternoon, they all went to see the new house. Maddy didn't know exactly what the Taj Mahal was like inside, but it must have been a jeweled and exotic version of this house: sunken living room, three-sided open glass fireplace, picture windows and all.

They moved during the Christmas break, during a Nor'easter typical to New England in January. Maddy and Robin held hands in the back seat of the family station wagon as it pulled from the driveway and headed down the hill to Westham. There was usually someone between them, but Kevin had been sent to Florida—"one less child to have to deal with during the move," she'd heard her mother say—and, although it felt strange, they sat firmly, albeit a little stiffly, alone together. As the wind blew the snow sideways and the movers slid up and down the loading ramp to the back of the long white truck, Katherine attentively supervised the activity from the front door, keeping warm by virtue of a fur coat, heavy scarf wrapped around her neck and wool hat pulled down hard over her ears. Jack had insisted they turn over their old house in the best possible condition, showing his attention to the details of it's upkeep, so he ran around after the movers wiping up any wet footprints that managed to miss the hundreds of yards of heavy brown paper and plastic he'd taped down all over the house.

When they pulled from the driveway for the last time, Maddy looked back at her house and knew it was empty of their belongings, cleared of everything but memories. Before they left, she'd walked around the house. *Goodbye bedroom. Goodbye my seat at the kitchen table. Goodbye special room under the stairs.* What Maddy secretly feared was that she was also saying, *Goodbye friends I've know since I was born. Goodbye feeling like a part of the fabric of my school. Goodbye neighborhood. Goodbye only world I've ever known.*

Once at the house, Katherine immediately sent them out to the back yard to play. She pulled a bag with their snow boots, gloves and jackets, and, before they left the car, had both girls wrapped and ready to sit in the snow in their new back yard. Maddy saw the old owners had left behind a swing set. The snow was so deep, they could stand on tiptoe and grasp the cold metal frame from which the swings, now embedded like fossils in the snow, hung. They did that for a while, but they had to stop when their fingers got numb.

While the movers were slipping in and out of the house and long after they were gone, Katherine made certain that every drawer and shelf had been thoroughly wiped down, practically sterilized, and lined with fresh white contact paper. Jack was the cleaner and secondary mover, taking furniture and boxes and putting them wherever Katherine told him to. The girls worked hard to stay out of the way, but nowhere felt like it was out of her way, and even though it was clean, nothing was comfortable or familiar. Maddy felt like she wasn't connected to anything—no friends, no new neighbors, no new schoolmates: *How could I be.* No one knew she was here. She hadn't even started at her new school!

For the rest of the school vacation, Maddy and Robin just tried to keep themselves busy: playing outside, in the box-filled basement playroom, or in their rooms. Their goal was not to interfere with Katherine as she re-established order as quickly as possible so life could continue as if it were normal.

Maddy started the second half of seventh grade in the Bayberry Middle School on a day so cold that when she boarded the 6:55 school bus her glasses immediately fogged, blinding her to the utter apathy on the faces that were her new social universe.

By the time she'd arrived in Mrs. Burke's seventh grade homeroom, however, Maddy could see quite clearly that she was "the new girl,' whose only crime was that she wanted to fit—or even just blend—in. People pushed into her in the hallways, as if they didn't see her. Told that the open seat at the lunch table was saved, Maddy watched from a table she had all to herself as, not only did the table fill up, but, wanting to join in, another girl was invited to bring a chair from another table. In gym they picked her last, and then only by a finger and a shrug, not by name.

In the first three and a half weeks, only four kids in her grade even spoke to her. It was like she was invisible, only worse, because she knew the other kids knew she was there. One of them was Wendy. There were just ten houses between them, so they would meet at the bus stop, and Wendy would let Maddy sit next to her on the bus—unless Amy was on the bus too. Then Wendy would sit with Amy and pretend that she didn't know who Maddy was.

No one from her new school called Maddy to hang out after class, nor did anyone call her from her old school, which was only a few miles away. There was no room for her in her new school, and she couldn't help feeling that now that she was gone from Newfield, the space she once filled had closed up behind her, as if she was never there.

Maddy was freezing by the time she opened the front door, having walked extra slowly from the bus stop to avoid catching up with Wendy, Amy, and two other girls Wendy had invited over after school. Katherine was at the kitchen sink, washing potatoes. Without looking up, she asked, "How was your day?" *It was lousy, thanks. I got teased for getting a good grade on my quiz, I was picked last in gym, I sat alone at lunch. I hate this place. I hate you for making me move.*

"Why did we ever have to leave Newfield?"

"Now Madeleine, living here is absolutely not a punishment. This is an excellent town. It has an outstanding school system. And it can't feel like a punishment living in this house! I mean, look around at all this space! A sunken living room, a two-car garage! Three-season porch. You must admit that you like your room, right?" Her mother had apparently already forgotten that Maddy didn't even want the room she ended up getting.

When Katherine had taken them to see the house the week before they moved, the three children ran upstairs to claim their bedrooms. Robin picked with the corner room, the largest and brightest of them all: a vast ocean of baby blue shag carpeting, a crisp field of blue and white daisy wallpaper, and matching, lined drapes that ran across transom windows that ran the length of two whole walls.

Maddy and Kevin both wanted the same room. It was the smallest of the four bedrooms, no bigger than a closet, really. It had a built-in bed with drawers underneath and built-in desk, dresser and shelves that wrapped around the room. Neat and utilitarian, not an inch wasted, it reminded her of a ship. But the real reason Maddy wanted the room was that there was a pass-through to the attic at the back of the closet, where, like her space under the stairs in her old house, she could have a place to go and be alone.

It was decided that Maddy should have the larger of the two rooms—"girls have doll collections, lots of clothes. Kevin doesn't need so much space"—and, in an effort to pacify her, they promised to redecorate it as soon as they moved in. She would get to pick out her own wallpaper, bedspread and draperies. Reluctantly, she agreed.

Her father brought Maddy to the hardware store where he bought the materials for the shelves, and Maddy could pick the color paint she wanted the shelves to be. Within a few days, he had painted the whole room white and put up a whole wall of bookshelves, where she rearranged her doll collection, her photo albums, her stereo and her few albums. He hung three large hooks, one in front of each long, high transom window that ran along the wall that faced the street. It reminded her of Mrs. Kaplan's classroom. *But back in Shangri La,* she thought, *I felt safe.*

It wasn't bad, but whenever she went into Kevin's room, she felt a little jealous.

"I'm asking you a question, Maddy! You *do* like your room, *do you not?*" Katherine's attempt at diversion was futile, as was Maddy's attempt to ignore it.

"Mom, I don't get to spend my day in my room! I have to be at a school which…"

Katherine straightened up, and Maddy saw a look she knew too well. It stopped her mid-sentence: there would be no point in discussing it any further.

"School which is the main reason we moved to Westfield?" Katherine nodded, finishing Maddy's sentence. Maddy said nothing. Katherine couldn't understand how it felt to be invisible all day, to be an outsider, excluded from the small but so important conversation between classes, on the bus and in the cafeteria. To be the one nobody knew well enough to invite to their Bar or Bat Mitzvah parties. To be *nothing.*

Missing out on the Bar and Bat Mitzvahs was hard for Maddy. American Jewish children "come of age" by preparing and practicing for months so that on a given Saturday morning, a twelve-year-old girl or a thirteen-year-old boy, can come to their synagogue, and, in front of family and friends, recite blessings and chant from the Torah. They do this, from what Maddy had learned so far, as a symbol of their acceptance of their adult obligations.   The only other requirement is a "festive meal." In some cases, and in many cases in Westham, the meal is much more than "festive:" it is an all-out extravaganza. Starting in sixth grade, children start to prepare for their part in the service. From what Maddy had been hearing her whole life, parents must start preparing financially for the celebration shortly after the child is born. The parties can be as simple as homemade lunch for a few close friends back at the house after Saturday morning services, to a private event at Madison Square Garden with the Big Apple Circus, luminaries and gourmet food flown in from France. Most were something in between, but Maddy wouldn't know: she wasn't invited, and only imagined what they were like based on what she'd overheard on the bus, in the hall, and in the cafeteria.

Finally, after too may parties that didn't include her, Stuart invited her to his Bar Mitzvah. Actually, her whole family was invited, even Kevin and Robin, but she didn't care. His parents had moved to the same neighborhood in Westham as Maddy's parents had. They were in none of the same classes in school, so she would only see him a few times a day as they passed each other in the hall, but they were friends. And at Hebrew School they were in the same class, learning the prayers they needed to know for their service. They sat next to each other and Maddy was excited to be celebrating with her friend. Maddy was was also looking forward to Stuart's Bar Mitzvah because Stuart had become friends with Robby Myers, a lanky boy with rich, dark skin and thick, curly black hair. His teeth reminded Maddy of Chiclets, straight and white and square, and when he smiled at her, blood rushed to her belly and her legs felt wobbly—buzzy, but not unpleasant. She didn't know what was causing it, but she hoped she was the only one who could tell it was happening.

The Saturday morning of Stuart's Bar Mitzvah was cold, even for February, so Maddy wore her flowered maxi skirt with a white ruffled bottom and a white peasant blouse that had long, flared sleeves. She put on her platform shoes and, after putting in her newly-acquired contact lenses and fussing with her hair until it was half up/half down with no bumps, she was ready to leave, hoping that she looked like someone who should be invited to more—even one more!—of these parties.

The whole family entered together, but once they got to the sanctuary, Maddy dashed off to sit in the rows reserved for friends of the Bar Mitzvah, leaving her parents to sit with their old friends from Newfield. Maddy was excited to see that Robby had already arrived, but sorry she hadn't come a bit earlier; the seats on either side of him were already taken. When he saw her, he smiled and shrugged his shoulders as if to say, "Oh well." Maddy's stomach fluttered. She smiled back as she took a seat near to, but not next to him.

The rabbi was not their regular rabbi: Stuart's parents flew Rabbi Gold, their rabbi from back in Newfield, in from Arizona to officiate at the Bar Mitzvah. Shortly after the two families left Newfield, Rabbi Gold also left the small town. He decided to take over the congregation of his ailing father, also a rabbi, who lived in Phoenix. But, here he was, blessing Stuart in front of all his family and friends, using words and a tone that made Maddy quite sure God was listening.

After the service, everyone got into their cars and went to the banquet hall of downtown Hartford's newest, largest hotels, where three hundred guests were treated to a five-course luncheon, complete with individual baked Alaska for dessert. The room was decorated with giant balloons, as big as a person, tethered to the floor by colorful ribbons and a profusion of flowers on each table. The kids were all seated together at a long table, and when Maddy found her place card, she saw that she was seated next to Robby. The music started as Robby came to the table.

"I love this song! Hey, you wanna dance?"

Maddy nodded, afraid she'd say something stupid if she opened her mouth. He put his arm across her back and walked her to the dance floor, and Maddy noticed that where he touched her, the skin under his hand tingled.

They danced the next song and Maddy was ready to sit when a slow dance played. He pulled her to him and started to sway to the music. Though there were many people, including her parents, surrounding them, she felt like they were the only two in the room. She closed her eyes, rested her head on his shoulder and moved to the music, intently in sync with his rhythm. When it ended, they separated only slightly and looked at each other. Robby leaned closer. Maddy, realizing he was going to try to kiss her, pushed him away. "My parents are right there!"

He looked like she'd slapped him. Softening her tone, "Follow me."

She took his hand as he led her from the dance floor and out into the hall. He opened the door to the small chapel, where they were met by cool, musty air. Memorial lights illuminating plaques of deceased relatives were the only source of light in the room. As Maddy closed her eyes, excited—and a little anxious—for her first kiss, she felt his lips touch hers. It was nothing like she'd imagined. Her heart sank: it felt like she was kissing her grandmother. Her eyes flew open and she jumped back, pushing him away for the second time in as many minutes. He must have felt it too, but only shrugged his shoulders in wonderment. Her back was cool as he guided her through the maze of tables to their seats, but her cheeks burned.

Stuart's Bar Mitzvah was only slightly less disappointing than her own small celebration. Most of the Westham kids that she had invited were going to Amanda Roth's, and Amanda—pom-pom squad, kiss-you-under-the-bleachers, soloist in the chorus Amanda—had invited practically the whole grade.

It was at a small Friday night service on a chilly and rainy evening in May when Maddy did her best to sit and stand when she was supposed to, trying to look like it was something she had done many times before. She was careful to recite her prayers and responsive readings slowly and with feeling, even when she didn't understand what she was saying. And then it was done: she was a Bat Mitzvah. Everyone went back to the Berger house. The bartender they'd hired for the night made Maddy a Shirley Temple, which she sipped while wandering through a sea of colorful dresses, lipstick, blue suits and yarmulkes. She made her way past her parent's friends to the back of the living room where Stuart and Wendy were sitting.

"If one more person tells me that I look just like my mother, or that they remember me when I was only two years' old, I think I'm going to scream!"

"Oh come on Maddy, it's not so bad. We pull in good money for an uncomfortable suit and a couple of prayers."

Having tried to navigate the groups of adult conversations, Robin, Kevin and the few other non-adults were back in the kitchen, bored and looking for something to do. Maddy, feeling unimportant even at her own party, thought about Amanda's party and what the cool kids were probably doing. Maddy convinced them all to play "find the abandoned drink and drink it." They had taken half of a woman's Whiskey Sour—her lipstick was still imprinted on the glass—and had each taken a sip, and were about to take what was left of a gin and tonic when, from across the room, Jack put an end to the game with a look that stopped Maddy cold. They decided to go to the basement, where they would not get in trouble. They played Ping Pong and listened to the hum of adult conversation punctuated by the cackle of women laughing upstairs. Maddy wondered what the kids were doing at Amanda's.

Over the next few days, as Maddy thought about the two parties that she'd attended and all the parties she didn't, she grew frustrated, then angry, that her mother was more concerned with living in a good school district than having a happy daughter. To Katherine, having close girlfriends and being social with boys was not as important. To Maddy it was more important.

At least classes were easy. Maybe too easy. Maddy had gotten all A's, and on one test, a score of 107. While this pleased her mother, who would proudly tape the perfect paper on top of the small pad of tests and quizzes already taped to the refrigerator, it rubbed her new classmates the wrong way. It was clear that nobody likes a smarty pants. The final straw was when the teacher told the class there would be no curve, because it would not be fair to the student who'd scored perfectly. By noon, the whole class knew it was Maddy.

"Teacher's pet! You're all wet! Teacher's pet! You're all wet!" one student started the chant, and soon everyone, even the few kids sitting at the far end of her lunch table joined in. Maddy wanted to ignore them, but watching the whole room chant and bang their trays to the beat, her eyes filled with tears, blurring the sandwich she held suspended in front of her face, until a teacher on lunch duty made them stop.

By then it was too late. Maddy knew what she had to do. Only because she drew a page full of doodles for most of the next period, scribbling "I don't know" and "I forgot" for as many answers as she could, did she manage to keep herself from answering any of the exam questions correctly.

The following afternoon, Maddy came home, put her book bag on the kitchen floor, and pulled the test from her notebook. She held it out for her mother, careful to fold the pages just so, and hold it so the thick red "F," circled, at the top, wouldn't show, but the "X" and the "Parent Signature," underlined at the bottom, would. Maddy also handed her mother a pen.

"Oh, could you please sign this?"

Katherine pried the paper from Maddy's awkward grip, snapped the test paper over. Maddy tried not to laugh as she watched her mother register the red felt-tip "F." Maddy thought her eyes were going to pop right out of her head.

"My God Madeleine! What did you do?" Maddy shrugged. She knew, but couldn't say it out loud. Katherine stepped closer, pointing to an "I don't know" she'd written in response to a question.

"You know this! There is no reason on earth that you should have gotten an F. *An F!* What's wrong with you?"

"Well, mom,"—she hated that her voice cracked, and she swallowed hard to push against the constriction in her throat, which she involuntarily cleared before continuing— "The kids make fun of me when I get hundreds or A's on tests and quizzes…so I figured out how to get them to stop." She crossed her arms and smiled, trying to look confident, though she felt less so as Katherine glared at her. While Maddy hoped that the truth would finally wake her mother to how her situation affected her, that she would feel understood and supported, she knew better.

Each staccato syllable, hissed through clenched teeth. "Who. Do. You. Think. You. ARE?"

Not waiting for an answer, Katherine curtly signed the paper, then threw it, and the pen, at Maddy, before she turned hard on her heel, and wordlessly left the room.

The following afternoon, Maddy was surprised to see her mother's station wagon parked across the street, just outside the school. Maddy usually walked home from school unless she had an appointment. Since her mother had not mentioned anything, she couldn't imagine why she would come to pick her up.

As Maddy shut the door, she asked, "Do I have an eye doctor's appointment?" Katherine had pulled out of the space and was on her way to somewhere, when, without looking up from the road, Katherine said tightly, "No, Madeleine, you don't have a doctor's appointment." Period. End of discussion.

Maddy knew they weren't going home; the car was heading in the opposite direction of their house. It occurred to Maddy that perhaps she was going to get some kind of surprise. Somewhat buoyed by optimism, she asked, "Are we going somewhere special?"

Her mother smiled. Maddy thought she looked smug. Nodding, she said, "You have an interview at Queensfield-Eaton."

While she didn't know anyone who actually went there, Maddy knew the name. Everyone in town did. Queensfield-Eaton was a local private school, every bit as stuffy and proper as its name implied. Pronounced in "Connecticut Valley lockjaw," which meant it was said without separating the top teeth from the bottom, the school was the product of a merger between the prestigious all-boys school, Eaton and the prim preparatory all-girls school, Queensfield. The school was renowned throughout New England for its magnificent campuses, its rigorous curricula and its exclusive, WASP-y student body.

Maddy turned to her mother hoping to see she was joking. Did her mother really expect her to start all over at a new school *again*? Katherine's eyes were fixed on the road, like she was mad at it. Her jaw was clenching and releasing over and over. Manicured hands gripped the wheel so tight her knuckles were white. Maddy knew the answer without asking.

They continued in silence until they reached the entrance to the school. Gryphons, creatures with a fierce lion body, head and wings of an eagle, and plated, pointed tail of a dragon, crouched atop the tall stone columns on either side of entrance. Maddy had learned about these menacing beasts when they studied Greek mythology, and as she passed them she couldn't shake the feeling they were guarding the campus from unwanted visitors.

Katherine parked the station wagon in front of an ivy-covered brick house that had a well-tended flower garden running along a tidy brick walk. The building had a green metal roof, which her mother told her was aged copper, and a small plaque designating it as the "Langley P. Sutton III Administrative Offices." Looking around, Maddy noticed the brick building was the first in a necklace of cottages and larger brick buildings encircling a grassy square. Maddy would later learn the small quad was called the "senior green," as it was reserved for use by seniors only. All other students had to walk around it, using the sidewalk.

Maddy had to admit it felt *substantial*. At the far end of the green stood an imposing white two-story structure. With stained glass windows and large wooden doors with heavy iron hinges, it looked a lot like a church. Projecting from the steeple, there was a flagpole flying the American flag over a gold banner with a maroon crest, which she assumed was the school flag. She also assumed the steeple was once home to a cross.

Students walked between the buildings, dressed in identical uniforms, carrying similar canvas monogrammed book bags. The picture was so perfect, that the idea crossed Maddy's mind that the students were put there as part of some marketing ploy for prospective students. She could hear the director now, "Okay. Two blonde girls, exit the church, giggle and head towards the library. Great! White-haired teacher in round glasses and bow tie, leave the small white cottage with green shutters and catch up with the young boy in blue blazer and a well-worn canvas book bag. Good, good, now take the pipe out of your mouth, ruffle his hair and continue on toward the lacrosse fields…..aaaaaannnnnnd, cut!"

Entering the administration building, Maddy and her mother were promptly greeted by an older woman with immaculate posture. Her chin-length gray hair was held in place by a tortoise shell barrette. She wore sensible, soft-sole tie shoes, a beige sweater with pearl buttons and a long brown wool skirt. She introduced herself as Mrs. Parkridge as she graciously escorted them to the waiting area. Maddy and her mother sat in the two maroon leather wing chairs. The rest of the chairs in the room were black wooden spindle chairs with motto and crest painted in gold on the backs. Her mother picked up a copy of the school paper, *The Gryphon*, and flipped through it. Maddy chose a yearbook. She noticed many boys names were followed by "III," or "IV, or "Jr." The girls also had names that conveyed history—Alden, Churchill, Witherspoon, and Goodspeed. Maddy looked around. There were pictures of past headmasters lining the room, from paintings to sepia prints to color photographs. Each portrayed a gray-haired man in a dark suit, sternly—maybe aristocratically—looking at her.

The room smelled a little musty and was not-quite-cluttered with what Maddy believed were antiques: vases filled with dried eucalyptus branches, bookcases, cabinets and chairs, worn, yet polished to the point they looked wet. Heavy paisley draperies, trimmed with thick gold tassels, were tied back with slightly faded satin cords. Through the small window, a dusty ray of diffuse light fell onto a worn oriental rug. Maddy imagined corseted women and men in waistcoats waltzing across this room to music that emanated from a crackling Victrola, but there was hardly any sound at all. Only the ticking of the grandfather clock standing in the corner tapped out the continuous passage of time.

Two girls walked through the sitting room. Peeking over the yearbook, Maddy tried to look at them without being obvious. But she'd never seen anything like them, and it was hard not to stare. They both wore long gray skirts and white shirts. Each was carrying a large beige book bag with a blue monogram on the side. They were both tall, and very thin. Maddy thought they looked like dancers: backs straight, chins held high, long graceful strides, and long blonde hair pulled into tight ponytails.

Three boys came bounding down the sweeping, circular staircase into the foyer, and ran out the front door before Maddy could get a good look at them. What she glimpsed was tall, thin, and blonde: they looked just like the girls who'd just passed through, only with jackets and ties, and nothing like the thick, dark, fleshy-featured family and friends who had surrounded her all her life.

"Mrs. Hautain will see you now."

Mrs. Parkridge waited for Maddy at the entry. Though she wanted to believe that Mrs. Hautain would be warm and kind, Maddy was immediately nervous in the presence of the well-coiffed woman in a crisp, white button-down shirt and long plaid kilt pinned at the knee with what looked like a giant brass safety pin. Maddy watched as she pushed a hairpin back into her stiff gray bun; the tendons that ran down the sides of her neck were so defined that Maddy was sure she could hang a heavy coat on a hanger off one and the coat would hold.

"Well dear, your mother tells me that you would like to attend Queensfield-Eaton. In your own words, please, might you tell me why?"

Maddy wanted to tell Mrs. Hautain that she didn't want to attend Queensfield. She wanted to tell her that it was all her mother's idea and that she was okay staying at her new school, where things were finally starting to come together for her. Okay, not really, but she'd become adept at blending in, and had even made a few friends, and most of the others had moved on to other pursuits, most of the time. She wanted to say that as out of place as she felt at Bayberry, looking down at her worn, brown, buckle shoes, she was sure she didn't belong here at all. At the same time, while she didn't want this school, she didn't want to hear that the school didn't want her.

She tipped her chin up, hoping she looked more like the woman in front of her, and with enthusiasm she hoped didn't sound as forced as it was, she smiled, and trying to sound proper, said, "Mrs. Hautain, I think this school will grant me an opportunity to develop myself—in mind, body and spirit."

Her answer surprised even her. Maddy knew that the school prided itself of the Greek ideal of "Mind, Body, and Spirit." It was the motto that was plastered in Latin on everything from chairs, rugs and flags, to book bags, newspapers, and, conveniently, the yearbook she had picked up in the waiting room. All she did was restate the school's mission, word for word, to the lady in charge.

She thought she saw Mrs. Hautain's thin lips press into what could be taken for a smile, jotting something down on the pad in front of her, nodding slowly.

This small bit of encouragement prompted Maddy to continue, hoping to impress Mrs. Hautain again. "I would be a good student, and I'd try very hard."

She didn't see any reaction on Mrs. Hautain's face this time.

Three weeks later, Maddy received a thick envelope from Queensfield. They wanted her, and she was being offered endless electives: photography, ceramics, drafting, yoga, and theater to name a few, if she enrolled.

All during the summer, Maddy tried to convince her mother that she was okay where she was; she didn't want to change schools again. Yet, the first day of school arrived, and as she fixed her uniform, a gray knee-length skirt, Peter Pancollared shirt and tie shoes, she tried to imagine what it was going to be like in a place where the clothing she was wearing was the only thing she had in common with everyone else.

Pulling up to, but not through, the gates, Maddy realized she had destroyed the English muffin her mother had wrapped in paper towel and insisted she take on the ride to school. As she was too nervous to eat, she'd twisted and squeezed the small packet for the full fifteen-minute car ride, rendering it not just unappetizing but inedible. She tucked it in between the seat and the door.

"Maddy, it says on the orientation letter that the whole school is meeting in the Mayfield Assembly Hall first thing."

Katherine had dressed for the drop off as if she were going to a tea.

"Great." She took a very deep breath, blew it up through her bangs and shrugged, "Thanks for *ruining* my life. *Again.*" She shut the door, hard, but it didn't slam. Katherine smiled, then turned to the rear view mirror to check if she could pull away. Maddy wondered if she'd even heard! She started to storm away, but was pulled back almost immediately. She opened the door to release her grey wool skirt. Katherine looked at her, smiling, kind of, and said, "I hope no one saw that klutzy move. And that you don't have grease on your new skirt." Katherine reached over and handed Maddy the paper towel-muffin. "Don't forget your breakfast!" Maddy looked around, relieved to see no one seeing her, then, without looking back, started toward anywhere but her mother's car. As she passed the gryphons, she felt like there should be a sign on the gate, "abandon hope all ye who enter!"

She felt nauseated. She tossed her breakfast into a black iron trash barrel just inside the gate. Maddy pulled the map that had been included in the welcome packet from her monogrammed canvas book bag, a gift from Grandma and Grandpa Berkowitz, and "Mayfield Assembly Hall" on the map corresponded to the steepled building she saw at the end of the quad.

As she sat in a pew looking up at the stained glass windows and high archways, Maddy couldn't help feeling like she was doing something wrong by being in a place that felt so *Christian*. She shivered, accidentally bumping the elbow of the boy sitting next to her, who, like all the boys Maddy had seen so far, was dressed in chinos, a blazer and a knit tie.

"Are you cold?"

Maddy looked at him, long, straight, blond hair and clear, blue eyes, fair skin and a perfect smile. Maddy's breath caught in her throat. She tried to make it into a cough, and shook her head, trying to signal she was okay. Then, not wanting to seem rude, she asked, "Was this place ever a church?"

She was afraid to look at him for fear he'd think she was staring, but she couldn't make herself look away.

"As a matter of fact it was a church, but now that we aren't an all-Protestant school anymore, we use it for assemblies."

She couldn't tell if he thought it was a good thing or a bad thing that it was no longer "only for Protestants." He had smiled, so he probably didn't mean it as anything against the change. Or at least that was how she wanted him to mean it. She felt out of place, but couldn't bear the thought that she was unwanted as well.

"Two years ago, when my sister Margaret was in the third form they changed the rules here." His arm leaned against hers on the shared armrest. She felt something electrical, but it wasn't so much a shock as a gentle hum, a buzz that ran from his arm, around some butterflies in her belly, then deeper. It was the same feeling she'd had when she'd danced with Robby—before the kiss.

Anxious to keep the conversation going, she asked the first question that popped into her head. "So…um…is she the oldest in your family?"

"Yes, Gigi is the oldest, and I'm the only other….um…how about you?"

Was he also looking for more to say?

She gave him her best smile, "I'm the oldest in my family. My brother Kevin is three years younger than me and my sister Robin is three years younger than him." As an afterthought, she added, "And I'm Madeleine"

"Hi Madeleine, I'm Christopher Philip Dana the Third. People call me Chip."

He put out his right hand and she shook it firmly. When they touched, Maddy felt more than his soft, muscular hands—she felt a shiver run through her body.

He abruptly stood up, and, again, Maddy was struck at by how blonde he was, and how his thinness was athletic, not sickly. People in her family just didn't look like this: while he looked like he stepped out of a Norse Opera, she felt like she looked like she came from a tribe of Eastern European Pygmies.

"Who'ya talking to Chip?"

A striking girl with long, thick brown hair that hung past her shoulders in loose curls was wearing the uniform, but she'd flipped the collar up, rolled the sleeves to the inside and tied a bright Fair Isle sweater around her neck, making the bland uniform look fashionable and cool.

"Madeleine, this is Victoria Fairchild. Victoria, say hello to Madeleine."

Victoria looked down at Maddy, but Maddy couldn't see that she was nodding and smiling at her. She was blinded by the refraction of sunlight streaming through one of the stained glass windows off one of Victoria's giant silver hoop earrings. Chip slid over to make room for her, pushing up against Maddy, who moved over slowly, savoring the sensation of his body touching hers. Chip and Victoria started to talk about going to "The Center" after school. There was an air of adventure and fun about them, and Maddy wanted them to like her. But they were so cool. So, trying to act as sophisticated as the woman in the Viceroy ad, she put her fingers into a "V" and took an imaginary puff on a cigarette. Exhaling, she asked, "What do you do for fun in a school like this?"

Victoria and Chip both burst out laughing. Victoria said, "It isn't easy, my friend, but we try. Stick with us and you'll find out. Maddy considered it an invitation, and her first social victory since moving to Westfield. *Maybe it won't be so bad here*, she thought.

The rest of the first day was one long orientation. Cafeteria, library, science laboratory and office procedures were explained in painful detail by a series of teachers that all reminded Maddy of the headmistress. Whether they were taller, older, or even male, most of them spoke in an almost British accent that Maddy hadn't ever heard before.

The first time Maddy went home from school with Victoria was not long after they met. The house was a lot like the Queensfield admissions building, but much, much bigger. There was a maid and a gardener, there were many works of art hung on fabric covered walls, sculptures standing in halls and gardens, and there was a musty room filled with leathery, old-looking books, all proof to Maddy of their prosperity and permanence.

Victoria introduced Maddy to her mother, "Mummy, this is my friend Madeleine Berger."

"Well, good afternoon, Madeleine. Victoria speaks so highly of you, dear."

Maddy smiled and looked at her friend. Mrs. Fairchild continued, "Berger… Berger… What kind of a name is that, dear?"

Maddy didn't know what to say, but she knew what *not* to say.

"Well, Mrs. Fairchild, Berger is a German name."

"Oh, how lovely, and so very nice to meet you."

She wasn't sure why, but she knew that her religion was something she needed to keep in the background. It made her feel a little more apart—like she had a secret—from Victoria and Chip. *Would they still like me if they knew I was Jewish?*

Maddy and Victoria spent most afternoons together. Over the next year, they would often just hang out at Victoria's house, but sometimes they would go to a diner, to a movie, or shopping. It was during Christmas break, and a combination of boredom and big sales drew them to the mall. Victoria found two silver necklaces: one said "Best" and the other said "Friend," and when put together, they made a heart.

"Oooh Maddy! Let's buy them!"

Maddy turned the tag to see that they were fifty dollars. Each. "Well, I don't know…"

Victoria looked hurt. "Aren't we best friends?"

"Of course we are!" Maddy didn't want to tell her that she didn't have the money to buy a silver necklace, but she didn't want Victoria to think she wasn't a good friend. And it wasn't like Maddy didn't want it either—it was a sign to everyone that she had a best friend!

"Then let's get them!" And with that, Victoria went to find a register. Maddy stood there holding the necklace. While she couldn't afford it, she couldn't afford not to get it either. Her heart was pounding as she put the necklace in her jacket pocket. She picked up another just like it and went to find Victoria. When she did, the clerk was just finishing.

"Would you like a box for that?"

"No thanks, I'm gonna wear it!" Turning to Maddy, she handed her the necklace, "put it on me!" Maddy did, though she was sure the clerk could see her hands trembling. She was afraid to speak, afraid if she opened her mouth, she'd confess to being a thief—or at least start crying.

But Maddy needed Victoria to be away from the register, so she sent her to see the first thing that caught her eye.

"Hey Victoria, go look at the purple scarf hanging over there by the hats—do you think it matches your new sweater?"

As Victoria went to investigate, Maddy put the necklace on the counter. After the woman started ringing it up, Maddy said, "You know what? On second thought, I don't think I want this. Thanks anyway." She wiped her now-sweaty hands on her jeans, "Want me to put it back?" She hoped the sales woman would be less suspicious of her change of heart if she was in no hurry to leave.

"I'll get it, hon." Maddy tried to look up, but could only turn to find Victoria.

"Hey, I'm done here. And your mom will be here to get us in a few minutes, anyway. Let's go." Maddy tried not to sound too anxious to leave, but she was already a good ten steps ahead of Victoria, and couldn't slow herself down even if she wanted to. She was fighting every urge to run. But she couldn't run from the real problem: she was a thief now, and crossing that line made her anything but a best friend; friends were trustworthy. She was ashamed she didn't admit she couldn't afford the necklace, and she was even more ashamed at what she did to get it.

Once out in the parking lot, Maddy turned back toward the store to see if anyone was coming after her. An elderly couple came from one set of double doors and a woman with a large shopping bag perched on top of a baby stroller entered another. Through the open door, Maddy saw a security guard coming toward the exit. Her knees gave way. She wanted to run away, or to casually walk to the trash barrel and toss the necklace. But she could do neither. Her pulse pounded in her ears to a quick rhythm, "Thief. Thief. Thief!" It felt like she was watching the scene unfold in slow motion: the guard, holding open the large glass door, and looking up and down the curb, fixing his gaze straight up the main aisle of parked cars. *He's looking directly at me*, Maddy thought, and, as he reached into his hip pocket, she was sure he was getting his gun!

As he stepped out onto the sidewalk, Maddy tried to think about what she was going to say to her parents when they learned of what she'd done. She regretted her decision and wished she'd had the courage to tell Victoria that she couldn't afford the necklace in the first place. She wished Victoria was really her best friend, because then she would tell her the truth. And that it bothered her when she said things like "Jewed him down" or "cheap Jew." She was about to throw the necklace at him, while explaining her mistake, when she saw that he had pulled a pack of cigarettes from his pants, and lit one as he leaned back against the glass. As he looked up at the sky, Maddy turned to see Victoria's mother's car making its way toward them.

When they got in the car, Victoria offered to clasp Maddy's necklace. Maddy let her, but no matter how loose she set the clasp, it felt like it was choking her.

CHAPTER SIX

2:46 P.M.

As Maddy floated through memories she became aware of the faint sound of voices. She couldn't quite make out what they were saying, but there were many voices and Maddy could sense urgency in their tone.

She felt a very slight chill as the blanket that lay on top of her was removed. She sensed many hands on her body—along her back, arms and legs. Lifting. A dull thud as her head fell back and hit the headboard. No pain, but the noise echoed through her like footsteps in an empty corridor.

In her mind, she was surrounded by hurt, though she felt no physical pain at all. As she felt the warmth of hands leave her body, she was still again, her back supported now by a solid surface, the weight of a heavier blanket, maybe even a belt, on her chest. There was another sensation of pressure on her legs, and then she felt like she was moving.

As she came to understand what was happening, Maddy panicked. She tried to pull herself away from them faster, like when her nightmare ghouls chased her. She wanted to scream out to them to leave her alone.

The pills were doing their job well. She couldn't make a sound or a movement to break out of her own sleeping shell. Yet, the pills weren't doing their job well enough. (What if they save me??!!) She needed to move beyond the reach of the paramedics. She had to beat them to the finish line in a race Maddy desperately wanted to win.

Spring 1976

Thinking about the big race, Maddy wasn't nervous. Though she wasn't the fastest girl on the track team, her 'secret weapon' was her endurance. Two years ago, in third form, the school-wide Field Day had revealed Maddy's potential as a long-distance runner. The track coach, who was also her calculus teacher, Mr. Hughes, was not blasé when he discovered her ability.

Mr. Hughes wasn't low-key, even under normal circumstances. He was wiry and nervous. He'd absently and vigorously twirl his bushy mustache as he taught: the theorems and proofs clearly exciting him. His passion for higher mathematics was contagious. He would long be remembered as the teacher who jumped up on the desk in a review lesson on exponents. Hopping from leg to leg like Rumpelstiltskin, he shouted over and over again, "Raise a power to a power, multiply the exponents!" until the entire class was up on their desks dancing and chanting with him.

Mr. Hughes' passion for math was matched only by his passion for running. When he saw how Maddy handled the long-distance run, he recruited her for the cross-country team on the spot. Maddy tentatively agreed to try it out.

The first day was warm and sunny, and the group went for a run over Talbot Mountain. They traveled in a pack, which, over time spread itself thinner and thinner, until the thread of maroon singlets finally snapped, becoming sporadic dots on the road. Maddy ran at her own pace, enjoying the sights and smells as she passed farmhouses, woodlands, a reservoir. This piece of New England was at its peak of fall foliage brilliance. The colors reminded Maddy of a paint-by-number project, where every leaf was a different color. As the sun shone through the trees, Maddy marveled at the beauty all around her. Before she knew it, she was back at school.

She finished somewhere in the middle of the group, but, unlike those who finished in front of her, when she returned to the upper field, she didn't feel the need to lay on the track, limp like a wet towel. She watched as the remainder struggled to finish.

The cost associated with that first day's exertion was that her leg muscles, unaccustomed to the strain, were so sore the next day they barely worked. Sitting, walking up or down stairs, even crossing her legs was an effort that threatened to tear what was left of her muscles from the bones in her thighs. It was so bad for a few days, she was worried she might never walk normally again.

She wondered if maybe her ability to run so far with relative ease was just beginner's luck. Actually, her mother suggested it, and she couldn't disagree. She limped up to Mr. Hughes and tried to explain away her success as exactly that, but he would hear none of it. He saw that with training and dedication, she could learn to be a real runner. He taught her how to stretch, and told her to buy Tiger Balm, and showed her how to rub it into the offending muscles. He brought her back-issues of running magazines so she could learn about training, strategy and good form. When Maddy got very sore, the school's personal trainer would rub out her aching muscles in his small office behind the towel room.

Over time, hard, thin muscles started to give shape to her calves, thighs and abdomen. She was overall thinner, and she had gotten some freckles as well as a little color on her face. She was also able to work things out in her mind when she ran.

Problems seemed to lie down in the road and fall behind her as she worked through them, a step at a time.

Not everything was a problem she could resolve. Her father had his second heart attack over the summer and was still recovering at home. He was even more removed from his old self than before, and Maddy was worried his heart still wasn't working right. Like it had broken a little more, Maddy also worried that his heart problems were something she could have inherited. Running could help keep her heart strong.

She'd run year-round now for two seasons. As she became familiar with the training routine and her opponents, the meets were more exciting and less nerve-wracking. As Maddy prepared for this race, she wasn't nervous, even though her toughest competition was present and looking intensely focused. Jennifer Whitten, a junior at Sage-Worthington Academy, was a formidable foe. She was tall, almost five foot eleven, her legs were muscular, and even the bones in her cheeks and brow were strong. As all track team members took on a field event as well, Maddy did the long jump. Jennifer threw the shotput.

They were about to compete in the two-mile event. Each had beaten the other twice this year. Though unstated, this was a personal rivalry for the both of them, and each was intent on winning. As they lined up for the race, Jennifer casually strode in front of Maddy and whispered out of the side of her mouth, "I win, or Bear's gonna kill you."

At first Maddy didn't think she heard right. She played the tape over in her head, and her heart sank. "Bear" was Carl VonBaer, a six-foot-six, three-hundred-pound track and field legend. He was the state champion shot put thrower, and, not inconsequentially, Jennifer's boyfriend. Maddy could either lose this race or deal with Bear after the meet. As she thought about going to the coaches, the starter called out "set," and they had to toe the line. The race was under one second from "go."

The adrenaline that normally propelled her legs in these events was chaotically pulsing through her body, and her mind was so tangled up in the immediacies of *what to do*, she almost didn't hear the gun. They started off and Maddy ran hard. It quickly became a two-woman race, and judging by the look on her face, Jennifer couldn't believe that Maddy wasn't backing off. Twice Jennifer hissed at her the warning, "You're dead meat!"

It didn't help matters that this event was the last in the meet between the two rival schools, or that the teams were only six points apart. This race would determine the winner of the competition.

Final lap. Maddy realized that she could only lose. If she won she'd lose because Bear would pummel her, and if she lost, she'd lose because she'd bring her team to defeat. And Jennifer would break their tie, winning the year. As she frantically contemplated her options, out of the corner of her eye, she caught sight of Bear on the sidelines cheering Jennifer on, and as Maddy passed him, he growled and lunged at her. Her blood, racing through her veins, turned to ice. *I'm going to faint!* She looked back at him—*maybe I just imagined it!?*—and with that one small deviation in her form, she was off-balance. Her left toe caught her right heel and she went hurling to the ground.

Jennifer flew past her, spitting on the track just inches from Maddy's head. Maddy was sure she heard Jennifer say, "Good choice, loser!"

She got to her feet and tried to catch up, but with less than two hundred yards to go, she was too far behind to recover. She finished sixth. The team was supportive in spite of their loss, and on the bus ride home, many shared their momentous mishaps, offered to help ease the pain of what many knew to be a long, lonely ride home. She wasn't sure, even now, whether she'd fallen purposely or accidentally, only that the threat of Bear was unsettling, and that her concentration at the finish line wavered. In that tiny breach, an error that cost her—and her team—the meet.

Sitting with her boyfriend Dave Babcock helped. She met him when they were paired up in science lab. He was a sixth form star soccer player, sprinter, and one of the most popular guys in school. Maddy was still not sure why he'd asked her out, not that she minded being his girlfriend, just that she didn't know why, when there were so many girls who liked him—*beautiful girls*—he'd picked her. They'd been going out for over a month, and as he put his arm around her, she sighed heavily and settled into him. He sensed that something wasn't right, beyond her defeat.

"You okay?"

Shaking her head, she made him promise not to tell a soul. The threat. The growl. The lunge. The fall. When they'd arrived back at Queensfield, Maddy was feeling a little better, mostly because, the whole time she was whispering her story to him, David kept turning his ear away and kissing her. Somewhere in northeastern Connecticut, she found she was repeating herself, recounting irrelevant details, feeling more electric every time their lips met.

Back at school, the dark, empty hallways felt and sounded different. Maddy's parents weren't coming to pick her up for another forty-five minutes. David had a car. He took her hand and without saying anything, led her to the auditorium. Behind the stage, it was dark, darker than the halls, and it smelled like musty fabric. It didn't surprise Maddy when he pulled a flask of peppermint schnapps from his backpack. Even though he drank and occasionally smoked Marlboro reds, he never got caught. *Maybe*, she thought, *because it never got in the way of his winning.* They each took a sip, and as the liquor started to warm their bodies, they started kissing again, but this time, something was different, and she knew they both felt it.

Maddy loved his hair—blonde, soft, and slightly curly. It reached past his collar, and his bangs were past his eyebrows. Both were, strictly speaking, against school rules. As his hair brushed by her neck, her stomach jumped. As she ran her hands through his hair, he kissed her lips, her neck, her arms. Kisses mixed with alcohol were electric. Their touches grew stronger and lasted longer. Maddy was on her back on a pile of mats, and David, moving to a fast song only he could hear, was on top of her. Maddy could hear only the pulse in her ear, and realized she could barely catch her breath. David sat up and took off his shirt. Then, both gently and very, very intently, he removed hers. The lightest touch of David's hands brushing her bare skin left Maddy nearly desperate for what she had never known before.

She pushed his pants to his knees. He in turn pulled at the tie at the waist of her running suit, rolling her bottoms down until they caught on her running shoes, their bodies touching, a single knot of nerves and heat. She couldn't quite catch her breath, and the rest of her hummed like it was plugged in, "Mmmmm…David…" She was looking at him through eyes half-closed, heavy with anticipation. His hardness against her thigh sent a tidal wave of want right through her.

Though they'd gone this far before, they'd both always understood that it was as far as it was going to go. He would be her first, and Maddy had stopped him, saying she wanted her first time to be special. "Everything but" had been enough for them both. Especially Maddy. Until now. "Not here, Maddy. Not like this." He kissed her again, sure she would agree. But Maddy pushed him away, and stood up, as if he'd slapped her. In a single movement, she pulled up her running pants and straightened her hair. She picked up her book bag and ran from the auditorium.

Later that night, David called her at home, trying to explain himself again. He told her that he'd wanted to do everything to her she wanted and more. He also reminded her she was the one who wanted her first time to be special. He cared for her and didn't want her to have any regrets—even though it was hard to stop, ha-ha. She only regretted that he stopped, and what she had wanted him to do to her was not connected to her rational plan for how her first time was supposed to be. Behind the stage, all she could think about was what it would feel like with him inside her and she wanted to feel it in a way that was beyond her brain.

He told her that if she still wanted to, on Saturday night there was a party at Jimmy Sullivan's. His parents were at their place in Palm Beach for the week, so the house was all theirs. Maddy and David were invited, and—David lowered his voice when he told her—they could use one of the bedrooms, *wouldn't that be special?* They wouldn't be on a pile of old mats in the school theater or in the back seat of a car. No, they would be in a queen-size bed, like in the movies.

She couldn't tell David, but it didn't need to be special for Maddy anymore, mostly because she couldn't concentrate on anything but the throbbing ache between her legs, and nothing could make it go away. Well, only one thing. Excited and a little nervous, Maddy agreed to go.

When Saturday came, she wanted to calm down, and remembered that since her father's heart attack, there was always a ready supply of Valium in his medicine cabinet. She took ten pills from the oversized vial, knowing no one would miss them, like the packs of gum she'd purloined years before. She put the pills, wrapped in a tissue, in her book bag, along with a number of heavy textbooks, and told her mother she was going to study at Victoria's. Katherine, sitting square in the large wing-back chair in the living room, waved to her from behind a fashion magazine.

She met David at the party, which was already well underway. She didn't want to take the Valium alone, so she donated six to the lucky winners of a heated game of quarters, saving two each for her and David. They each took a pill and drank a beer to wash it down. They danced close to the hard rock music. Maddy felt life's corners grow round. Dancing and kissing, and pressing and rubbing. Wordlessly, they left the dance floor and, arm-in-arm, they walked toward the large staircase leading to the bedrooms. To a bed. As they passed by, Jimmy raised his beer mug, foam slopping over the top, "Don't do anything I wouldn't do!"

Her only response was a weak laugh and a shrug. Dave quipped over his shoulder, "Yeah, Jim, that doesn't leave much!"

He turned to Maddy, "Jimmy's had so many girls, and he's so fucked up, he doesn't know how special this is."

The truth was, Maddy hadn't heard a word. Her whole body throbbed, and she could think of nothing else as they made their way upstairs.

From the landing, they could hear the music through the floor, which was vibrating to the beat. *This is special*, she told herself, *this is how I'd always wanted it to be.* The pills and the beer made everything thick and move in slow motion. They rocked gently to the music from downstairs. She kissed him hard as they stood by the bed. He sat her on the bed, kissing her, unbuttoning her shirt, unzipping her jeans. Pulling off her panties. Whispering words of passion, of love, of forever and always. Gently at first, then with more intensity as they were lost in their single rhythm and heat. They lay wrapped around each other until overwhelming thirst and the desire for fresh air overtook them both. They got dressed and went downstairs.

They passed the living room, where three members of the football team were funneling beer into the mouth of a girl, whose top looked like it had been ripped open: the overflow was caught by the running back, whose head was pressed between her naked breasts, while the linebacker, quarterback, and defensive end cheered him on.

In the game room, a couple was making out on the pool table. The girl pulled away to sing to the music and to take a sip from the fifth of Jack Daniels hanging from the hand that wasn't down his pants. A whole group of kids was standing outside on the back deck, smoking a joint; the sweet smell, drawn by the cross breeze of open front and back doors, filled the house.

In the kitchen, David grabbed a big plastic cup of punch for Maddy, and took a beer from the garbage can filled with ice for himself. She sucked down one, then two, glasses. As he put his arm around her to head outside, she stumbled.

"Dave, wait…. wait…something's wrong….I'm dizzy…" She sat down on the floor, right in the middle of the foyer.

"Hey, baby, what's up?" Trying to pull her back to her feet, "You okay?"

She shook her head, making all the blood inside her brain slam from side to side. "No…no…Dave, the room is melting and spinning, and I'm….not…okay."

He held her tight, kept rocking her, saying, "It's okay. It's okay."

The rocking made it worse. She needed to lie down flat. David's face grew large and distorted like in a fun house mirror. She whispered, "What's happening to me?"

"Its okay, baby. I'll bring you back upstairs to rest. You'll be okay." He half-carried, half-dragged her up the stairs. Looking upside down through the banister, Maddy thought they looked completely different. He put her back down on the bed, kissed her, and left. As she lay there, she could still feel the music pulsing under her, but now it sounded manic, frightening and dark. She spun into a bizarre and fitful state, neither awake nor asleep.

Some time later, she was roused by the sensation of someone kissing her hard on her mouth. And pinching her nipples. Still trying to process what was happening, she gagged as his tongue reached deep in her mouth. She pulled hard to separate her heavy eyelids. What she saw was blurry, but unmistakable: bloodshot, half-open, hazel eyes. Jimmy Sullivan's eyes. Jimmy Sullivan's hand up her shirt. His prying fingers trying to unbutton her pants.

"Hey…hey! Stop it…stop…" Though she was screaming, her voice was only a croak. She was still painfully dizzy and thirsty, and in her half-sleep, she felt unsure whether the dark and the loud and the smell of marijuana and stale beer was real or if she was dreaming.

"Hey yourself. Now Jimmy's going to have some fun too…" He wrangled her pants down to her knees and he was poking into her through her panties. She tried to pull away. She shook her head side to side violently on the pillow. She cried out, but all that came out was a hoarse plea.

"No!!" She swallowed hard and tried again. "Come on Jimmy, stop it, it isn't funny…stop!" Her words were swallowed whole by his mouth coming down hard on hers, his tongue snaking down her throat. She was awake now. Dizzy and slow. Nauseated and terrified, she tried to roll herself off the bed.

"Where are you going, you little slut? You came up here with David, and now it's my turn!" He let out a loud harsh laugh, "Yeah, you're gonna fuck Jimbo, all right. I'm calling it a house tax!" As he held her arms tight over her head with one hand, he tried again to wrestle his way into her with the other. He kissed her hard again, and, for the second time in as many hours, it was all about sex, but the words Maddy spoke were punctuated differently. "Don't stop!" was now "Don't! Stop!"

When he thrust his tongue deep into her mouth again, Maddy bit down. Hard. As hard as she could, stopping only when she felt the flesh of his tongue give way between her teeth. Salty, thick blood filled her mouth. He jumped off her, falling backwards off the bed when his foot got tangled in his pants which were bunched around his ankles. "What the fuck?!" He tried to catch the blood as it gushed from his mouth. "Get the fuck out of my house! Fucking whore!"

Jimmy staggered out of the room and down the stairs, leaving a trail of expletives and blood in a crooked path behind him. She spit out a mouthful of blood and tried to get up off the bed. Her head was so heavy, she could only manage to pull up her pants still lying down. She was trying to pull herself up by the heavy wooden post at the foot of the bed when Dave came rushing in.

"What's going on Maddy? What did you do to Jimmy?! He's screaming curses—and your name—and bleeding like a stuck pig. They're taking him to Hartford Hospital!"

"*Me* do to *him*? He was trying to open my pants. He was kissing me!" Shivering, like she'd been outside too long without a jacket. "David, he called it a house tax!" David pushed her hair out of her face. Wiping blood from her mouth with the corner of a sheet, "He's just a little too wasted for his own good, Maddy. I'll bet tomorrow he'll be sorry he got out of line."

Maddy thought he'd be sorry alright. *Every time he moves his tongue.*

Maddy struggled to remember what happened, and she wanted to know for sure that Jimmy hadn't…but everything was so fuzzy. "He didn't……I mean, I don't think he…."

"Its okay, baby. I'm here now. I'll take you home."

He held her tightly as he steered her, pale and shaking, down the hall, down the stairs and out the front door.

"It's okay, Maddy, you're safe now."

I don't feel safe, she thought.

They drove along in silence, and a friend followed them in David's car. He brought her up the steps to her front door, but neither of them wanted her parents to associate him with her present state, which looked bad and felt worse. As she leaned against the door, he rang the doorbell, ran down the walk, hopped into his car, and drove away. Maddy was not sure how she'd ever imagined her first time ending, but she was sure that this wasn't it. As the thought pricked at her, Katherine, her silk bathrobe and slippers sparkling in the light from the foyer, opened the door. Maddy, leaning hard into the door as it opened, fell into a near-fetal heap in the front hall.

"You weren't studying at Victoria's, were you?" The look, even through eyes bleary with tears and exhaustion, was unmistakable. Pure disdain, and fury for lying, intended to finish what was left of the red-eyed, pale and limp girl curled up on her foyer floor. Maddy felt, like a shipwreck survivor washing up onshore, too tired to move from the encroaching tide. In light of what had really happened to her that night, Katherine's rhetorical question was so absurd, the lie so many lifetimes old, that a laugh bubbled up from her, as involuntarily as the first gasp of breath from the newly-landed survivor.

She lay on the floor laughing uncontrollably. Then she was crying. Katherine was clearly not amused, but she realized there was no point in trying to let her have it, it would be like trying to stick a pin in a glass of water.

Still, "Well, young lady, as far as I'm concerned, you can stay right there until your father sees you in the morning!"

With that, Katherine left Maddy, still laughing like a hyena, on the foyer floor.

In the morning, she awoke to the fur of her sister's slipper tickling her nose and her sister's voice, like an ice pick in her ear, "Mo-om! Why is Maddy on the floor in the front hall?" Then, without the slightest touch of concern, "Did she die?" From the kitchen, over the violent scrambling of eggs, her mother's answer was loud and terse.

"No she didn't, Robin, but when she gets up she'll wish she had!" Maddy stayed in her pseudo-sleep position for as long as she possibly could. Finally, when every cell cried from thirst, and when her bladder was going to burst if she waited another second, she started moving. Very. Slowly.

She climbed the five wide steps and closed herself in the bathroom, her heart pounding in her ears from the effort. After she peed and brushed the sweaters off her teeth she thought about taking a shower. Her body was rank with sweat and shame, but a shower was more than she could manage. Instead, she had to satisfy herself by scrubbing the whole night off her face. She opened the bathroom door and braced herself for the confrontation. It was waiting in the kitchen.

"Well, well, how nice of you to join us." Her mother slammed the silverware drawer with what Maddy felt was excessive force.

Maddy tried to look better than she felt by pulling her shoulders back and putting a smile on her face. Both adjustments required tremendous effort. Every noise was amplified in her ears, which were filled with a hollow ringing, like it was coming from the end of a long, empty hall.

"And what exactly did you do last night young lady, since you obviously weren't at Victoria's studying?"

Katherine, meting out her wordless punishment, was pulling every pot and pan out of the cabinet and dropping it onto the floor, where each landed with a heavy metallic clang, until she feigned finding the frying pan she had been looking for.

Maddy had time to think about what she was going to tell her mother, but when the time came to actually explain herself, she didn't know what to say. She started with the truth—a truth she thought her mother would believe.

"I did go to Victoria's to study like I told you I would. We got invited to a party, mom. We'd finished our work and thought it would be no big deal. It was a little wilder than we'd thought, and I guess I can't handle my liquor, because I got so silly on two beers, well… you saw."

Maddy went to the cabinet and took a glass. She went to the fridge and poured herself a glass of orange juice. Mercifully, one long sip sent coolness through her veins saturating every dried out, cavernous space in her body. As she drank, she watched her mother over the top of her glass, hoping, *praying*, that her innocent confession would put the matter to bed, which was where she desperately wanted to go herself.

Maddy had poured and almost finished a second full glass of juice when, finally, Katherine spoke. "You should know better." Dishwasher door slam. "I know we've taught you better than that." Silverware drawer slam. "And lying to me about where you're going?! Who do you think you are?!!" Cabinet door slam. "And you can forget about those new shoes I promised you. Wear your old ones—and remember that was your choice!"

Maddy just shrugged her shoulders.

Katherine really couldn't argue with no response. "Fine. Go to your room, and stay there until I tell you to come out."

Maddy, secretly triumphant and barely able to hide her elation, tried to look contrite. She gently set her empty glass in the sink, turned and left the room.

CHAPTER SEVEN

2:59 P.M.

The ambulance siren's scream worked its way dully into Maddy's ears. It was far away and fuzzy like the voices that wafted upstairs that night with the tainted punch. She was aware of the pressure of the straps across her chest, thighs and feet holding her down against her will, like when Jimmy...

Unlike so many years ago, Maddy wouldn't resist. The drugs were taking her away, and she was going to let them pull her, stretching ever more taut the cord that held her to life, until, mercifully, it would snap, letting her go.

Fall 1977

The student secretary handed the crisply folded blue note to Maddy, who was right in the middle of dissecting a frog's stomach. "It's from Mrs. Hautain."

Maddy knew who it was from: she recognized her perfect Palmer script and her trademark blue fountain pen.

"Dear Madeleine, please come see me in my office. Sincerely, Mrs. Hautain"

"Do I go now?" Maddy wasn't sure if she was asking the secretary or the teacher. Both responded, "Yes."

Maddy didn't mind leaving: the smell of formaldehyde was making her nauseated, and it didn't help that the team next to them pulled a whole fly out of their frog's stomach, causing the girl right next to Maddy to throw up in their shared lab sink.

When she got to the office, Mrs. Hautain, silver-gray in a heather tweed skirt and jacket, a pair of large, pearl-button earrings and a tight pearl choker, brought her into her office where an attractive, well-dressed woman was seated.

"Madeleine, this is Denise Harding, admissions officer from Rome University in Atlanta, Georgia. She is here for interviews today, but, due to the long flight, and the timing of her meetings with our students, she would like to go for a run first. Could you please take her out? She is unfamiliar with the area and would feel better if she went running with someone who knew her way around. I thought you wouldn't mind. Was I correct?"

Maddy thought about the options: biology lab, where she was sitting in the piercing, malodorous reek of formaldehyde and vomit, dissecting a dead frog with flies in its stomach, or running, where she would be set free outdoors on this clear, warm spring day, surrounded by the scents of cut grass, flowers, fresh air and pine bark mulch.

"I'll get my sneakers."

She trotted to her gym locker and changed into her running clothes. Maddy returned a few minutes later to find that Denise had also changed into running clothes and was stretching out against a gryphon at the school's entrance. They ran across the lacrosse field, then off campus, Maddy leading the way toward Talbot Mountain. As they ran, they chatted. New England. The weather. Queensfield.

Denise asked Maddy how she did on her SATs, which schools she'd applied to, and why. Maddy told her that she'd done pretty well on her college entrance exams. Maddy went on to explain to Denise how her mother had taken a compass and drawn a neat circle radiating two hundred miles out in every direction from Hartford. It was her mother's wish that Maddy apply to schools in the area. But Maddy had other ideas. She wanted to go to school farther away. She told Denise it was so her parents could never wake up on a Sunday morning missing her and decide to pop over for a visit, but that wasn't really it. She had the feeling that even if she went to school close to home, her parents, both busy with their own lives, wouldn't come to see her.

As they ran, Maddy pointed out landmarks: Mark Twain's house, Noah Webster's birthplace and the reservoir. Denise spoke about Rome, the city of Atlanta, and the South. She painted a picture of an intimate, genteel city that housed a well-regarded, lively, liberal arts institution. Maddy was enchanted by the sound of it. Rome offered a warm climate and was a lengthy and fairly expensive plane ride from her parents. Denise promised it would provide her with a liberal arts foundation on which she could build any career. And it was made all the more enchanting because Denise spoke in a slow southern drawl, every word coated in honey. Denise invited Maddy to come take a look during Rome's 'Senior Weekend,' which was coming up. Maddy agreed to think about it.

As they stretched out against the gryphons, Denise offered Maddy a piece of advice: the application deadline hadn't passed; Maddy should apply for Earl Decision. And that she'd be remiss if she didn't come see what Rome was all about before making up her mind.

She flew down to Atlanta in March for Accepted Senior's Weekend. High school seniors who've been accepted to Rome visit for a long weekend to help give them a taste of university life. Though she'd flown before, usually to visit her grandparents in Florida, this trip was special, as she didn't know what awaited her at the other end.

Her mother deposited her curbside at the American terminal at Bradley International Airport—a grandiose name, thought Maddy, for an unimpressive, small building with two threadbare gates attached to an airstrip, wedged between farms of dense tobacco covered in white gauze and fields of grass, still dormant, bounded by stone walls, dotted with cows.

Even though she was wearing the warmest coat that science had to offer: a blue down jacket with fabric designed by NASA, a neon orange quilted lining, and a gray and white fake fur trim collar, the cold rawness of the day was still a shock to Maddy. She pulled her hood tight around her head, picked up her small buckskin Samsonite suitcase, and made her way to the gate where she sat, people-watching, until her flight was called. Maddy was anxious to see what Rome had in store for her—for the weekend, but also for her future. As the plane took off, she looked down at Hartford: a bleak sea of gray and brown. She opened a puzzle book.

The first thing she noticed when the plane descended into Atlanta was that it looked like another planet: deep red clay was visible through random breaks in the vast expanses of green trees and grass. The city of Atlanta was a cluster of glass and granite buildings emerging from the middle of the gently rolling, clay-dotted hills. Maddy noticed how the city sparkled in the sun. And how new everything seemed. As she moved through the airport, she was amazed at how many people said 'hello,' or more often, 'how y'all doing.' Even if these strangers didn't speak to her directly, they would acknowledge her with a nod, or by tipping their hat. People were wearing hats! Unlike in New England, where if someone spoke to her on the street, her first reaction would be to hold her purse closer and stare harder at the ground, here she was all alone and felt perfectly safe.

She rode by cab to the school, never closing her passenger window. The whole city smelled damp and green. She smiled when she glanced down at the parka on the seat next to her and realized if she went here, she would never need again—which, to her surprise, felt just fine with her.

The cab dropped Maddy off in front of the administration building, where a student guide, dressed in overalls half-masking a Grateful Dead T-shirt, checked her name off, gave her a "hello my name is" tag and a marker, and sent her to stand with several other accepted seniors. Name tag firmly affixed to her now too-heavy crew neck Fair Aisle Dean's of Scotland, she joined the group as he led them to their assigned dorms, depositing her and a few others outside Alabama Hall.

The pale pink limestone building, complete with terra cotta tile roof, was nestled coolly in the shade of several very large pecan trees. It reminded Maddy of the Ante-Bellum mansions in *Gone with the Wind*. She'd only been standing for a minute when she was approached by the two freshman girls who'd agreed to share their room with her for the weekend.

"Ma-dah-laihn!" She was immediately taken with the deep southern drawl and the petite, sandy blonde girl who held out both her hands in warm greeting. The other girl, whose accent was also southern, but different, offered to take her suitcase.

"How'd y'all know it was me?" Maddy liked the way the 'y'all' tripped off her tongue.

"Your name tag, silly!"

They all laughed and headed up the stairs. After putting her things on the cot the school had delivered to their already-cramped room, they brought her back to the lobby, where the tour was to continue. Though she'd only known them for a few minutes, she hugged them and told them she'd be back soon. They smiled and waved as she left, making Maddy feel like they'd been friends for years—or like family.

The main quad was a verdant expanse surrounded by regal oak and pecan trees that shaded red-roofed buildings that looked like Tara. Maddy thought that Queensfield's green paled in comparison. Students clad in T-shirts and shorts played guitars, read books, and sunbathed. A dog with a red bandana collar was playing Frisbee with what Maddy assumed was his master.

The tour continued to Fraternity Row, where over a dozen antebellum mansions stood watch over a shady tree-lined street on the northwestern corner of the campus. Guys were everywhere. They were out front of their houses, sitting on porch swings and rockers. Walking the Row. One ATO fraternity brother was washing his car while rock music blasted from speakers set into the house's front window.

Maddy felt like she could have entered the set of a promotional film. She could almost hear the producer, scripting this prosaic scene—"Ready camera one! Okay now two handsome shirtless boys, leave the TEP house, wave to the group of students on the upper road, get into the metallic blue Camaro, blast Led Zeppelin, and leave. Good! Aaaaannnd cut!"

When Maddy went to dinner in the cafeteria, she was struck by how much better the food was here than at Queensfield. She went through the line, only to be greeted by a large black woman in apron and kerchief. Maddy thought she looked like she'd fallen off a bottle of syrup.

"Whashuwan, dahlin'?" Half a day in the south, and Maddy already understood.

"May I please have the fried chicken, and some corn?"

The woman smiled broadly, and served her up some of the crispest, most un-institutional chicken she'd ever seen or smelled. "Okra, dahlin'?" Maddy wasn't sure.

"Try it honeychil'." Without waiting for an answer, she scooped a spoonful of fried okra onto Maddy's plate, 'Sgood!" Then she added a thick yellow slab of corn bread with a wink, "Ah made it mahself. Y'all eat up now, y'heah? And welcome to Georgia!"

Maddy nodded. Her mouth started to water at the aromas emanating from her tray. *I could really get used to this!* Maddy sat down at a table with other visitors, where she proceeded to eat every bite.

Before she'd realized it, the sun was going down, and Maddy watched the sleepy campus come alive. There were parties that night and Maddy went with her roommates and other visitors to taste a slice of Rome's social life. The parties were fun, and southerners—or was it college students, Maddy wasn't sure—really like their beer!

By the time she left on Sunday she had a list of names of people to look up when she came back, and the name of one girl with whom, Maddy thought, might be a good roommate. Rachel was from Charlotte, North Carolina. She was southern, genteel, and sweet. And while she didn't have a lot on the surface in common with Maddy, she was Jewish. It was a kind of baseline likeness that made Maddy think that living together would be okay. Maddy had heard the horror stories involving young nubile co-eds let loose—literally—for the first time in their lives. Kids who left roommates displaced for whole nights, lazy teens that lived in piles of dirty laundry and clutter, and dorm mates who "borrowed" things like cash and jewelry without express permission, or any intention of returning them whatsoever. From what Maddy knew about Rachel, she liked her. She was direct, intelligent and serious, and she thought it was better to go for the devil she knew over the devil she didn't. Almost on impulse, she asked Rachel to room with her.

Just before she left for home, Maddy went to the upper floor in the admissions building, which sat majestically, its long granite stairs running the length of the building, at the far end of the quad. There she found Denise, the interviewer she'd taken running at Queensfield.

"Hi Denise. I don't know if you remember me…"

"Of course I do—a beautiful Talbot Mountain run. Maddy Berger, right? How are you?"

"I'm great—I love it here. It feels more like home to me than where I've lived all my life…" The decision was made as she was speaking, "I'm coming here!"

Denise smiled knowingly, like it was clear to her that Maddy would attend all along. They hugged goodbye, and Denise promised to take Maddy for an historical running tour of Atlanta when she returned in the fall. Maddy couldn't believe she'd have to wait until the end of August to come back.

It was a long wait. The seniors, knowing they were going to be dispersed far and wide for college, started drifting apart. Over the next few months what had been a fairly cohesive group—or more accurately, many small groups that somehow all fit together—slowly disintegrated. The loosening of ties made the transition to the next phase of their lives easier in some way. Though by doing so, many senior rites of passage were merely a charade for those, like Maddy, who had moved on and were just going through the motions without caring anymore who won the "big game," or who the prom king and queen were.

At the end of a great summer, Maddy's parents help her fill the station wagon with everything Maddy owned—stereo, clothes, plants and keepsakes. She'd also bought a fan, a hot pot and a new comforter that she and Rachel had color-coordinated with each other over the summer.

The three of them started the long drive in high spirits. Maddy sat in the back and said goodbye to her house, her street, her town. Unlike leaving Newfield, she didn't feel sad about the life she was leaving behind, and was excited for what lay ahead. She read a book and chatted absently with her parents, who felt it was their duty to announce road signs, landmarks and interesting people, most of which blew past Maddy before she could look up. It really didn't matter; she was already mentally at school, unpacked and ready for a new life.

After two days of driving through rainstorms that did nothing to dampen the smell from the nearby paper mills, they arrived at the school. Katherine and Jack helped Maddy unpack, while all the time looking around, commenting on the beautiful surroundings and kind people, apparently pleased. They had never been in the South before—southern Florida wasn't so much the South as a warm suburb of New York—and were not quite sure what to expect. Maddy thought that her father seemed relieved it wasn't like a scene from the movie *Deliverance:* no 'crackers' with toothless grins and torn overalls leering at his oldest daughter. He had to admit: Atlanta was a modern city and the campus was beautiful.

They loved meeting Rachel, who was already unpacked, hanging posters while chattering away excitedly as they brought the last few things from the car.

As they prepared to leave, her mother looked her in the eye and said levelly, "Do your best—and don't do anything that would embarrass us." Maddy noticed that her mother, while serious, was smaller and less threatening than she'd seemed in the past. Her father smiled, winked at her, and said, "Don't go upstairs in any of the frat houses!"

They hugged and kissed her, then left her to meet her dorm mates and to unpack. For the first time since elementary school, she got to start at ground zero forming new friendships at the same time as everyone else. She was assigned to live in Alabama Hall, coincidentally the same dorm she'd stayed in for Senior Weekend.

Her floor quickly gained the reputation for having a close-knit group of fun-loving girls. They formed a softball team, which they called the "Bama Bombers." They had shirts made up with their nickname and number on the back. There was "Goose," Marie Geise, who took "00," goose eggs. Debbie aka "Doobie," was the cross-hatched number sign. Angelina Sanchez, called herself "Amante," lover, and the number "2." Maddy settled on "Mad Dog" and "69." When one of their games made the underground newspaper, including a photo of "Mad Dog 69" at bat, Maddy wondered if her mother would find it embarrassing. While she didn't send a copy home, she did tuck the clipping into her journal.

Rachel quit rushing a sorority just a few days in, saying that even if she had to spend the rest of her college weekends

in the library, it was better than subjecting herself to such
scrutiny, letting others decide if she fit in or not. Maddy didn't
like the idea of being talked about, about having things she said
and did and wore dissected to determine if she fit in. But she
liked the idea of having nothing to do and no one to do it with
less, so she pretended she didn't care who said what about her
and pledged the less dressy of the two Jewish sororities on
campus.

Her pledge class went to dances, parties, movies,
scavenger hunts and intramural games with the fraternity
pledges. There was a house for almost everyone, Good Ol'
Boys, Party Animals, Jocks, Nerds. Maddy saw that most of
their parties were with either of the two Jewish houses.

She first saw him sitting at the far end of the quad.
Actually, she heard him. He was playing guitar, surrounded by a
small circle of people. She was drawn to him, and wanted to sit
with the others who'd gathered around him. He was muscular
but lean. Blonde curls peeked out from under the bandana he
wore like a kerchief, but tied at the back. As she crossed the
quad, she saw that her Big Sister was one of the women
listening to a mellow version of what she could now recognize
as the Grateful Dead's "Panama Red." Patty waved her over
and introduced her to the group, and to Ricky Hellman. Trying
not to look as attracted to him as she felt, she forced her eyes
around the circle, looking at the others who'd gathered around
this magnetic and very good looking guy. Everyone but Ricky
was female. She realized that while she felt a strong attraction
to him, the others, including Patty, did as well.

Maddy had many friends in common with Ricky, and so
she saw him often. She was thrilled when, on a few occasions,
he invited her to his house to hang out with him and his four

Roman roommates. Hoping each time for him to finally realize that she was the one for him. Each time she was disappointed.

She learned that Ricky was taking a girl named Monica to the semi-formal fraternity dance when Monica came to her room asking to borrow a pair of dress shoes. Maddy had turned down several invitations in anticipation of Ricky asking her and a few more once he didn't.

When the night of the dance came, Maddy spent it in the library. She sat in a carrel, telling herself she needed to study, practicing formulas for her statistics class, but she kept looking at her watch, trying to figure out whether Ricky and Monica had finished hors d'oeuvres, or started dancing, or what. She was making herself miserable, and decided to bum a cigarette and take a break.

She was sitting on the front steps of the library blowing smoke rings, trying to get one ring inside another, when one of Ricky's housemates wandered by. She remembered him from Ricky's house the night of the "Red Party." He was in charge of the music, playing Grateful Dead, Bob Marley and the Wailers, and Little Feat concerts, while a few hundred Rome undergraduates, or Romans, dressed as devils, red crayons, and Clifford the Big Red Dog danced and partied all night long. His name was Ben Gold.

"Hey Maddy." Ben veered off the sidewalk and came over to where Maddy was sitting.

"Hey Ben, what's up?" Maddy drew hard on her cigarette, trying to make a perfect smoke ring. She looked at him, noticing for the first time, that though his frame was smaller than Ricky's, he was lean and very muscular too. He shrugged and showed Maddy his backpack. "Nothin' much. P-Chem midterm on Thursday."

As he spoke, he seemed to become distracted. Maddy knew the look: many a student was terrorized by the specter of the weekly exams in physical chemistry, known to all to be the toughest class in the whole school. In Ben, Maddy thought, it made his big brown eyes bigger. While he had left the fraternity the prior year, he'd remained friends with many of the brothers. But tonight he was on his own.

"Why aren't you at the semi?" As he spoke, he sat down next to her, and watched her smoke, waiting, she guessed for an answer.

She tried to make it sound like it didn't really matter. "I didn't want to go with anyone, and anyway, Ricky took Monica."

She thought of Tep and Rich and Steve who'd all asked her to go, and wasn't sure why she'd said no to them. "No biggie. I figured I'd spend the night studying statistics."

She would have rather been with Ricky, but she didn't mind spending the night with statistics. The numbers and patterns were always a solvable problem, which was a challenging kind of fun for her. When she got an answer that didn't make sense based on her intuition, it pricked at her temples. More often than not, on a quick recheck, she'd find a mathematical or other silly mistake.

"You know? I'm done studying, Ben. What are you doing now? How about I buy you a drink at the tavern?"

"Sure Maddy, I'm game. I was only going to go home."

She stood and turned around to retrieve her backpack. Her back to him, she heard him whisper, "Ricky's not your type." Maddy smiled, not sure whether he had been talking to her or to himself.

They walked and talked to the edge of the campus, crossed the street, and sat down at a table in the popular, just-off-campus pub/restaurant. While they waited for the waitress to return with their pitcher of beer, Maddy suggested they play in the arcade. She reached into her backpack for her wallet. She reached deeper, and then she started unzipping all the pockets, searching hard for something that clearly wasn't there.

"Oh my God, Ben, I am such a loser! I invited you out for drinks, and I don't even have my wallet!"

Maddy felt that if the floor would open up and swallow her whole—chair, backpack and all—it would be a blessing.

"Hey, don't worry about it, I have mine, and I'd love to buy you a drink, a few games, and anything else the night might call for."

Even though the room was dark, Maddy was pretty sure he was blushing.

They drank, played Centipede, Asteroids and Pac-Man, and drank some more. Maddy realized she was having a good time, and told Ben so.

"Me too, Maddy! You wanna come back to the house? I have something there I think you'd really like!" Maddy thought this sounded like that weak "come see my etchings" line, and said so, not sure that would have been so bad.

He leaned in a little closer, so their heads touched and Maddy caught a trace of his cologne. She liked it. He lowered his voice.

"My brother is a medical resident in Miami. And he just sent me a package of pure cocaine. We could try it and then maybe go hear some music?"

She'd tried it once before and liked it. It had made everything clearer and more alive. It was at the Red Party, with Ricky. Ricky, who was at the semi-formal gala. He was probably through with dinner by now, maybe even dancing a slow dance. The whole idea that she was thinking about him depressed her. She looked at Ben, considering carefully his generous offer and trying not to consider Ricky at all.

"Maybe just a little? Then we can definitely go out. I think it's Southern Rock Night at PJ's Pub…"

Walking back to Ben's car, Maddy smiled to herself. *Maybe this night isn't going to turn out the way I thought it was going to after all.* He opened the door for her. Again, Maddy found she was smiling.

Riding to the house, she was not surprised to learn that he'd bought the dark green BMW 2002 with earnings from his part-time job as a University Hospital medical researcher. She liked watching Ben shift gears, his taut clutch press and precise gear shifting made it clear he was driving the car and not the other way around. He was controlled and serious, not like Ricky's carefree playfulness at all, but attractive in a different way. He made her feel like she was in capable and mature hands. And here she was, comparing him to a guy she knew she'd never have. *Get over it,* she thought, *get over him. Why do I keep thinking about someone who doesn't want to be with me?* She couldn't help feeling that maybe it was because somehow she didn't *deserve* more.

She was looking through the communal album collection that covered the entire fireplace wall from floor to ceiling when Ben returned from his room. He carried a framed picture of five guys standing with their skis all lined up, like a male version of the Rockettes, against a snowy mountain; each young man, smiling and tan, except around their eyes—where goggles had been. In the framed picture, she saw Ben on one end, his arm around his brother. Sitting on the frame was a razor blade, a dollar bill and a little folded triangle of paper that looked like a finger football.

"Wait till you try this—it's really good stuff. Practically all rock." Maddy wasn't sure what that meant, but it was clear it made it better. Using the razor blade Ben shaved a little bit of white powder off the solid rock, chopping the bits into a fine powder.

"We'll only need a little taste." He and Maddy alternated hovering over the skiers, snorting up thin, short lines through the rolled up dollar bill. Maddy, not wanting to seem too inexperienced, watched him carefully, touching her finger to the tiny flecks that remained on the glass, then rubbing it on her gums, just like he had. They put on a Grateful Dead album. As the cold metallic taste dripped down her throat, she sat back against the couch, enjoying how the drug froze up her insides and made her feel so *sharp*. Chatting easily, if not a little frenetically, they had listened to several album sides—*Skull and Roses, Eat A Peach, Dark Side of the Moon*, when Maddy, not wanting the intensity of energy and sensation to fade, asked, "Can I have just a teeny little taste more?"

Ben shaved off a little more for Maddy, who loved the way it made her feel—the clarity was intoxicating. She was sure that if she could get enough of this into her system, she would be able to cure cancer or disarm a bomb. They laughed, and talked easily, and as the night wore on, the lines on the mirror got fatter and longer until there was no more. Licking the creased magazine paper that the coke had come folded in, Maddy was surprised at how strong her desire for more was.

"Hey Ben? I was just thinking that we should get some more of this stuff. I mean, not for right now, but for later." As she said it, she knew that she meant later, but not much later. Maddy realized at that moment she didn't care what was happening at the dance.

"Well, we could call my brother and see what's up in Miami..." Interrupting him mid-sentence, she picked up the Princess phone on the night table and handed it to him. "Definitely!" She sat back, trying not to look as anxious for more as she was feeling. He called his brother, and though it was just after midnight, Jake was not only awake, he was throwing a party. It was so loud on the other end of the phone, his brother's speech so slurred, Ben could barely hear or understand him. After a short back and forth, Maddy understood from Ben's side of the conversation that Jake had invited him—them—to Miami.

When Ben hung up the phone, they rationalized that Miami would be a good break for the both of them. Ben threw a bag of weed on the couch, along with a Bob Marley album, and some rolling papers, asking Maddy to roll a few joints for the road, while he put a few clothes into a duffel bag. Ben then brought Maddy back to campus to pack up what she needed.

Opening the door to her dorm room, Maddy was hit with the stench of pepperoni pizza and cigarette smoke. Her roommate, Edna, was sitting on her bed, solitarily polishing off three slices of a large pizza at once—a pizza sandwich. They were matched in the housing lottery. The fact that they had nothing in common convinced Maddy that no one read the request form she'd dutifully filled out the prior semester. By the end of the first week, it was clear they were not only mismatched, they were also incompatible. Maddy drew an imaginary Venn Diagram of each of their traits and there was zero overlap. Two separate circles. For the whole year.

On a small campus, there were only a few students that weren't part of the fabric of the community. These loners clung to the corners and, loosely, to each other. Edna was a loner. She didn't want to be friends with anyone; she wanted to be left alone. Which was impossible because the dorm rooms were tiny and Edna was large. It was crowded in their room, and Maddy was neither happy nor comfortable, but at least Edna didn't get into her stuff or her business. But a good roommate, the kind of confidante and cohabitant Maddy had hoped for, the kind she'd still be friends with long after graduation, was definitely not Edna.

Standing in front of her closet, trying to pull out the few things she'd need for a weekend in Florida, she was trying to imagine what she'd be doing, but she could only picture sitting on a beach and eating at Morrisons, as she used to do with her grandparents. A bathing suit. Her toothbrush. A Rome T-shirt and a pair of shorts. Contact lens case. On her way out, she realized she had almost forgotten her glasses. *And God knows what else.*

She slung her backpack over her shoulder, and turned to leave.

"If anyone calls for me, tell them I'm in the library, okay?"

Edna looked up from her pizza absently and brushed a few crumbs off her dingy Abba T-shirt. She narrowed her eyes conspiratorially, "Where are you going, really? You just dumped all your books from your backpack onto your bed and packed clothes and stuff."

Maddy really didn't want to tell her anything, but figured that *someone* should probably know where she was. *In case of an emergency.* "I'm going to Miami. With Ben Gold."

The conversation had taken Edna away from her snack long enough. Turning back to the pizza box, she picked up the last slice and folded half of it into her mouth. With a strap of mozzarella hanging off the corner of her mouth, and without looking up, she said, "Yeah okay. Bye." Maddy closed the door behind her, not sure what lay ahead, but certain it was better than going back to Edna.

Ben and Maddy rode for several hours in relative quiet. Maddy was having some regrets about what she had packed. *Did I bring beach shoes? Pajamas?* Maddy sighed heavily. Ben asked her if she wanted to stop at the next rest stop for a quick break. They'd been driving a while and were still in Georgia. They'd heard two whole cassettes all the way through and Maddy was getting tired.

"How far away is Miami anyway?"

"I told you before, it isn't too close. Door to door, it's about an eleven-hour drive. Speaking of which, you wanna take over the driving when we break?

Maddy bit her lower lip. "Remember when I said I could drive a stick? Well…." She looked at him as he nodded.

"I guess you're going to learn right now." He pulled off at the next rest area. They stretched, used the bathrooms, grabbed a snack, and returned to the car. Ben met her on the passenger side.

"I'll help you." He smiled at her and handed her the keys. "Go on."

She got behind the wheel and listened as Ben explained the theory behind driving a stick: disengaging the engine by pressing in the clutch, shifting into larger gears as the car gained speed, which helped her understand what she was trying to do. This was nothing like learning to drive for the first time, no yelling or crying, just a kind and gentle voice guiding her through the steps as she shifted gears and the car got up to speed.

Once she was in fourth gear, it was just like every other car. She drove for a few hours and when it was time to switch, she put the car in neutral, pulled over to the breakdown lane and stopped. They alternated like this every few hundred miles until the sun started to peek through the trees.

Ben was not what Maddy would have expected for someone who was raised in the Five Towns of Long Island, New York. He was less a product of the materialistic and ostentatious community than he was a practical and down-to-earth second son of German and Romanian parents who had immigrated from eastern Europe to Israel before coming to America. He knew his story well and told it with pride. His mother's family had come from Berlin to Palestine when she was only three years' old. Her older brother, her only sibling, had fought in the Israeli underground army, the Irgun. Ben's father was born to Romanian farmers and had trained as a doctor in France before coming to Israel not long after the Jewish State was founded. They met at a rally for young Zionists, and were soon married and working to fulfill their obligation to populate the country. They had Jacob, and, after some years of trying, Benjamin. When Ben was four, they gave up the pioneering life of Israelis and moved to the United States, where they believed they could make a new life for themselves, in a land safer and more full of promise for their sons than where they were.

Unlike all his Long Island friends who were shipped off to sleep-away camp every year, his parents would bring him to visit their family in Israel every summer, usually after visiting someplace they'd never seen. By the time he graduated high school, Ben had been to countries in Africa, Europe and Asia. Maddy attributed his keen sense of direction, of world geography, and of history to his first-hand experience of so many varieties of people, places and cultures. She was impressed, maybe even a little envious; Maddy had gotten lost many times, sometimes even on the way to places she'd been before. But more than anything, she felt safe around him, sure he knew where he was going.

Though the night was gone, they were still mostly in party mode. By the time they hit the Florida border, they'd smoked both of the joints Maddy had rolled and listened to a bootleg Grateful Dead concert tape so many times through, Maddy and Ben could sing it all, including the part where someone in the audience yelled, "Aiko Aiko!" Finally, just before noon, they pulled into Jake's apartment complex.

They got out of the car, stiff from sitting so long. Ben led the way to the entrance and buzzed Jake's apartment. No answer. He looked nervously at Maddy and buzzed again. This time a woman's voice came on the intercom, "Hu..hu..hello?" It was Marci, Jake's wife, and it was clear from the confusion and sleepiness in her voice that they had woken her.

"Hi Marci, it's me. Ben."

"Ben?"

Maddy shot a nervous glance at Ben. Ben was calm, assuring her it was just that Marci forgot, or that Jake forgot to let Marci know that they were coming. *Maybe because Jake didn't think we'd really come.* "Ben, we should go."

He laced his fingers in hers and together they pressed the intercom. "Um, hey Marse, we called last night, during your party, and uh, Jake said we should come down." Standing there in the light of day, shifting uncomfortably from sandal to sandal, Maddy was embarrassed to admit to herself that she'd just driven twelve hours for drugs. *This is exactly what my mother warned me not to do!* Remembering, or maybe just happy they were there, Marci laughed and buzzed them in.

Empty glasses and bottles covered every horizontal surface. Leftover food crusting over in serving dishes and on platters was piled on the kitchen floor. Dirty plates and balled-up paper napkins were overflowing trash bins, carpeting the floor. Maddy quietly followed Ben and Marci through the maze of people sleeping on the couches and on the floor. A hazy aura made the room hard to figure out. It seemed to Maddy, though, that if it were clean, it was probably very nice. What furniture she could see was modern and sleek.

In a whisper, so as not to wake the remaining party-goers, Ben made introductions and then , Marci told him to put their bags down in the bedroom—which, she added, had a locking door and a *waterbed.* At this, Ben and Maddy both smiled at each other and laughed—they knew that they were just friends and that they were here for another reason altogether, even if they were now too tired to party anymore. They figured they'd set Marci straight a little later, maybe when Jake came home.

Over the next half-hour or so, the various revelers woke and slowly made their way out into the day. Maddy and Ben helped Marci clean the small apartment, then Marci took them to the beach for a little afternoon sun. They spent the afternoon sleeping on the beach, dipping into the ocean every so often to cool off. As the sun started to set, they headed back to the apartment, where Jake was sitting on the couch still in his scrubs, newspaper on his lap. The TV was on, but music was playing on the stereo, drowning out the sound. A glass of red wine sat on the coffee table, next to the rest of the paper, a copy of *National Geographic* and a stethoscope.

Jake explained that as medical residents, they both had heavy work schedules, which rarely allowed for the two of them to be home at the same time. When they'd learned they had twelve hours off *at the same time*, they threw a party, "Work hard, play hard," he said, as he refilled his wine glass.

Their whole existence seemed to Maddy to be electrified, buzzing with an intensity, which, while not familiar to her, was exciting, kind of *sexy*. When Jake told them he didn't remember Ben calling, or even that he'd invited them down, he'd laughed it off as unimportant. They were together now, and that was all that mattered: they would make the most of the time they were together.

Maddy noticed that Jake's dark brown eyes and smooth, olive skin were strikingly similar to Ben's. Jake was a bit shorter and a little thicker than Ben, but they were clearly brothers. They even sounded the same. Maddy liked him immediately.

In Coconut Grove for the night, they were at the restaurant bar splitting a pitcher of beer before dinner, when Jake whispered something to Ben. Ben nodded then tipped his head and looked at Maddy.

"What?" Maddy didn't know what they were talking about, but she was sure it had something to do with her.

Jake pulled out three white pills from his shirt pocket. "Quaaludes, fresh from the pharmacy."

"It's like drinking a six-pack, but without the fullness or the queasiness of that much beer." Ben took one from Jakes outstretched hand, tossed it into his mouth and washed it down with his beer.

"Well…"

"This is a completely safe dose, it'll just give you a really mellow buzz."

He placed one pill in the center of the ring Maddy's beer left on the cardboard coaster and popped the other into his mouth.

"I am a doctor who prescribes medication all day long, so you can trust me."

She washed the small white pill shaped like a baby aspirin down with her beer. Before she knew it, they'd finished dinner and returned to the bar. When Ben slid his hands up her back, Maddy felt a charge run from each of his fingers right through her. He held her gently, and pulled her close. Whatever was happening was evolving in slow motion. *Probably the Quaalude*, she thought. Slow enough to realize they were going to kiss. And to dismiss the idea it was the Quaaludes that made it feel like the most natural thing in the world.

"Ben…" Exerting the slightest resistance to his frame-at-a-time movement toward her, Maddy didn't want to stop, but she didn't want to change what was so calm and easy with him: their friendship lacked the drama found in the "serious relationships" she witness up close in some of her sorority sisters. She liked how it felt to be with him, and was afraid of what would happen if they were more than friends.

His gaze steady and intense, he looked straight into her eyes, "Maddy, I don't know what we're doing, but it feels so right with you. I want to be with you, not just tonight but tomorrow and the next day and the day after that."

Maddy's arm slackened. There they kissed, and Maddy knew her world was changing forever. He led her from the dance floor, and, claiming they were tired, got Jake to take them back to the apartment.

As she lay close to him, matching his breathing without trying, she wondered: What were they going to tell Ben's housemates, her roommate, and her sorority sisters—especially Patty? Surely, the people they'd left behind just a day before would expect some explanation. She decided not to worry about it. It felt right, and they'd just have to cross those bridges when they got to them. They ate a quick breakfast, packed their bags, and headed back to school. It wasn't until they'd left the state that they realized they had no drugs. Somehow, it didn't seem to matter to either of them anymore.

Within days of getting back to school, Ben helped Maddy move in with him. She gladly left Edna behind and brought all her stuff to Ben's house off campus. As if his room were made to accommodate the two of them, her clothes, music and plants mingled easily with his. Not only did her stuff fit, but she fit in. It was like a family. Ben and his three housemates took care of each other. Food shopping. Laundry. Dishes. Best of all she was out of the dorm, away from Edna, who, Maddy was sure, was as glad to have the small, smelly sty all to herself as Maddy was to leave it to her.

They studied well together, quizzing each other for tests and proofreading each other's papers. Ben was pursuing medicine, while Maddy concentrated on business, hoping one day soon to become an accountant—a job she understood paid enough to get her off her parent's financial support. The older she'd gotten, the more she realized how they had used money to control her—it had been that way since she cleaned the basement for a quarter, when she was in reality being paid off to stay out of the way. Her parents would not support her unless they agreed with her. Mostly it was her mother: Katherine wanted Maddy to do and be what made her look like a successful parent. Maddy could hear her yelling *how do you think that makes me look?* Maddy would be forced to take tennis lessons, and Katherine would bring home tennis skirts and cute tops, which Maddy had to wear to the lessons she hated. Katherine didn't care when Maddy told her she really wanted to paint. Maddy wanted a guitar, but her parents told her she wasn't musical, so she babysat for two years to save enough to buy one for herself. Being away at school had opened her eyes to the many other, much more honest, ways parents related to their children, and she suddenly felt anxious to get out from her parents' financial control.

While she'd told her mother about Ben, she hadn't told her *everything*, only the stuff she thought she'd want to hear. The stuff Katherine would be sure to repeat at book club, or her weekly bridge game. She omitted the part where she'd moved from the dorm and was now living in a house off campus with Ben and three of his friends.

Katherine would call Maddy early every Sunday morning. Edna would tell her the same thing every time: Maddy was already at the library. Then Edna would call Maddy at Ben's. Maddy would call her mother from Ben's bedroom. Maddy's friends couldn't believe that her mother didn't suspect something, but Katherine never brought it up, and Maddy played along.

One Sunday morning, the phone rang at Ben's. Maddy picked it up, expecting Edna. It wasn't, and Maddy immediately assumed the worst. "Mom, what's wrong?"

"It's your father, Madeleine. He's had another episode and he's in Hartford Hospital."

"Episode?"

"Well, yes, he had a heart attack on Friday, and they performed another quadruple bypass on him yesterday."

Maddy's mind flashed back to his first heart attack, and his subsequent operation. This time, she wasn't even surprised to hear about it two days after the fact. As much as Maddy wished it were different, that she could be trusted and feel included, she was not. And would never be. She tried to tell herself it was just how her mother chose to handle these matters, but the dismissal was hurtful. She pushed the feeling down, as she had so many times before, in order to deal with the issue at hand.

"I'll come home today, okay?"

"You don't need to, Madeleine. He's supposed to come home the day after tomorrow and everything is under control. I just wanted you to know, and I really didn't want you to worry."

She hung up and told Ben, who'd understood enough to already begin mobilizing. He got her a flight while she packed. He drove her to the airport and she was in the hospital before dark that evening.

"Dad?" The first time she'd seen him like this, she had emerged from her grandfather's coat. Unlike the last time, four years ago, the doctors were predicting a good recovery.

"Hi Pumpkin." His voice was weak, but his color was good, and his hand, though filled with tubes and tape, was warm in hers.

"I can stay for a week. Ben said he'd talk to my teachers for me. The doctors say that you'll be home in a few days. I can help mom and keep an eye on you." She told him how Ben had helped her that morning, and was surprised at how much love she felt for him at that moment.

"You can keep away from that boyfriend of yours for a whole week?" He winked.

"Sure. It's not like we're engaged or something."

"Not yet, Pumpkin. But seeing how well you two of you get along, it wouldn't surprise me one bit."

Two days later, from his bed at home, Jack insisted that she returned to her classes, but Maddy was pretty sure he was sending her back to Ben.

CHAPTER EIGHT

3:06 P.M.

The feeling of being pulled away from things that had once grounded her was physical, but it was more than that. As she slipped further from the grasp of the paramedics, like a kite caught in a cross breeze, she was being pulled away harder and faster by a force she could feel, but couldn't see—tethered to her own existence by a single, fragile thread.

Fall 1985

"I'll get it!" By the second ring, Maddy knew that Ben was not going to pick up the phone. Since they'd been married, he rarely did, claiming it was never for him anyway. As usual, he was right.

"Hey Kevin, what's up? Where are you?"

"I'm home. What's up with you?"

"Me? Nothing much—I'm just doing the Sunday puzzle."

The New York Times magazine's crossword puzzle was one of Maddy's weekly activities. For years now, every Sunday she'd sit for a couple of hours and devour the puzzle. This week's was easy. She'd figured out the puzzle's theme, so she was almost finished. She was happy to work the last little corner of the puzzle while shooting the breeze with her only and beloved brother.

In their collective memory, Maddy and Kevin had fought only once with one another. Only once. They were seven and ten years' old. Maddy had won a dollar bet and Kevin refused to pay. She wanted her money and she wasn't going to let him welsh. They went from trying to get or keep the bill to yelling, then to pushing, then to wrestling each other to the ground and hitting. At one point, one of them slammed the other into a wall.

Jack was had been sitting upright in his armchair in front of the TV, green-side at the Masters. In one swift move, he flew off the couch, grabbed them by their collars and smashed their heads together like cymbals. End of argument. Maddy realized they both cried—not because they were hurt, but because each feared that their father had hurt the other. It was an epiphany. They were not rivals, nor were they jealous of one another. They cared deeply for and about each other, and knew they always would.

She remembered a time on her parent's boat that her brother closed his finger in the hinged door to the head. While he cried in pain, Maddy screamed, inconsolable, until her father could assure her that Kevin was okay. She was hysterical at the thought that he might have lost his finger, and she calmed down only after her brother showed her his finger, purple and swollen, trying to smile through teeth clenched in pain, bending his finger as best he could, so she'd know he was okay.

"Well, Tony's friend Michael is making him a surprise thirtieth birthday party in Boston tomorrow night. I thought I'd stop over on my way up if you're going to be home."

Maddy and Ben had moved to Massachusetts a few years ago so Ben could attend medical school. Just a few months ago, they moved to Southwood, a tree-filled suburb south of Boston. Though they had no children, it was a family-oriented town where housing was affordable. They'd bought a house and were in the process of making it a home.

"Sure, Kev. We're here. Do you know about what time?"

Noon-ish?"

"Noon-ish is great." Maddy smiled to herself, knowing he'd show up anywhere between ten and four. She pressed the star key on the phone down and held it down-making the phone beeeep on his end. He replied by beeeeping back. They hung up laughing.

Years ago, and Maddy swears it was by accident, her earring hit a button and beeped while she was on the phone with Kevin. It had cut him off mid-sentence, causing him to forget what he was saying. She apologized, and, true to his sweet nature, he said "no problem." But then, just a minute later, he beeped her while she was talking. He said "Sorry!" but she knew he'd done it on purpose. She couldn't let him get away with that, so she pushed the button down again, interrupting him while he was talking.

"Stop it!" Beeeep!

"No you stop it!" Beeeep.

Neither wanted to be the last one to get cut off, so they kept talking. Though both were now adults, they wouldn't— they couldn't—let it go. It was as close as they would come to fighting as adults, this confrontation of wills, and the certainty that neither would let the other beep last never failed to make them giggle like children. Over the years, they'd each sent and received more than one answering machine message that was nothing but a beeeep—neither tiring of the joke.

The next afternoon Kevin did arrive, and he had a friend in tow. He introduced Maddy to Christopher, who, like Kevin, looked sharp, dressed for a party.

"Did you go to college with Kevin and Tony?" Maddy was half joking, there was no way she wouldn't remember meeting a six-foot-four-inch muscular African American who Maddy believed she had seen in a Gap print ad, hanging out in her brother's dorm room. Kevin interrupted her thoughts, with a poke on the shoulder. She realized she'd been staring.

"Where's Ben?"

"Hey Kevin! I'm down here in our bedroom wiring our new TV." There was a thud, a grunt, and then, "Uh, could someone give me a hand?"

Kevin practically dove off the couch, and like a synchronized swimmer, Christopher followed. Other than their like-timed movement, the two were physically mismatched. Kevin was small and square and strode casually, his Wallabies, jeans, black belt and black mock turtleneck creating a clean, classic look. Christopher was long and lean and he seemed to skim the floor. His body smelled of a spicy cologne and the silver points of his ostrich cowboy boots were sharp and shiny like a new dime. Maddy found his gracefulness a little unsettling. Maddy followed the trail of his scent down to the bedroom with her eyes closed.

The TV they'd just bought for the bedroom was sitting in front of the armoire that was to house it, a cable running from it up into the front of the open cabinet, and out a hole in the back that was punched out of the particleboard. By the time Maddy got to the room, Kevin and Ben were on each side of the unit trying to get it off the ground. Twice they 'one-two-threed' and nothing happened. They stepped back, not wanting to admit defeat, but needing a minute to catch their breath. Ben pushed the empty cardboard carcass out into the hall as if that was what had kept them from success in the first place.

Christopher stepped forward through the pile of Styrofoam and plastic, and in one fluid movement he bent down, picked the set up and placed it in the armoire. As he straightened, he checked his fingernails for damage—palms down. Seeing none, he re-tucked his Armani shirt into his pleated pants, ran his fingers over his hair, and checked the final product in the mirror over the bureau. What he saw was the reflection of Maddy and Ben gaping in amazement. And Kevin beaming with what could only be described as pride.

They headed back down the hall to the living room. Maddy turned toward the kitchen, pulling Ben in with her by the elbow, as Christopher sat down next to her brother on the love seat.

"Lemonade or iced tea?" Maddy tried to sound casual as she called to her brother and Christopher from inside the refrigerator. She opened the freezer and started to fill a pitcher with ice. Their answer, uttered in unison, was drowned out by the sound of ice crashing into the glass. She stuck her head into the living room to repeat her question, "You guys want something to drink? I have lemonade or iced tea."

What Maddy saw was insignificant, yet it changed everything. As she peeked around the corner, she caught a look between Christopher and her brother. Christopher had all of his attention focused on her brother, his eyes almost yelling what he could barely keep to himself, an 'I-am-so-in-love-with you!' look that Maddy saw and couldn't un-see. Christopher was leaning on the arm of the sofa; his crisply-pressed sleeve rested on a heavy, woven chenille throw. The sun was sending off rainbows from the diamonds at the ends of his Tiffany's twist bracelet. Like she'd taken a snapshot, Maddy's eyes saw the look, her mind captured the image. Her stomach jumped, as the whole picture was processed. Not only was she certain that Christopher was gay, she now understood he was her brother's boyfriend.

She felt like she had leaned up against the theater backdrop to the story of her life and it had just crashed to an unrecognizable pile on the floor. *How could I not have known?* Maybe her memories of growing up were nothing more than impressions and interpretations of what she saw and knew. There was so much more she felt she must have missed.

She was filled with a strange sense of loss. Her brother was still alive. She adored him. But now he was not going to have a wife who wasn't good enough for him, or terrific kids whose pictures he carried around in his wallet. She realized that she'd never have the sister-in-law to share family vacations and holiday cooking, nor nieces and nephews that she would spoil rotten.

The four of them talked about life: Ben's trials as a medical resident in a busy Boston hospital, and Maddy's stresses of heavy travel and grueling hours in public accounting. Kevin recounted recent challenges stemming from his role as second-in-command to their dad, and Christopher animatedly described vicious backstabbing and infighting that he confronted daily working in the design department of downtown's largest high-end men's clothing store. It wasn't too long before Kevin looked at his watch and stood up.

"Well, Maddy, Ben, it's time to go. As always, it was great seeing you!"

Maddy walked them to the door, and hugged Kevin and Christopher as they left. Once the door had closed behind them, Maddy leaned her head against it, trying to process what just happened.

"Boy, that Christopher is really…" Maddy was hoping Ben would finish her sentence so they could discuss the issue that was causing her to feel the ground shifting under her feet like it was made of snakes. Ben and Maddy did talk, but, since there was nothing concrete Maddy could point to, and since Ben was uncomfortable with the subject to begin with, the conversation was brief. Maddy decided that she would call her brother Monday morning, and just ask him outright. There was no reason to speculate or to jump to conclusions.

"Hey Kevin, it's Maddy." She thought about pushing the star key, but she didn't really feel like joking around. She kept seeing the image in her mind's eye, and playing out what it meant to her idea of what her family was supposed to be.

"Um, so, I have a question for you."

Unsure how to proceed, she knew only that she needed to know. She also knew that she'd always been able to talk to her brother and that he'd always be her brother.

"What's up Maddy?" *Just say it*, she thought, *whatever it is will be fine.*

"Well, it was great to see you and to meet Christopher on Saturday. He's a really nice guy…" She was finding it difficult to get to the point. No easy way to jump from the mundane to the question she'd called to ask. "I have a stupid question, and you don't have to answer it if you don't want to." After a deep breath, she said, "I couldn't help noticing that Christopher was, well, meticulous. I don't know, I got the sense that maybe he is, I don't know…gay."

The silence lasted forever.

"Um, Maddy, are you asking me to *out* him?"

"What does that even mean?" She'd never heard the expression before.

"It means to take him out of the closet."

"Hey, if he's in the closet, I don't want to 'out him' but if he's gay and people know, I'd like to be one of those people."

When Kevin finally answered, his tone was serious.

"Well, Maddy, yes, Christopher is gay."

Okay! Thanks and good-bye! She really wanted to hang up.

"Well, Kev, can I ask you another question?"

"Sure."

Before she spoke, Maddy realized she did and did not want to ask. More precisely, she didn't want to know, but she had to. To do otherwise would be living a lie.

"You went to a party of two gay guys with another gay guy…it made me wonder, are you gay too?"

The pause that followed was even longer than the earlier one.

What will he say? she thought. She knew. Deep down, she already knew, but she wanted him to know she knew.

A sigh. So soft, Maddy could hardly hear it. Then in a whisper filled with relief and nerve, "Yeah, Maddy, I am."

She sat down to keep her legs from shaking.

"Are you healthy, Kevin?"

So many programs and articles she'd seen addressed the high incidence of AIDS in the gay community. Since there was no cure, "unhealthy" was synonymous with 'dying.' And while she'd lost the brother he'd always thought she had, he was still alive, and Maddy prayed he was okay. She shut her eyes tight, an attempt to squeeze out the tears that had involuntarily sprung at the thought he might not be healthy.

"Yes."

Overwhelming relief caught in her throat. It sounded like a cough.

"Are you happy?"

"Happier than I've ever been, Maddy. You can't know how hard it's been to know, and not be able to tell the people who you love, and who love you the most."

That was virtually an answer to her third question, but she asked it anyway.

"Do Mom and Dad know?"

Even as she thought about them, she felt ill. Dad. Two massive heart attacks, bypasses, and a medical regimen that had made his body a breathing house of cards: this bit of information would be all that was needed to blow the house down.

And Katherine. Maddy laughed. She thought back to a discussion she'd had with her a few months back. Both Kevin and Robin were dating Christians. Robin was dating Ernie Roberts, a fellow law student, and Kevin was dating a woman named Maureen O'Shea. Katherine had made a comment that she would have really preferred her children to be involved with Jews. Maddy had spoken in defense of her siblings. She told her mother that in this day and age, it is a miracle to find someone whom you can love and trust, and who will love and trust you back. She told her that while a common religion arguably makes life easier, it shouldn't be the bottom line determinant of a relationship's validity. Maddy laughed, Maureen O'Shea is going to look pretty damn good to Katherine now!

"No I didn't tell them—yet. I was going to tell them at the beginning of the summer, but there was never a good time. Then they went on this vacation to Montana to fly-fish, and I promised myself that I'd tell them when they got home. Which was four days ago. The time has come. It wouldn't be fair for you to know and not to tell Robin and Mom and Dad."

Why couldn't she have kept her observations to herself? Then, maybe her brother wouldn't have felt he had to come out to their parents.

"Don't tell them, Kevin. You really don't have to say anything, you know. I don't mind being the only one who knows. I won't say anything! I promise."

"I do have to tell them Maddy, I do. Like I said, I have to tell them, for myself. It's been a long time coming, and I can't keep it to myself anymore."

Maddy knew he would do the right thing. He always did.

"Oh God, Ke—" Maddy was cut off as her brother beeped her.

She smiled. Everything had changed, and yet, nothing had changed at all.

Their parents were disappointed, as Maddy had expected. However, he was their only son and the chosen heir to the family business, so they couldn't bring themselves to sever their relationship with him. Over time, they came to accept his "lifestyle," as they called it, but without asking too many questions. They were actually relieved when he broke up with Christopher and started to date an adorable blonde named Chad. They had known Chad for years—he was a Queensfield grad—and in a true-life talk show twist, happened to be the boy that took Robin to her senior prom.

Kevin and Chad built a home together, and shared the responsibilities of dozens of houseplants and a female cat named Gus. When Robin announced her engagement to Dale Green—now a fellow law student, but on track to become a partner in his father's law firm—it was Katherine who suggested that Kevin bring Chad to the wedding.

"Just don't do anything…physical," Jack didn't direct his comment to anyone, not even looking up from his plate as he spoke.

Robin seemed genuinely happy. Katherine's firm-yet-unrelenting financial and emotional pressure on Robin had successfully steered her away from a serious relationship with her Lutheran boyfriend, and for a while it seemed she would never find someone who was like him, who loved her the way he did, but who was also Jewish. The way Robin tells the story, when she first saw Dale, she felt like she'd been hit in the head with a frying pan, and that instead of seeing stars, little hearts flew around her head. She claims she said something incoherent, by way of introducing herself, and was snapped back to reality when he told her his name was Dale. She'd just broken up with a man because he wasn't Jewish, now here she was, already falling for a guy she knew Katherine wouldn't allow.

They talked for a while but Robin realized every minute she spent with him made him more appealing, which could only lead her to trouble with Katherine, so she tried to excuse herself. He insisted on knowing why she was leaving, and feeling like she had nothing to lose, she told him. He laughed in her face.

"Robin, I'm Jewish!"

She didn't believe him. He explained that it was a family tradition to pick untraditional first names. She still didn't believe him. He chanted what he remembered from his Bar Mitzvah. She kissed him hard on the lips and, from what she said, they'd been together ever since.

Maddy and Ben had been married for six years when Robin got married to Dale. Though Maddy was once where Robin was now, she'd come a long way from living like a college student. When Maddy looked at the lifestyle of a newlywed she wondered how it was that she and Ben had come so far so fast. Whereas her sister was living in a small, Spartan one-bedroom apartment with mismatched pieces of screw-together and donated furniture, Maddy and Ben were settled into their first home. It was furnished with sofas, tables, lamps and rugs, and Maddy had sewn many of the window treatments herself. All of Maddy's loving touches made it homey and comfortable. They were both working, allowing them to save for their future while enjoying meals, theater and travel. Maddy couldn't really explain how sometimes she felt a force at work, helping her succeed. She didn't take that sense for granted, but she didn't know where to direct her gratitude either.

Just after Robin and Dale's wedding, and maybe a little on account of it, Maddy swore to Ben that she heard her biological clock ticking. Not one to doubt her intuition, he agreed that although he was still working to buy into a group practice—while it wouldn't be easy—they could probably afford to have a child. Maddy reserved a table at a romantic restaurant for the weeknight, when, according to all her reading on the subject, she was most fertile. They ate oysters, had a little champagne toasting their soon-to-be family, and they went home. They fantasized about how much fun they were going to have "trying," and realized that for the first time, sex would be purposeful.

Maddy woke up in the middle of the night with a pang in her abdomen, like Cupid had shot an arrow in her belly. *Or maybe an egg had just been pierced by a sperm?* She knew that while it seemed too easy, and impossible to know for sure, she was sure she was pregnant. The next morning she bought a two-pack of home pregnancy tests, which she couldn't even use for a couple of weeks. She somehow managed to wait through the rest of her cycle, and though she wasn't even due to get her period for another day, she took the test, hoping for a "+" to appear in the little window of the stick that claimed to be able to "detect the hormone present with pregnancy as early as the first day of a missed period!" She watched as the blue line formed in the middle of the "test" window. Nothing changed in the middle of the "actual" window.

Two more days went by. She still didn't have her period, her breasts were swollen and sore, and she had since bought and peed on three more sticks. On the morning of the third day, just after the blue line formed on the test window, showing that the test was working correctly, a faint blue line broke through on the "actual" window.

Her hands were shaking as she put the toilet seat lid down and set the test on top of it.

"Ben, something is wrong with the toilet! Can you come look at it?"

"Be there in a minute."

He didn't sound enthused. She sat on the bed, waiting for what felt like forever until Ben finally came down the hall, plunger in hand. Maddy pointed casually, apologetically, towards the bathroom. Maddy watched him learn what she'd suspected for two weeks.

"You'll be a great mother, Maddy."

She nodded, hoping he was right.

"We'll be great parents."

Ben's parents were anxious to finally be grandparents. They had already decided on the names they wanted, shunning the too American "grandma and grandpa" as well as the too old world "bubbe and zayde" for "mimi" and "poppy." Miriam started knitting. Maybe it was because Maddy's parents were younger by ten years than Ben's, but they weren't nearly as enthusiastic about their impending "grand" status. When Maddy confided in her mother that she was pregnant, Katherine said, "But I'm not ready to be a grandmother yet!" And it was true. Maddy's parents were always busy with their friends playing golf and bridge, eating out, taking in movies and theater. It hurt that they didn't offer to baby-sit, or claim any names at all.

"Madeleine?"

The voice was her mother's, but Maddy knew something wasn't right by the way it caught in her throat.

"What's the matter, mom?" Since she got married, Katherine's mother rarely called on Sundays anymore. She preferred to wait until Maddy called her, where she would barrage Maddy with updates on family and friends. She would apologize, saying that she would have told her "the news" sooner, but since Maddy hadn't called, she hadn't been able to. Maddy often wanted to remind her mother that the phone was a two-way device, but deep down sensed her mother already knew this, so said nothing.

"Grandpa Berkowitz is in the hospital."

Maddy wasn't sure if that was to be the entire report, but when her mother didn't elaborate Maddy whispered, "What happened?"

"This sounds silly, Madeleine, but he has had the hiccups for a week, and he hasn't been able to sleep or eat, and the doctors can't make them stop. He's been in the hospital since Tuesday, and they don't know why he has them or how to get rid of them. They were supposed to leave for Florida last week, but couldn't go, on account of his hiccups."

Maddy thought about it for a minute, greatly relieved that her grandfather was alive, and that "hospital" wasn't a euphemism for "morgue." She remembered only a few months ago when she'd danced with him at Robin's wedding, he'd seemed so healthy and vital for a man in his early seventies.

Maddy sensed the underlying reason for the call was that her mother didn't know what to do next.

"We'll come down this afternoon, okay?"

Her mother seemed relieved to have the moral support, and maybe a free medical consult, from her son-in-law.

"That would be great. Thanks Madeleine."

That evening, Ben and Maddy were in Hartford Hospital visiting with her grandfather, who was grateful for the company. Bess sat stoically by his side, chewing her cheek. Maybe because Sam had only daughters, Ben had been like a son to him from the day they met. Ben and Sam would talk about life and business and sports as if they'd known each other forever, as if there weren't almost fifty years between them.

"I remember when you brought me here to visit my dad. You snuck me in under your coat." She took his hand, "You know that made a big difference, Grampa, right?"

He smiled. She didn't tell him that she was as worried for him now as she was for her dad back then.

Maddy and Ben returned home to Southwood, but the specter of Sam hung over them. His condition persisted for days, hiccupping even as he slept. All the while, doctors worked furiously to figure out why. Two weeks later they found the hiccups were a symptom of a larger and more serious problem: an inoperable and malignant tumor in his stomach, pressing on his diaphragm and causing his incessant hiccups.

Once again, Maddy and Ben returned to the hospital, but this time they knew better than to expect him to get better. He was already exhausted and growing thinner, and when they rose to leave, Sam broke down in tears, certain that he wouldn't live to be a great-grandfather. Maddy told him that he was a *great* grandfather, and that she would always remember the wonderful things they did together. She held his hand and retold the stories about going with him to the track in Florida and driving with him while he sang old songs. Out of nowhere, she remembered the time she'd gotten a "gold" prize ring from a box of Cracker Jacks stuck on her finger. She remembered sitting in the back of his car—her grandparents were taking her out to dinner—and when she tried to take the ring off, it was tight and it wouldn't move. She broke off the tiny pink stone set in four tin prongs, pulling and twisting, but the ring held fast. She had no choice but to tell her grandparents, who responded by pulling over and taking turns trying to pull it off. When it was clear they wouldn't be able to—her finger had started to swell up around it—Sam drove to the police station. An officer tried to soap the ring up and pull it off her finger. When that failed, he attempted to cut the ring off with huge wire cutters, but they were too big to fit between her finger and the ring. As a final resort, he put her finger into a drawer, and holding her finger firmly in place, he slammed the drawer closed with all his might, shattering the ring, and much to Maddy's surprise, doing no damage at all to her finger. They unceremoniously tossed the ring pieces in the trash can, and the three of them continued on their way to dinner, where both Bess and Sam laughed about the incident. Maddy laughed along with them, mostly from relief that they weren't angry with her. Rubbing the red, swollen knuckle, it wasn't as funny to her as it seemed to be to them.

Sam, who had been holding Maddy's hand while she reminisced, squeezed it, pulling himself almost to sitting. He put his other hand on her belly and spoke right to the baby, "Listen, you. I may not live to see you be born and grow up, but you should know that I'll be watching you!"

Although Maddy and Ben had committed to being strong on the outside, while Sam spoke, they exchanged a glance that made it clear they were both broken on the inside. They tried to be positive, insisting Sam would be the "sandek", the one honored with holding the baby during his *bris*, the ritual circumcision that would take place on the eighth day after birth. Or, if it turned out that the baby was a girl, Sam would be the one they'd honor by having him carry her into the sanctuary of the synagogue for her ritual baby naming. Privately, they discussed names for both boys and girls that would honor Sam's memory by using the first letter of his Hebrew name.

They spoke at length with Sam about the plans that necessarily included him, but no one was convinced that by speaking it, it would be so. They visited him many times after that day. Each time they left the hospital, Maddy and Ben kissed Sam and joked about sneaking him out, but they all knew it was just a matter of time. He'd grown so much thinner and older in the time he'd been there, and the cancer was still eating its way through his body. It was inconceivable he would be able to hold out much longer.

At the beginning of Maddy's sixth month of pregnancy, one day after a short and difficult visit to Hartford Hospital, Maddy got the call: her grampa was gone. Even though it had been expected, when it actually happened it was still a shock. Maddy tried to pack but she couldn't see her clothes through her tears. She had worked so hard to convince Sam he'd live till the baby was born she had come to believe it herself. In a calmer moment, she called the rabbi of the large conservative congregation in their town. They'd never joined the synagogue in Southwood, as they planned to become members once they needed to send children to Hebrew school, still many years off.

Instead, they went to their parents' synagogues in Connecticut or New York.

Though he was a very busy man, and though the Golds weren't members, the rabbi took the call.

"Rabbi Modine?"

Maddy felt funny addressing a man she knew by reputation to be highly intelligent and forward thinking with a question as superstitious and plebeian as hers, but she didn't know who else to ask.

"My grandfather just died, and..."

"I'm so sorry."

The strength of his sympathy made her certain that the biggest issue was her loss, not how the logistics of the funeral were to be handled. It made it easier for her to continue.

"Thank you. He was a great man and a wonderful person and I'll miss him."

She paused and tried to work up the courage to ask him the question she'd called to get answered.

"Um, I'm really sorry to bother you with this, but I'm six months pregnant, and..."

"Oh! Mazel tov! His interruption emphasizing what was the *most important thing*.

"Thank you. But there seems to be some question as to whether I can go to his funeral or the cemetery. Some relatives and a few friends have told me that pregnant women are not allowed. Is that true? I mean, I loved my grandfather, and don't see why I can't go to his funeral..."

"Maddy, is it? There is actually nothing in Jewish law that says that you can't attend either the funeral or the cemetery. The prohibitions you are citing are *meises,* or stories, from a time when people feared that in the extreme state of grief that one feels at a time like this, a pregnant woman might cause injury to the baby. We know, of course, that this isn't exactly how miscarriage works, and that sometimes it's worse for a mourner, even if she's expecting, not to be at a funeral than it is for her to attend. The prohibitions on going to the cemetery weren't based in Torah law, but medieval eastern European superstition."

"Oh, so I can go, right?"

"Well, maybe." He laughed, and cleared his throat, "Judaism seldom provides a single answer to any question. Rather it offers us a way of seeing the world and understanding our responsibilities for caring for the earth and her inhabitants. The way we tell the story, the world was created for us for this very purpose. There is also one very good reason why you would not be permitted to go to the cemetery. If your grandmother is a superstitious woman who believes in these *meises*, your presence would likely upset her. In that case, Maddy, you need to stay home."

The sensitive answer resonated with her. For him the issues centered on life and loss, and not on following the traditions blindly and without regard to their impact on a real person's life. His answer was a great source of comfort, even though she still didn't know whether she was going to the cemetery or not. She thanked him and hung up, but she found herself playing out the implications of his answer not only for the funeral, but also for her questions about life after the funeral. For the first time, Maddy was exposed to an intelligent and modern Judaism, with plenty of space for tradition without dismissing the real world.

As it turned out, not only did her grandmother not mind if she attended the service and the burial, she wanted Maddy there. And not just there to sit and hear the service, either. Bess wanted all the family to *see* Sam before they sealed the lid tightly onto his brass-lined mahogany coffin. Even though Bess knew very well that a Jew was supposed to be buried in a plain wooden box, she couldn't bear the thought that he'd get dirty—he was always so immaculate.

Lying in his coffin with his eyes closed, his arms folded gently across his chest, it looked to Maddy like Sam was sleeping. She was greatly relieved to see that he no longer wore a paper-thin mask of pain on his face. Makeup had returned him to his healthy, pre-hiccup color, and he looked at peace. Maddy had never seen a dead body before. Looking at grandfather lying there, his mouth and eyes shut tight and straight, unmoving and unbreathing, she was reminded of the figures in Madam Tussaud's Wax Museum. She stared hard at his chest willing it to move. *Come back to life and be my grampa just a little longer!*

The family watched as they attached the heavy brass top onto the coffin and carefully wiped all the fingerprints off with a chamois cloth. It was Bess who laughed aloud at the thought that Sam would appreciate that chamois wouldn't leave scratches or smudges on brass. Laughing, but really crying, they began the service. Sitting among friends and family, they remembered him as the rabbi eulogized Sam using words like "moral," "fastidious" and "successful." They rode to the cemetery in three limousines, Sam alone in his, and his wife, their two daughters and their families following behind. On a chilly and damp New England day, they buried him.

The next three months were filled with name balloons for the coming baby being floated over the family. Maddy and Ben knew they were going to use the initial "S" in memory of Grandpa Berkowitz. Scott, Seth, Stephen, Simon, Samantha, Sophie, Sydney, Sarah. Every day the list grew. They quickly discovered that almost all the names they picked came with a story attached. Sarah was a mean girl in Ben's fifth grade class. Simon was a kid who Maddy knew in college who had a strange attraction to what seemed to be S&M films and leather clothing studded with metal. Seth was the name of an old boyfriend, a West Point cadet, who had broken up with Maddy so that he could date Mary, which wouldn't have been so bad if Mary hadn't been the friend that Maddy had brought up to West Point for a weekend to double date Seth's friend John. So many names just brought up issues; it wasn't easy to find one that suited both Maddy and Ben.

Over two weeks past her due date, and having gained significantly more than the recommended thirty pounds, Maddy delivered a boy. They finally had decided on a name—Stephen. Though they were not religious, the birth of a child, especially a boy, called for certain rituals that were as much cultural as religious. They gave him the Hebrew name Shmu'el— Samuel—after Maddy's grandfather. Their son's Hebrew name was given in memory of a man who'd been a model for morality and success and was someone whom Maddy had loved with all her heart. In naming Stephen for Sam, Maddy hoped her son would be blessed with those same qualities.

Eight days later, Stephen was brought into the covenant of Israel by what Maddy considered to be the most barbaric ritual ever inflicted on a new mother: circumcision. At the bris, Ben's father Saul was honored as the sandek. By this time,

Maddy had become a hormonal bouillabaisse, laughing one minute, crying the next, panicking, then calm, energized then exhausted. The very thought that her home, which had been blanketed in palpable peace and wholeness ever since Stephen came home, would soon be overrun with many of their closest friends and relatives, left Maddy slamming into unfamiliar and uncomfortable feelings. A lioness, she unceremoniously told a friend who showed up at the bris with her three-year-old daughter who was just getting over chicken pox to leave. Protective and vigilant for her defenseless child, yet she was about to subject him to circumcision. It didn't make sense, but somehow, as barbaric as it was, it meant something, not just to her family, but to all the Jews who had or would ever live.

Maddy's sister, Robin tried to help keep her calm.

"Here, Mad, put on this lipstick. It'll make you feel better."

She pulled the cap, twisted the tube and handed it to Maddy.

"You remember what mom always says—it's better to look good than to feel good!"

She was actually relieved to have someone telling her what to do, even if Robin didn't—couldn't—know any better than she did. Also she was exhausted. Just the day before, she opened the fridge only to see a box of breakfast cereal on the top shelf. She stared hard at it, as if by watching it, it might offer up its reason for being misplaced. When it hit her, she laughed out loud to no one there. She went to the pantry, where, sitting on the cereal shelf was the milk carton. Up until that moment, she'd thought she was doing well, having gotten showered and dressed before noon. According to all her reading on new parenthood, she knew not to expect very much—at least not for the first few weeks.

"Hey Maddy, you want a banana?"

Maddy nodded. She hadn't been able to eat all morning. Robin, smirking, asked, "Do you think I should get the mohel to peel it for you?"

It wasn't funny. Maddy was nervous about the mohel they'd hired to perform the circumcision. Cantor Abraham wasn't their first choice, or their second, or even their fifth. There weren't too many people qualified to perform ritual circumcision to begin with, and since May was historically a very busy month for births, they relied on the recommendations of friends to find someone available on Stephen's eighth day of life. All the younger, more popular mohels were already committed. Maddy was actually sorry she didn't have a C-section: those families could call and book a mohel well in advance. Finally, they succeeded in hiring Cantor Abraham. He sounded old on the phone, but they weren't prepared for the stooped, wrinkled man with unkempt gray hair and beard, in a worn, black suit and a yarmulke fraying at the edge who showed up at their house an hour before the ceremony.

Cantor Abraham came to Stephen's room and told them it was time to begin. They put the baby on a pillow and followed the mohel down the hall in a processional to the living room. Though his voice and gait were weak, Maddy was slightly comforted to note that his hands didn't shake. Her Uncle Daniel met them her in the hall, whispering a commentary into his video camera. She was glad he came. Even though Jack and his younger brother Daniel hadn't been in close contact, the importance of family events such as these served to bring the whole family together. Daniel had offered to be the videographer and Maddy was grateful. He was a free spirit, following his passions and the paths of peace. This personal liberty and concomitant happiness was probably the basis of the fundamental difference between him and his brother, saddled with work and family and living with a heart condition, thought Maddy. In any case, Daniel was an excellent photographer. Maddy tried to smile at him and the camera, but felt her eyes tear up instead.

The entire ceremony was recorded on the videotape for posterity: a slow pan of Cantor Abraham entering the room while chanting a Hebrew prayer, a close up of Stephen, cradled in a pillow as he was transferred literally from generation to generation, a pan of the men standing in the back of the room, each with his arms clasped in front of their belts as if the mohel might finish with Stephen and then come for them. The camera focused on Saul's face shining proudly, then panned to the baby, quiet, completely unaware of what was about to befall him. Then Daniel leaned in closer to get a good shot at the actual circumcision: the cut, a baby's scream, followed by a blur of shoes, a pan of the ceiling and concerned faces and frantic voices cutting in and out of the camera's view. While Daniel was a good photographer, he wasn't very good around blood.

The spirit of the moment was only temporarily diminished. Daniel revived, the service continued. As with all Jewish life cycle events, it was followed by food—the symbol of communal acceptance of the religious ritual that preceded it. They ate.

Many of Katherine's friends came up from Hartford just to bear witness and to share in the joy that comes with a new life. Six of her best friends, mothers of Maddy's childhood friends, made the trip in one car. Each lady was immaculately dressed and genuinely thrilled for Katherine's status as first grandmother in their group. *More excited than*

she is, thought Maddy. Mrs. Davidoff was sitting on the living room couch wearing a light pink suit, holding a glass of seltzer water and lime and a small plate of kugel, salad and tuna. The refined and elegant wife of a successful lawyer, she assumed an air of authority as she questioned the efficacy of hiring such an old man to perform this ceremony as Mrs. Levinson—a plate of bagel, lox and creamed cheese, whitefish salad and apricot Jell-O mold perched on her lap—tried to argue that, though he was old, the mohel had done a wonderful job. They were interrupted by Rachel, the eighteen-month-old daughter of a friend from their neighborhood, dressed in her party dress and Mary Jane patent leather shoes, who approached them. With a poise and vocabulary that rivaled many adults, she marched right over to the two women seated on the couch.

"Lookit!"

Mrs. Davidoff smiled at the young precocious child and put her glass down on the coffee table so the small girl could come a little closer.

"Oh honey, what did you find?"

Rachel shrugged and told them, "I found it over there." She pointed and a small, whitish, wrinkled wad dangled from her dimpled hand. Instinctively, Mrs. Davidoff put out her hand to take it from her. It wasn't until both ladies had given it a good examination that they realized they were holding Stephen's foreskin. The mohel must have dropped it on the floor. Rachel was standing in front of them, hands on her hips, waiting for an answer.

"Well, uh, dear, uh, I…"

"Oh, my... Yes…mmm"

"Oh...uh... I think this is, uh, trash, yes, trash, and I'll just wrap it up and put it right in the barrel." Mrs. Levinson winced as she clamped her napkin around Rachel's find. Mrs. Davidoff put her plate down. Shaking her head, "Honey, tell your mama to wash your hands. Mrs. Davidoff smiled too brightly as she rubbed her hands into her napkin.

CHAPTER NINE

3:08 P.M.

Maddy could hear beeping, buzzing and humming, but it was very far away. The muffled sounds were punctuated by agitated voices shouting sounds that Maddy couldn't quite make into words. She knew people were touching her, but she wasn't feeling their hands so much as sensing a dull throbbing their hands were radiating into her. She couldn't fight them. For a moment she felt powerless, but then she remembered. And knew they couldn't win. She clung to the hope that the force that was pulling her away from them was powerful enough to keep them from pulling her back.

Winter 1987

Two years of "firsts" with Stephen were all recorded on videos neatly labeled "Birth to Bris," "Stephen and the Snickers ice cream bar," "Stephen and Mr. Bubble" "Shhh—nap time," and "First Steps." Maddy wasn't sure what to do with "Swimming Lesson in Boca," the video of Stephen learning to swim. Watching her then thirteen- month- old shivering, crying, and begging "out!" only reminded Maddy that drown-proofing, at Katherine's insistence, was something she should have done differently. First of all their friends' children to be out of diapers, Stephen slept in a "big boy bed." He could also feed himself and brush his own hair and teeth. Maddy could see how fast Stephen was growing from infant to toddler, and how quickly these precious moments would be memories. She didn't want it to end, and realized maybe it was time to have another.

While Ben agreed, he made it clear that while he wanted another child, he wanted two kids and no more. Maddy realized that while they'd talked about having children, they never talked about *how many* until now. Maddy had always seen herself as the mother of at least three—ideally five—children. Many times in her life she imagined going to the supermarket with one child holding every finger on one hand while she easily pushed a cart filled with the week's groceries with the other. She knew it was unrealistic: even shopping with Stephen took both hands and even then, it wasn't easy, but dreams weren't required to subscribe to logic.

She understood she was only going to have three children if this next child was twins. From that moment, she imagined nothing else; Maddy could already see the fraternal pair: a boy and a girl. He was bigger than she was and a few minutes older. He protected her fiercely, and they shared that special relationship exclusive to those who share a womb. Stephen should have a little brother. And a little girl would make the family, mostly Maddy, feel complete.

This time it took several months, but considering Stephen's uncanny knack for picking the precise moment to demand a hug, juice or to be tucked in again, she considered herself lucky. Luckier because she knew she was having twins.

"Did you say that you did or didn't want to know the sex of the baby?"

The question was innocuous enough, but Maddy felt its impact like she was hit by a car.

"Baby? You mean there's only one there?" She had been running through the list of items she'd need two of: crib, car seat, high chair, when the doctor abruptly ended her fantasy. *He's wrong.*

"Check behind! Don't you sometimes miss a twin because it's hiding behind the other?"

The doctor was puzzled and unsure why she was so insistent.

"No, Maddy, there is only one baby here. And from what I can see, it is a healthy baby too. My question was whether you want to know you what it is?"

"No. It's the only surprise I have left."

As she spoke, she turned her head from the doctor, ashamed she was crying. In the process of turning, her eyes passed over the screen. At that precise moment, even though her vision was blurred by tears, there was no mistaking what she saw for anything else.

"It is a boy, right? I just saw boy parts, didn't I?" Maddy was asking, but she didn't really want to know. Unconsciously, her hand stroked her belly as she tried to process the loss of a daughter she'd never had. If she were only going have two children, one of them was supposed to be a girl: her shopping buddy, constant fashion consultant, sharer of secrets about boys—then men—and the one she'd school in cooking, needlework, make-up, braiding hair. There was supposed to be a balance in the house; Ben brought his love of sports trivia, history, and science. She saw herself cultivating their softer sides with art projects, gardening, and sewing.

The doctor tried to brush it off, aware there was more going on than he could see. "Oh, that? No Maddy, that was the baby's umbilical cord. Anyway, quit looking at the screen. You want it to be a surprise, don't you?"

She turned her head farther from the source of her disappointment. Maddy knew what she saw. One baby. A boy.

She tried for months to adjust to the prospect of life without a daughter. Then, just shy of three years after Stephen was born, his brother Brandon completed their family.

As she held him, she realized she only ever wanted him. Her thoughts of twins and a daughter dissipated as she smelled the sueded skin on his head and watched his tiny movements as he slept. And she loved him with all her heart.

Life in the Gold house was busier and more chaotic and before Maddy knew it, Brandon was three and Stephen, six.

"Where is Brandon's other flip-flop?"

Maddy was rummaging through the toy box, hoping to be able to finish packing for their first summer trip to Cape Cod. They were excited to be going away with the Englemans. Friends since their older boys were in preschool, Carrie and Maddy found the same things funny, and managed to make it feel like a party whenever they were together. Both were accountants-turned-recruiters, so they shared business acquaintances and work experiences. And of course, their boys.

One big difference. While Maddy grew up with a father whose poor health meant he could exit the picture at any minute, Carrie grew up without a father in the picture at all. From what Maddy had gleaned over the years, it was a snowy Christmas Eve, and her father was driving back from a shopping trip to downtown Boston, his trunk full of Christmas presents. He was killed by a drunk driver. Carrie was only two years' old when he died, which was too young to recognize the enormity of the tragedy of a young father senselessly killed, leaving behind Carrie, her three sisters and a young mother to raise the four girls alone.

Carrie was married to a man who had a daughter from a previous marriage, so she had a stepdaughter with whom she was very close. Maddy didn't begrudge her friend anything, but she couldn't help feel a twinge of jealousy that she had a girl in her life.

She pushed those feelings aside as she pushed aside a play workbench, revealing the missing flip-flop.

"Got it!" She threw it in her beach bag and ushered everyone to the car. "Let's go!"

The two families spent a fantastic week on the Cape playing on the beach, hiking, swimming, biking, mini-golfing, eating local seafood and lots of ice cream. They took turns watching the kids so the men could golf and Maddy and Carrie could hike. They each went out to dinner as a couple: free, for just a bit, from the rigors of parenting young children. They all agreed, it was the fastest week of the year.

A few days later, Maddy got out of the shower and a funny mark on her thigh caught her eye in the mirror. It looked suspiciously like a target lesion. She remembered reading about a new threat to New Englanders called Lyme disease. It was carried by a deer tick, and its bite caused a rash that looked like an archery target: a red spot, surrounded by a white ring, surrounded by a red ring. Untreated, the damage from these bites to a person's immune and nervous system was devastating. Maddy called Carrie and made her come over to look at it. They both examined the mark closely, but found no tick. Neither was an alarmist, but Carrie made Maddy get out her Polaroid camera and they snapped a picture of her leg,

"Just in case you need it." Carrie left, and Maddy tucked the picture in her night table.

A few days after it appeared, the mysterious rash faded. Maddy was relieved that the mark was gone. But, two days later Maddy woke up feeling like she had the flu. She was tired, stiff and she had a fever and chills. There must have been a connection and, though not one to go running to the doctor, she made an appointment with an allergist for that same day.

Once in his office, he made her feel foolish for even calling him with the "disease-du jour"—self-diagnosed, no less. He was quick to point out several reasons that would also explain her illness.

"Of course you're tired, you have two active young boys, don't you?"

She nodded slowly.

"The mark was probably from an insect a bite. You did say you were at the beach, right?"

Again, she nodded.

"Well, there are about a million biting and stinging things out there, and chances are a sand flea, a spider, or even a mosquito bit you. And you might even have had a slight reaction. I also believe you're the type who won't be satisfied unless I test you for Lyme—even though I'm pretty certain it's just a bug bite."

Not wanting to seem like the type of patient who would not be satisfied, she pushed the Polaroid back into her pocketbook. He left the room and returned with a thick, loose-leaf notebook. Thousands of pages on rashes and skin diseases printed on the thinnest onion-skin paper Maddy had ever seen. He dropped the tome on the table next to her and flipped it open to a page on Lyme disease. His tone made it clear he was trying to be nice but she was wasting his time, he pointed to a paragraph and sighed, "Here, if you read this, you'll see you don't have Lyme disease."

Maddy read as the nurse drew her blood, and convinced she had overreacted; thoroughly exhausted by the effort, she went home. The results of the blood test came by letter one week later—she was Lyme negative. She should have been relieved, but she wasn't. *What else could be making me feel so lousy?*

Her joints were very stiff, getting out of bed was the worst. Each morning she would look at the clock and calculate how many hours—and minutes—before she could get back in bed. Once she did get up, it felt like she was walking on glass. Her eyes were itchy and red: she looked like she had a bad case of conjunctivitis, but it didn't respond to treatment. Some days her eyes were red, some days they weren't. Some days her joints were more swollen than others, and she didn't know which kind of a day she was going to have. It was nearly impossible to keep up with her boys. Most days attending to their basic needs was the best she could manage. Now, instead of going to the park, she'd park herself on the couch and let them watch a movie as she watched the mantel clock tick off the hours until Ben came home from work. Mercifully, every day did end, and she would crawl back into bed, falling asleep within minutes.

She tried to chalk her exhaustion up to the cumulative effect of mundane, quotidian chores and the depression that can accompany going from having a high paid, well-respected, downtown professional career as an accountant-cum-headhunter to being an at-home mother of two, whose daily schedule went from juggling ten executive meetings to squeezing in errands between nap time and kiddie classes.

On a day Carrie had asked Maddy to watch her kids so she could help her mother move, Maddy was in so much pain she had to cancel. Carrie had been counting on Maddy, and maybe out of frustration, but more likely out of love, she made a suggestion.

"Hey, don't be mad at me for bringing this up, but do you think, maybe you should talk to somebody?"

Maddy, feeling guilty enough about her inability to help her best friend, didn't want to hear she needed psychological help.

"Listen here, Care, I don't need to go on Prozac. I don't know why I feel so lousy, but I'm only depressed because I'm just tired all the time. I'm probably dying from some horrid disease, and I just don't know it yet!"

When Maddy hung up the phone, she wasn't sure that she still had a best friend. And while it upset her, and she knew she should go over to Carrie's or at least write a long letter, but she was too tired to do anything at all.

For the next many months, Maddy grew increasingly depressed, as she grew certain she had an as-yet-unidentified terminal illness. It was just a matter of time until the symptoms were recognizable. The end would be quick to follow. It would happen smack in the middle of something mundane, she'd fall into a heap as her whole system shut down at once. When the doctors finally checked her out, they'd discover that she had only weeks.

One of Stephen's teachers finally said something to Maddy. She'd witnessed Maddy's shorter fuse, and her new wardrobe made up entirely of old sweatpants. She told Maddy that she was surprised that, as the wife of a doctor, Maddy had held onto a cold and cough for most of the winter. Maddy confided that she thought she was seriously ill. Aches and sharp pains, utter exhaustion and now depression plagued her, but no one seemed to understand. Not even Ben, who understood that she was tired, and tried to relieve her when he got home. But he was so busy building his practice that he tended to trivialize her symptoms, treating them individually, rather than try to find out what was causing them in the first place. He had reviewed the Lyme test results and would occasionally prescribe a medication so she wouldn't have to pack up the kids and go to the doctor. He'd listen to her complaints, then respond with stories of patients he'd seen during residency or in the ER that were similar, but worse. Maddy felt that unless she was spurting blood from her eyeballs or in several pieces, Ben wouldn't think it was anything to worry about.

Stephen's teacher listened patiently, then suggested Maddy see her sister, an internist whom she promised Maddy would help her. She explained that her sister was a young athletic woman herself who would at least understand where Maddy was coming from. Maddy made the appointment, suddenly terrified that as she got closer to the answer, she was also closer to the end. She was panicked at the thought that she wouldn't live long enough to see her boys grow up.

Maddy liked that classical music played quietly in the green and maroon paisley waiting room with large brass planters filled with lush green plants in the corners and by the window. *It's calming*, she thought. There was also a subtle incense or potpourri reminiscent of musk perfume she'd dabbed behind her ears and on her wrists back in high school. Flipping through the current edition of a women's health and fitness magazine, she thought, *just maybe I've come to the right place.*

After a short wait, a petite and soft-spoken woman came to the waiting room. "Madeleine? I'm Dr. Brown."

Maddy followed her back to her office, where they both took a seat, Maddy in a soft and well-worn club chair and the doctor in a brown, high-backed leather swivel chair that looked like an old catcher's mitt.

"Maddy, it says here on the new patient form that you are tired, and that your joints ache. Why don't you tell me what's going on?"

Maddy didn't know where to start. As she reached for a tissue on the corner of the desk, Maddy started to speak and Dr. Brown to write.

"Back over the summer I got a red and white mark on my leg. It was so unusual I even took a picture of it. Do you want to see the Polaroid?"

Dr. Brown nodded. As Maddy handed her the photo, she remembered the last time she'd brought it to a doctor. She noticed her hand was trembling.

Dr. Brown took the picture and held it under the green-shaded lamp on her desk.

"It sure looks suspicious, Maddy. Would you mind if we keep it with your record?"

Maddy shook her head as the Polaroid joined the questionnaire she'd filled out in the waiting room.

"Okay. Well, a few days after that rash, I got achy and had night sweats. Now, no matter how much I sleep, I'm completely exhausted. I had to stop running because when I did, everything hurt. I've had to stop living so much of what was my life because I either have a cold or a cough, something hurts, or I'm just too tired…"

As Dr. Brown made page after page of notes on a lined yellow legal pad, nodding silently, Maddy cried out all the pain and fear that had been building up over the last many months. At one point, Dr. Brown replaced the box of tissues on her desk. When Maddy's story had finished, Dr. Brown folded hands together on the desk and looked down at the yellow legal pad she'd filled with notes.

"First, Maddy, I don't think you're dying, but I believe you feel like you are. Second, I think you feel this way because you have Lyme disease."

Maddy wiped her eyes and looked at her in stunned surprise. Dr. Brown, noting her reaction, continued.

"There is a known problem with the test you were given: if you are tested for Lyme disease too soon after a bite, there is a high incidence of false negative. I'm fairly certain that's what happened to you. Third, I think you also have developed secondary infections because the disease has weakened your immune system."

Maddy was struck by how upset she was at the news that her ailment probably wasn't life threatening. Shaking, she realized relief was overwhelmed by anger. She wasn't going to die, but Maddy thought, *even a long life is very short, and I wasted months!*

"I would like to do an exam now and draw some blood, okay?" Maddy nodded; it was more than okay. As she lay on the table, she realized this woman knew more about her before the exam than any doctor she'd ever seen knew about her after.

Dr. Brown continued, "I want to take enough blood so we can test you for Lyme, MS, ovarian cancer, thyroid malfunction, rheumatic disorders and the presence of anti-nuclear antibodies—and some other rarer diseases."

As she drew blood, Dr. Brown told Maddy, "I'm going to put you on a month-long, mega-dose of antibiotics. The drug will take care of the Lyme, if that is what this is, as well as your bronchitis. I think you will start to feel better very soon."

I already do, thought Maddy.

Dr. Brown handed Maddy another tissue as she put her arm around Maddy and escorted her back to the waiting room.

"It must have been a tough time for you. You're going be okay, though, I promise."

She handed Maddy a prescription she'd written out and Maddy took the paper with one hand and hugged her with the other.

Maddy picked up the medicine on the way home and took her first dose in the car. Three days later, just as Dr. Brown had predicted, Maddy felt her old self reemerging. It reminded her of the time she'd bought a new chrome switch plate at the hardware store. When she peeled off the dull blue plastic covering it, the chrome underneath was shiny and new. She was like that piece of chrome with the plastic peeled off. For the first time in nearly a year, she had energy, no pain, and was more hopeful than she'd been in a long time.

She wasn't surprised when, a week later, the lab confirmed that she did, in fact, have Lyme disease. By that point, the diagnosis was moot: she was already busy finding ways to spend the rest of her life. Since she was young, her father's precarious health had always been a reminder of what is not promised. As a result, Maddy had never taken life for granted, but now she understood how every day was a gift. Her eyes opened anew to the simple patterned beauty in nature, and in the smallest things she used to miss completely, like how soap bubbles on the dishes she washed each had its own rainbow. So much of what her contemporaries were striving to achieve was unimportant. Striving was a misplaced focus altogether. *Being* was more important that than *being successful.*

She would ask Ben every month if he'd wanted to try for a third child, but he would say that he didn't. He said it was for her health, but she knew it was because he was focused on providing for the boys' education and for retirement, and the way he saw it, a third child would set him back a calculable amount of dollars and years. Their boys were growing up. Maddy felt that if she continued to wait, she would miss her opportunity altogether. She would be unable to conceive, or, no longer able to endure the exhausting hours another child would require, even without the unknown long-term effects of Lyme disease.

Brandon went to preschool at the synagogue Maddy had called six years earlier for advice before her grandfather's funeral. It was loving and gentle, and Brandon loved being there. They found their home life increasingly affected by the Jewish calendar: Shabbat dinners, baby naming and brises. While not "believers" per se, the Golds were happy to participate, never expecting anything more than a sense of community to come from it.

It was certainly not in Maddy's mind to be anything but supportive when she signed up for the "Challah on Shabbat" fundraiser. Parents pre-purchased a challah for every Shabbat in the school year. Every Friday, their child would be sent home with a loaf of the sweet, braided egg bread. Though integral to the Sabbath meal, challah wasn't meaningful to Maddy or Ben since neither had grown up with any level of Jewish observance in their homes. They bought the bread thinking that, at the very least, they'd be helping out the school and as a bonus, they knew that challah would make great French toast on Saturday morning.

The challah, however, had a strange and unanticipated effect on Maddy, maybe, she thought, because of her post-Lyme heightened spiritual awareness and appreciation, but there was something else. One Friday afternoon, Brandon came home, carefully pulled the bread from his backpack, and reverently placed it on the counter. He told Maddy it looked lonely without the wine and candles. While Maddy looked for candles that weren't from a birthday cake, he told her he'd learned the blessings, and that when they lit the candles, he could say them. Maddy put two beige candles and a cup of wine beside the bread, thinking Brandon was right: it did look more complete.

Once it was evening, Ben, Stephen and Brandon stood by the counter as Maddy lit the candles and Brandon recited the three prayers. They ate dinner and for a few hours the light of those candles and the echo of the sound of his small voice reciting the prayers transformed their kitchen. It was something Maddy would never forget.

Each Friday night, Maddy would light the candles and Brandon would say the prayers welcoming the Sabbath. There was something about the sound of a small child reciting the Hebrew prayer, the light of the candles brightening and warming their kitchen, the feeling of being part of something timeless and completely in the moment. As the four of them would sit at the table and eat their dinner, the whole experience felt elevated—*holy. All*, thought Maddy, *because of a challah*.

They started inviting Brandon's friends from preschool and their families over to dinner on Friday nights. The Shabbat dinners became an integral part of their social life. Maddy loved cooking and preparing for the dinner party and, since some of the families they invited kept kosher, she'd have to think about what she would serve and how she could prepare it within the constraints of the Jewish dietary laws. While the law was simple—the Torah stated, "do not seethe a calf in its mother's milk"—the way that law played itself out in a modern American kitchen was anything but.

Kosher meat had to come from a kosher butcher, absolutely no dairy products were to be used in the preparation of a meat meal, and only certain meat was considered kosher. Pork was not kosher, nor was shellfish. Some friends were particular about the dishes the meat was cooked and served in. Glass was okay, but metal and ceramic pans that had cooked non-kosher food weren't. They even had separate pots and pans for meat and dairy food! Maddy worked hard to make the meals "right." While she didn't understand much about kosher laws, she knew that she felt different when she ate a dinner that had been prepared with such care and attention to detail. She was part of something ancient and enduring.

Soon it was Rosh Hashanah, and rather than face the daunting logistics of traveling with two small children to Westham to attend services with the Bergers, Maddy and Ben decided to stay home and attend the services at Temple Zion. It wasn't just the home of the terrific Rabbi Modine and the site of Brandon's preschool, it was also the center of the community where so many of their friends were now gathering for the holidays. Maddy and Ben could sit together and listen to the big sermon that the rabbi delivered on this Holy Day, while their kids would be in babysitting with their classmates and playmates. Even if they didn't attend any other day of the year, every member of the congregation was present to hear something inspirational. Rabbi Modine was known for giving each person something to think about.

The rabbi began, "The Torah is a finite work with infinite wisdom. While the stories contained within it may or may not be true in a historical sense, the Torah is filled with Truth. We read a little bit each week, and every week we learn more truths, which, over the course of a lifetime allow each of us to live in a higher spiritual place. At the end of every year, we finish reading the entire five books of Moses. We then re-roll the scroll on which this story is told, and start the process all over again. Each time we read it, something new appears to each of us!"

He leaned forward and spoke softer. Everyone leaned forward in his or her seat to hear.

"I'll let you all in on a little secret. You are all very lucky to be here today. I'll tell you now that we're almost finished with the scroll, and the very first Saturday after Yom Kippur, we'll be starting all over again at the beginning. I challenge you to renew your commitment to Judaism. You can show up for the first reading and maybe agree to hear the whole story through once. It is like those old-time serials at the 'the-ay-ter'." He paused for effect, and Maddy remembered her father talking about the weekly shows he'd seen as a boy. The rabbi continued, "You won't believe what is in it for you."

Maddy knew that she was sitting in a room with about nine hundred other souls, but she was sure the Rabbi was looking at and speaking only to her. He was giving her an opportunity to learn a little more about what made that Friday night challah feel so special, and she knew she'd already accepted his challenge.

The first Saturday after Yom Kippur she got up early and went to synagogue. Though no one greeted her to make her feel welcome, she still felt like she belonged. The whole point of her going was to hear the Torah reading—the first chapters of the book of Genesis, the story of creation. She listened to the Hebrew, and followed along in the English. She remembered the story of heaven being separated from earth, and of animals, including Adam and Eve, being created, from Hebrew school, but when the Rabbi spoke about it, it wasn't at all like from when she was a child. His interpretation was mature, modern and metaphorical. The whole story was the first piece in a puzzle of human morality that made up the Torah. She wanted to understand how the pieces fit together.

Maddy went almost every week for a year. Ben stayed home with the children: while he didn't mind freeing Maddy for a few hours, he had no interest in going himself or bringing the boys, who wouldn't go without him. On the few weeks they were out of town, or if Maddy really couldn't make it to services, Maddy read the portion on her own, going over her own interpretations with the Rabbi later in the week. At the end of a year, she'd read the whole story from the creation of the world and Adam and Eve to the death and burial of Moses just outside the promised land.

She met with Rabbi Modine in his office. "Well, rabbi, a year ago, you challenged me to read the whole story, and now, tah dah! I've done it. I wanted to thank you for the challenge."

The rabbi scratched his chin as he thought about it for a minute. "You read it in English, right?" A simple question. A gauntlet thrown. It implied that it was something less than reading it in its original Hebrew. "Maddy, any time a text is translated, it has been interpreted. You read someone else's interpretation of the text. Granted, a very educated and intelligent someone—but…" He paused to let her think about what he was saying. "There is so much richness in the Hebrew, Maddy. I mean, the first few words of the Bible you read are translated: "In the beginning, God created the heaven and the earth," but the words don't say that exactly, in Hebrew. In fact many other English translations try to imply something different. Some say, "In the beginning of God's creating," or "As God was beginning to create." All of these ideas have a slightly different valance, and many possible implications, right? Some seem to say God is still creating; some treat the act of creation as more of a process. And that is just what the translations do with the first few words. Think of the implications of interpreting translations to every single word."

Maddy did think, and given the fact that she had always loved languages, and that Ben's family was deeply connected to Israel, she decided that her next step would be to learn to read, speak and understand Hebrew. She would try to understand the writing of the five books, this time around with an appreciation for the subtlety of the ancient text. She thanked Rabbi Modine, who nodded and smiled, obviously pleased to see a congregant so inspired.

Maddy enrolled in a Hebrew course and was amazed to find out how sensible and logical the language was. She remembered the Alephbet—the Hebrew alphabet, named for its first two letters—from Hebrew school, but basically started from scratch and worked hard to try to master the language.

Her teacher, an Israeli woman who also taught at a local university, was impressed with her progress.

"Maddy, I know that you are good with math and languages, and I can also see that you intuitively understand how this language works."

Maddy nodded. Her teacher was right.

She continued, "Do you know how modern Hebrew came back into usage?"

Maddy shook her head; she had no idea.

"It was Eliezar ben Yehuda who revived the Hebrew language less than one hundred and fifty years ago. He lived from 1858-1922 in Palestine, and he brought the language of the Torah, which was used exclusively as a holy language, to the mouths of everyday people. He was a genius, with a tortured soul and torturous disposition.

"He created a language that was mathematical, logical and fanciful all at once. He was despised by his contemporaries for what they saw as profaning the holy language, yet his vision required him to toil without respite, earning him the simultaneous hatred of the Jewish authorities, as well as of his large, starving family."

Maddy understood the feeling of wanting to finish a puzzle, at the exclusion of everything else.

"He took the root of a word, usually made up of three letters, called the "*shoresh*,"and manipulated it into modernity. For example, the word for "going up," which was used in antiquity to refer to climbing a mountain, or to describe what happened to Elijah, who ascended to heaven, uses the same root for "stairs" and that is the same as the modern root word for "escalator."

Over time the secrets in the language revealed themselves to Maddy. Her love of puzzles drew on the same part of her brain she used for Hebrew language, except that in deciphering the Torah, she found more than meaning in the images and emotions the rich and beautiful words evoked, she found the words created a richness and beauty—more than that, a sense of *purpose*—in her daily life. She was a moth drawn to a flame: pulled by a force beyond the visible, she couldn't learn or incorporate what she'd learned fast enough.

"Ben, how did you like this Shabbat dinner?"

Maddy was asking for a reason. She had never been like the wives who secretly made meatballs out of soybean, or the ones who removed all the fat, testing to see if their husbands could tell the difference. But here she was, cooking a kosher meal, including the dessert, and after the fact asking if it was any good.

"Dinner was fine. Why?"

She didn't want to open a Pandora's Box, but she thought she needed to tell him how eating kosher all the time made her feel.

"No reason, other than it was all kosher. Even the dessert!"

He didn't seem overly impressed, or to mind, and she could never explain to anyone, except maybe the rabbi, why it made her feel so good, but it did. She waited for any indication that she had crossed a line. Getting none, she cleared the table, and washed the dishes. Encouraged by her small victory, she started to plan her next meal. Soon she was making meals either all meat or all dairy, only after the fact telling Ben that the meal satisfied the Jewish dietary requirements. She started ordering vegetarian or dairy food in restaurants. It was just like the vegetarian diet she'd adhered to throughout her teens and early twenties, but it was easy—easier now. It felt like she was

doing something *right* and *good*. It wasn't long until she had
evolved to the point where she had to take the next step.

"Ben, if I do all the cooking and shopping, and you
really don't mind all-meat or all-dairy meals, is there any reason
we can't keep a kosher home?"

Maddy was ready for him to dismiss the idea, not sure
what she could say to help him understand how important it
was to her.

"If it means that much to you, I guess we can have a
kosher home."

The next day Maddy, who generally disliked to shop,
went to the kitchen store and took tremendous pleasure in
buying another set of plates, a second set of silverware and a
few more pots and pans. She put everything aside for Passover,
which was only a few weeks away. Maddy decided to invite
both sides of the family up, as well as several friends who were
the Gold's surrogate family in Southwood, for the *Seder*—the
meal that marked the beginning of the holiday where Jewish
families and friends would tell the story of the Hebrews'
exodus from Egypt. Everyone agreed to attend, and Maddy
busied herself with all the preparations. This would be a special
Seder for Maddy. She was planning on making the kitchen
kosher, and then preparing her first kosher meal in it.

She had no idea where to start, so she went back to the
rabbi. First, he said, she had to clean everything—all the
cabinets, shelves and drawers. The she had to boil, burn, soak
or toss all the cooking pans and pots, bowls, and utensils. One
really strange side effect of the transformation—one that she
couldn't reconcile with her understanding of space and logic—
was that the pantry and cabinets in her kitchen, which were
pretty full to begin with, seemed to have more room *after* the

two sets of everything went in to them than they did before. The space must just work better, and though there were now double the dishes, silverware and cookware, everything fit. It didn't make any sense at all. She thought, *a lot of the things that I do that make me feel this sense of connectedness don't.*

When the house was ready, almost forty of Maddy's closest family and friends came for the Seder. She had been to many Passover celebrations growing up, but the holiday had been meaningless: a meal and some Hebrew read from a small booklet, the pages of which were stained with red wine and flecked with bits of matzoh. Preparations had basically consisted of her mother tossing out a bag containing the remaining slices of a loaf of branola bread and replacing it with a few boxes of matzoh.

In contrast, Maddy went all out. There were no crumbs of leavened bread in her house, all cabinets were scrubbed clean, and her freezer, which was usually stocked full, had been almost completely emptied over the last few months. When she looked into her spotless, empty freezer, she was reminded of the holiest space in the Great Temple—the *"dvir"*—the Holy of Holies. She laughed at herself, because a freezer wasn't supposed to remind you of a room in the Great Temple, which was destroyed in the year 70 CE, but hers did.

In addition to preparing a special meal, she had bought a special Haggadah made for children Stephen and Brandon's ages. It was a puppet show, and each member of the family would play a part. The traditional Haggadah is a book that recounts the story of, and explains the symbols that commemorate, the Exodus. It can be a daunting challenge to capture and keep the attention and interest of adults, let alone children. Maddy sent out puppets to everyone invited to decorate and bring to the *Seder.*

The meal was great, the story was told, and everyone felt that it was a spiritual high moment for the family, especially Maddy. She knew that she'd succeeded in bringing the joy of celebrating Passover to her family when her niece called her a few months later asking, "Aunt Maddy? Are you going to have us come for Passover again this year?"

Maddy was excited that her niece was even interested, "Sure Honey, why?"

"Well, I want to do the puppet show again, but now that I can read better, I want a bigger part!"

Maddy was elated.

As Maddy worked to bring herself and her family to a higher level of education and observance, she became a more active volunteer in her temple. In a short time, she'd chaired a few committees, then found herself in line for the presidency. If she stayed on her current track, she'd be the youngest president ever in the temple's seventy-five-year history, and one of only a handful of women to hold that highest lay position. It continually forced her to expand her knowledge and demonstrate commitment. She would get phone calls from people she knew only peripherally, asking her questions of Jewish law or language or history. Even if she didn't know the answer, she had built up an impressive library, and was thrilled when she could find the answer somewhere in her bookshelves. All her volunteering and praying and knowing made her feel like she was helping God. She gave serious thought to becoming a rabbi. At the very least she would become a steady presence at her temple.

Each act of charity, community building, or teaching filled her up. But not all the way up. *What's missing?* She knew, deep down, but tried not to think about it. Every time she was confronted with the source of her feelings of emptiness, she knew that no level of observance or depth of learning would fill her up. She was incomplete. Nothing could replace her need for another child. For a daughter.

Brandon was already eleven years' old, but she'd missed out on dance lessons, ear piercings, nail-painting. Not just those things, but all of it, the life of being mother to a daughter. When women she knew delivered girls, or when shopping with friends she would make her way through the sea of pink and ruffles to meet her friend in the girl's department, and she would ache for the female child she didn't have. She was brought to tears one night when she and Ben had dinner with another couple. Their friends had also had two boys, and when the waiter came around to pour them all a glass of wine, her girlfriend aggressively covered her wineglass, practically shouting, "None for me thanks!"

Jokingly, Maddy said, "What's up, are you pregnant or something?"

The woman leaned forward across the table, took Maddy's hands in hers, and in an excited whisper she announced, "As a matter of fact, I am! The amnio came back today—and it's a girl!"

Maddy squeezed her friend's hands, smiled hard, and congratulated her. Outwardly, Maddy was very happy for her friend, but inside she wished it were her announcement—and more scary, that her friend would have a miscarriage—so Maddy wouldn't have to watch another friend live her dream. She loathed herself for even having those thoughts.

What's wrong with me??

Not long after, in her Hebrew class, she learned that the root of the words "shalom" and "shalem" were the same. "Shalom" means "peace," "shalem" means "whole" or "complete." She understood why she had no peace: she was incomplete, her family was not complete. The ancient language had revealed a secret, and answer, to her. She decided that she was facilitating Ben's decision to have no more children by taking all the responsibility for birth control. She went off the pill and made contraception Ben's job, "You can either wear a condom, or get a vasectomy—but I'm done preventing us from having any more children!"

This lead to some pretty stupid games, almost as dumb as the rhythm method she'd used as a careless teenager, but Maddy didn't care, and secretly she hoped for an accident. Every month, she mourned the day she got her period, and when she was late, like holding a lottery ticket that could be the winner, just the thought of what could be was enough to send her spirits soaring. Though life went on, in some way Maddy was stuck, and she knew it. She couldn't reconcile herself to the fact that she had two terrific, healthy, happy and successful boys and no daughter. She even explored this in therapy and with her rabbi. No one had an answer for her; it was something she had to resolve for herself. Her yearning would give her no rest.

She begged Ben to reconsider his "two's the limit" decision. They argued and debated often. At one point, he completely convinced her that they should have no more, "What if something is wrong with the baby? Are you ready to accept that kind of challenge? Don't you know what the risks are of conceiving children once you are over forty? What if, even with the most advances technology they can only mostly promise you a girl, will you want a fourth if you have a boy? A fifth? Which would you rather have, retirement at sixty or seventy-five?"

The argument was made with such conviction, it was clear that even though Maddy didn't feel complete, Ben did. Backed by strong logical arguments into a very tough corner, she agreed with him and resigned herself to having no more children. To live with the want.

She immersed herself deeper in her volunteer work at the temple and took on numerous personal and community projects to keep herself busy. It still didn't block out the white noise of wanting. Then, when Stephen was fifteen and Brandon was twelve, Ben had a change of heart. To Maddy, it seemed to come out of nowhere, but Ben had his reasons. He'd gone to visit a friend and he was taken by the relationship of father and daughter. It wasn't the rough and tumble, suck it up, "c'mon son" kind of love he'd had with his boys. It was a sweet and adoring, delicate and nurturing love, and he finally realized he would love a daughter. He admitted to Maddy that it would be a mistake to put financial security before his wife's pervasive and unassuageable need.

Maddy was thrilled, but also scared: the idea of really starting all over again with an infant was an exhausting proposition. And balancing a third child with two other busy children promised to be a serious challenge. They met with many doctors and decided to proceed with the practice known to be the most successful in New England. She was shocked to hear that the first opening for an IVF procedure was not for three months. Disappointed, but undaunted, they remained optimistic. Even her friends noticed that Maddy seemed happier. When pressed for a reason, she'd say it was on account of new vitamins: she wasn't about to spoil the surprise by telling anyone about their decision until she had a due date.

She started to have dreams where she was caring for a baby girl. She'd wake in the morning and calculate how long before they'd meet with the doctor. As was the case every so often, the next month her period was late. At first she was unconcerned, but then she woke up one morning feeling fluish. She ran to the bathroom and splashed water on her face as she tried to stem the waves of nausea. *What is wrong with me?* She knew the answer even as she asked herself.

Simultaneously thrilled and disappointed, she had wanted to do everything she could do to ensure that their third child would be a girl, and here she'd just gotten pregnant, as if she were a teenager who'd skipped her birth control, or suffered a broken condom, and—as easy as falling off a log—conceived.

She wondered about her dreams of a baby girl. She bought a home pregnancy kit. This time, a single test. She didn't even wait until the next morning to take it. The plus mark was quite visible: pregnant.

She didn't know what she would tell Ben, but she drove to his office, something she rarely ever did, and waited for him to come out of his exam room. She looked at him as he looked back at her in puzzlement, she led him to his office and shut the door.

"Sit down, honey." She pulled out the pregnancy test from her pocketbook and unceremoniously put it down on his desk.

Unlike a thermometer, he didn't even have to look at it to know what it said. For a full minute neither of them spoke, or even moved. Ben just stared at the test. Finally, he stood up, walked around his desk and pulled Maddy to her feet. Holding her he looked right into her eyes. "If it isn't a girl, then we'll just have four kids—we'll keep trying! I can't even think of not keeping it just to be able to see a doctor to create the girl baby, could you?"

She hugged him, knowing that by even suggesting a fourth child he was putting his financial security dead last in the "what's most important in life" department.

She proceeded to tell him about her dreams of nursing a baby girl, so real she could smell the baby powder. Not one to doubt her intuition, he told her he hoped that she was right. They laughed at their "luck" and she went home, where she tried to figure out when exactly the baby would be born. She cancelled the appointment with the specialist, and made one with her obstetrician. Because of her age, the doctor suggested an amniocentesis, which wasn't for another two months.

Days passed slowly as Maddy tried to think about anything else. When the doctor called with the results, he confirmed that, in fact, they had a daughter on the way.

Maddy spent the next several months eating right, exercising, and following her doctor's orders to the letter. She cross-stitched her daughter a blanket, as she had done for both of her boys. She wanted it to be the one thing that comforted her, that she'd with her bring everywhere, and were it to get left behind, they'd have to go back to retrieve it. It was that way for the boys, and she put all her love into making her an intricate quilt filled with colorful animals and hearts. She would stitch her name and date of birth into one of the hearts.

She told her family and friends the good news and felt a special sisterhood with those women who had daughters. She started really watching, not as a jealous observer noting what she didn't have, but as a mother trying to learn how to raise the girl she'd always wanted.

The hospital experience this time was very different than her first two times. Whereas before she'd depended on better living through chemistry, namely epidurals, this time she decided on natural childbirth. She and Ben practiced all the birthing techniques with the assistance of a midwife, Maddy pushed and breathed and panted, and after six hours, a petite and perfect baby girl was guided into the light and love of the world. She began to cry immediately, but the minute she was placed in Maddy's arms, she was quiet. Reluctantly, Maddy permitted them to take her baby for footprints and a weighing, but only after they promised her that they'd come back immediately. When the baby was lifted from her, both mother and daughter started to cry.

Ben and Maddy wrestled with many names, but in the end, they decided to name her Elianna, Hebrew for "my God answered." Not only was Elianna the answer to Maddy's prayers, but she wanted God to hear and answer all of Elianna's prayers and dreams as well.

The next morning, they brought the baby home. As Maddy turned onto her street, she saw the balloons and streamers flying from every mailbox—all pink and white, proclaiming, "It's A Girl!" She looked at her husband, then at her sleeping little bundle, and she felt whole. Elianna was a sweet and good-tempered baby. Maddy enjoyed fussing over her, as did Ben, Stephen and Brandon, and any number of family and friends. As Maddy did for her other two children, she nursed Elianna, but this time the hours spent feeding and burping her baby bordered on a religious experience. As the baby took her nutrition from Maddy's breast, Maddy would fill up on the baby. She'd sit for hours just playing with her fingers and toes, and smelling her delicious head and feet. Tracing her downy ears with her finger. Whole-er than whole.

Though she never liked to shop, buying outfits and toys for her daughter gave her the greatest pleasure. She was ecstatic when Elianna turned two and a half, and enrolled in "ballet." Just looking at the tiny leotard and tights and pink slippers was enough to make Maddy happy. When she put them on her daughter, Maddy cried, overjoyed. In general, Maddy noticed that most mothers were more inclined to leave their younger children sooner than they did than their first. Maddy really didn't want to leave Elianna at all.

From the start, Maddy brought Elianna and her blankie everywhere. Her daughter loved the soft flannel-backed quilt, and couldn't fall asleep without it. Until Stephen went to college, Elianna had two built-in babysitters, but more often than not, Maddy preferred to keep her baby with her. Elianna completed Maddy, and Maddy loved having her by her side.

Each day, Maddy felt like she was finally part of *the sisterhood*. Without a daughter, the most feminine aspects of daily life had gone uncelebrated. So many of Maddy's friends had initiated their daughters into the rites of womanhood, buying them journals, having candle lighting ceremonies when they got their periods, and offering spiritual words of unity with all women. Now Maddy would be able to initiate her daughter into womanhood, and she promised herself that she'd never miss an opportunity to celebrate with her daughter.

When Elianna was four, Ben surprised Maddy with a twenty-fifth anniversary present—a trip to Paris. They arranged to leave the baby and Brandon with a preschool teacher from the temple. Maddy had known Mrs. Cohen for years. She had taught Stephen and Brandon and now was Elianna's teacher.

Elianna loved her. That fact, coupled with the fact that she had been the babysitter for so many of the Gold's friends when they went away, took all the worry out of leaving on vacation. With a prospect of rekindling romance, and the certainty that the kids were safe, Maddy and Ben left for the airport.

Maddy made it all the way to France before she had to call home from DeGaulle Airport just to see that everyone was okay, and to tell her daughter and son how much she missed them. In Paris, they were enchanted and reinvigorated as they soaked up the romance of the City of Light. They walked from one end of the city to the other, eating one fantastic meal after another and drinking bottles of mellow, rich wine.

Each morning they'd call home and Mrs. Cohen would update them on the events of the day. First they'd speak to Brandon, who at seventeen was still close to his parents, filling them in on school life, sports, and even occasionally girls. Brandon would put Elianna on the phone. Her sweet, small voice proclaiming her love for them, and relating stories from her day. Every conversation ended with a phone kiss, and their promise to be home soon.

On the fifth day, they had the kind of romantic and memorable day they were sure they'd remember always: they went to the Musee d'Orsay, a magnificent collection of their favorite Impressionist artists all housed in a state-of-the-art museum that was renovated from an old train station. They then lingered over lunch at a small café on the Rue du Rivoli. As they walked back to the hotel, rich tones from a cello lured them into a cozy, walnut-paneled bar, where they sat holding hands, sipping wine and savoring the simple perfection of bread and cheese.

It was late afternoon when they got back to the hotel, both of them feeling aroused by the wine and the gentle, sensual experience of Paris. As Ben opened the door to their room, a message dropped from the doorjamb. He picked it up, and read aloud, "Messeur and Madam Gold, please call home. Merci."

It was probably Elianna, thought Maddy, unable to wait to talk to her parents later in the day, she'd asked Mrs. Cohen to call. Maddy dialed the number, trying to imagine what delightful story her daughter wanted to tell her. She smiled to herself in anticipation.

"Hello?" The voice was unmistakably Katherine's. Maddy laughed at herself, feeling young and carefree, she must have inadvertently dialed the phone number of her youth. "Oh, hi Mom. It's me. I meant to dial my house, and…."

Katherine interrupted, "Madeleine, you did call your house…"

Her voice caught in her throat.

"Mom, why are you at my house? Is everything okay?"

Katherine's voice grew more shrill and staccato by the syllable, "No! There was a terrible accident! They dropped Brandon off at school, and on the way home, the car was hit head-on by a truck!"

"Where…where are they now?"

Her mother gasped deeply and Maddy's body went limp as the blood fell to her feet. Katherine was shrieking.

In a whisper and a wail, "They say it was instant. They never…I'm so sorry. I'm so sorry. I'm so…"

Maddy didn't hear it. She had dropped the phone and fallen to the floor.

Ben picked up the receiver, "Hello?? Katherine! What the hell is going on?"

Jack had taken the phone from Katherine and explained everything to Ben, who could hear most of what Jack said over Maddy's screams.

They flew home on a flight in which they alternated between being hysterical, crying—wailing really—and sitting, shuddering, dry-heaving, in shocked silence. People around them spoke but no words or gestures could comfort them. When they arrived home, the boys were sitting in the family room with Katherine, looking at a photo album filled with pictures of the baby. Jack had gone to the funeral home to act as "*shomer*"—a guardian over a body between death and burial. Jack and Katherine had decided that, though no family members had performed this holy act for either of their fathers, they knew that someone should be there for Elianna. She was too young to be alone. And so, as irreligious as he was, he went.

Maddy and Ben went to the funeral home and picked out a pine coffin, the smallest one they made, and sat with Elianna until the sun came up, but not out. The sky was gray and the sharp chill to the air was unusual for April. The mourning parents were sent home. As they drove, Maddy was overcome with the feeling that the whole thing was not real. As they passed by people, laughing or talking on their cell phones, Maddy couldn't believe that she wasn't in their world. She kept trying to wake up from the nightmare.

The Gold family slowly showered and got dressed. The limousine came and brought them back to Elianna. They were seated in a chapel room, which was off to the side of the room in which all their family and friends would soon be congregating. Over the next half-hour, the room filled with hundreds of mourners who'd come to pay their respects to the grieving family. Had Maddy not taken several Valium, and had she not been sitting between her husband and her eldest son—human bookends—she would have fallen off the shelf altogether.

The drugs helped to numb her from the reality, which was too much for her to bear. As she watched the small coffin, she was vaguely aware that the service had started. Rabbi Modine was officiating. He stood at the reader's table and surveyed the room, which was now filled to capacity. He looked over to the family and then at the small box. He seemed to be searching for the words that would reconcile unwavering faith with profound, unfathomable pain. He cleared his throat, and the soft whispers ceased completely. The room fell silent. He was an eloquent speaker, and everyone there wanted him to say something to help them understand this unforgivable loss.

"My friends, it isn't the length of days given to a person, but the joys those days bring to those who are touched by her. And so Elianna's life was painfully short in days, but it was a long life with regard to the joy each day brought to her family and friends, and to all who knew her."

The room was perfectly still, with the silence only broken by the sound of people sniffing or blowing their noses. The rabbi went on to tell a story about a Sage who lived long ago, named Rebbi Meir, who had a wife named Breuriah, who was also known for her wisdom.

"It happened that while Rebbi Meir was studying at the Temple on a Sabbath afternoon, both of his sons died. What did their mother do? She put them both on a couch and spread a sheet over them. At the end of the Sabbath, Rebbi Meir returned home and asked, 'Where are my two sons?' She replied, 'They went to the house of study.' Rebbi Meir shook his head, 'I looked for them there, but did not see them.'

"Then his wife gave him the wine cup for 'Havdalah,' the short prayer service formally marking the end of the Sabbath. He pronounced the blessing, then again he asked, 'Where are my two sons?' She replied, 'They went to such-and-such a place and will be back soon.' Then she brought food for him. After he had eaten, she said, 'My teacher, I have a question. A while ago a man came and deposited something in my keeping. Now he has come back to claim what he left. Shall I return it to him or not?' Said the Sage to his wife, 'Is not one who holds a deposit required to return it to its owner?' She responded, 'Still without your opinion, I would not return it with a full heart.'"

The rabbi continued, "She took her husband by his hand, led him up to the chamber, and brought him near the couch. When she pulled off the sheet that covered the boys, he saw that both children lying on the couch were dead. He began to weep. Then his wife came to his side and softly asked him, 'My teacher, did you not say to me that we are required to restore to the owner what is left with us in trust?'"

The rabbi's story was trying to tell them that God alone gives the gift of life, and that we can't question the why or the when a life is ended. On some level the story was supposed to comfort them, but as eloquent and Godly as he was, he knew there was nothing he could say that would make this tragedy okay with anyone.

The funeral ended and the limousine followed the hearse to the cemetery. It had started to drizzle. The mourners stood under large, black umbrellas, shoveling piles of earth back into the tiny hole in the ground. Everyone cringed when the hollow sound of the stones hit the box that had been gently laid inside. Then there was the sound of dirt on wet dirt, punctuated with muffled cries, until, in accordance with Jewish custom, the small hole was filled. Maddy and Ben stood at the grave, clutching each other in disbelief and despair. How could they go home and leave their precious baby behind?

When they finally returned to their house, their friends had prepared it for *Shiva*—the seven days of mourning that follow a funeral. As is the custom, food was served. However, few people could eat. Even the hard boiled eggs, which mourners and those returning from a cemetery are supposed to eat as an acknowledgement of the circle of life, sat uneaten, as if by shunning them people could express their disagreement with the premise.

The week passed slowly. There was a group assembled for prayer twice a day, morning and night, and there was an endless stream of deliveries of fruit and meals, of cards, phone calls and visitors—many of them children. Somehow the Gold family made it through, and at the end of the week, the boys and Ben returned with heavy hearts to their lives. Ben went back to work, both boys returned to their schools and their routines. No one but Maddy seemed to have trouble putting one foot in front of the other and Ben, himself consumed but not destroyed by this tragedy, had nothing left to give to Maddy, who was broken possibly beyond repair.

What started out as a mere disinterest in the pleasures of exercise, or eating, or even getting dressed, became her absolute reality. She shunned her friends, many of whom were at a loss as to what to say or do for her anyway. Even Carrie, who had managed to endure Maddy's bout with Lyme Disease, had no place in Maddy's misery. Maddy spent a lot of time at home. It was easier to avoid painful encounters with well-meaning friends, who, upon seeing her, would become somber, asking "How *are* you?" She wanted to yell at them. *How do you think I am? My daughter is DEAD!*

She used to be someone who had a life people would envy and admire—nice house, healthy and happy family—and now she could see how they only regarded her with pity. If they didn't want to be like her any more, why should she?

It was better to stay home, where she could comfort herself by going into chat rooms for people who were mourning losses. In the anonymity and safety of that environment, she would talk online with the only people who could understand the depth of her despair. One man, who went by the name "Adamsdad," shared his story of losing his son in a drowning accident. He tried to encourage her to accept the "new normal," assuring her that he knew she'd never be the same, but she would learn to live with the circumstances life had dealt her. He, too, was working hard to put order and peace back into his life, and he made her feel like she wasn't completely alone. Some mornings, only the promise of a conversation with him could get her out of bed.

Maddy knew the expression "misery loves company," but through endless days of unyielding grief, Maddy decided that misery really loves alcohol and sedatives. She found herself getting high often, *to stop feeling so low,* she would tell herself. While at the beginning, she'd take half a Valium to numb herself to the shock. It became a whole pill. Daily. At first a habit, it was soon an addiction. The unstructured days and sleepless nights were all the permission she needed to rationalize her abuse. She self-medicated day and night, but no matter how high or drunk she got, she couldn't make the pain go away.

As the weeks went by, she found more and more that daily life—sometimes just eating or showering—was more than she could manage. The few times she'd tried attending Shabbat services at her temple, it seemed to her that the liturgy had changed. Nothing resonated with her anymore. Even the rabbi's sermons fell short of satisfying her need for answers. Nowhere in the readings was there an answer to *why*. The problems of morality and ethics that were brought to light and discussed each week were so small and unimportant compared to the problem of the hole that had been ripped in her heart; she would leave temple sadder and more lost than she was when she'd come.

Like shedding clothes that are too heavy for hot weather, she slowly cast off pieces of her observance that no longer could be worn with any comfort or acceptance. The first thing she did was eat non-kosher food. As she ordered a plate of shrimp on pasta, she felt anger and satisfaction. She was confronting her God, *"Go ahead, take me to Hell. You couldn't even watch after my daughter, when I followed Your laws: why should I respect Your rules now? What difference would it make?"*

She had learned about the "slippery slope": when one act of observance was discarded, the rest followed right behind, like the whole ritual package was rolling down a steep hill. She'd experienced the phenomenon personally, but in reverse, taking on more and more observance as she became more knowledgeable, slipping easily into the rhythms and rituals of her religion. The result of falling into faith was not a descent but just the opposite. She saw now that it had elevated her spirit. But now, *after*, it was easier *not* to go to temple, *not* to keep kosher, *not* to want anything to do with a religion that could always pose more questions, and many answers—except *why*.

She lost interest in friends, food, fun, all the things that once brought her pleasure. Even sex now felt like an out-of-body experience, like she was there, but looking down at herself from the ceiling. She knew she was repelling Ben and it made her sad. Sadder yet when she realized that she didn't really care. Every night they'd kiss goodnight and Maddy would turn on her side and pass out.

It was at this time that she started having weird dreams. In one, Ben was standing on the lawn, which was undulating under his feet. Upon closer inspection, he was standing in a sea of snakes. She woke up feeling frightened and uneasy, but she wasn't sure whether it was the fear of the snakes or fear it symbolized the unsteady ground she and her husband were standing on.

In another dream, Maddy watched as Ben made love to several women, some friends, some strangers. At first, Maddy was sad and hurt. Then the women noticed Maddy watching them. They stopped loving Ben, got up and came over to her and tried to comfort her. Then to seduce her. She allowed them to kiss her, to rub her body and try to bring her passion back to life. As the women became more and more intimate, Ben, sitting alone on the bed, looked on, helpless.

CHAPTER TEN

3:11 P.M.

She was saddened that her love for Ben and all she'd invested in their marriage wasn't enough to override her decision to end her life. It wasn't that Ben hadn't tried hard to support or understand her. It was just that he couldn't support her or understand her <u>enough</u>. They'd tacitly agreed to disagree, but the ocean that separated them now was vast, more distance than she could possibly navigate in her lifetime. She needed the pain to end.

Spring 2004

Maddy and Ben were drifting apart. More precisely, Ben seemed to go on with his life and Maddy stayed stuck in place. Every morning Ben would get up, shower and go to work. Maddy didn't even get out of bed until after he was gone. One morning, though, she awoke early. Ben was out of bed, but not gone—she could hear the shower running. As she opened the door to the bathroom, she could see Ben through the water-spotted and steamy glass door, scrubbing himself vigorously. She realized what he was doing, and at that moment, she became painfully aware of how far apart they'd grown.

She'd grown away from men in general—including her own boys. Though they tried to be attentive to her at first, she repelled them with her despondency. Feeling powerless to help her, they retreated to their own lives, visiting and calling from college less and less frequently. Though she loved the men in her life, they just couldn't fill the void left behind by her daughter. Being around women helped a bit, if only temporarily, to fill the large hole that had been ripped in her heart. She found women to be more in touch with her pain, and as a whole, more sympathetic and soothing. She found herself fantasizing about having relationships with other women; the comforting thoughts of various kind and soft women ignited the only passion Maddy felt—the only passion she'd allow herself to feel—when she was alone. The comfort was short-lived. The pervasive hurt would come right back.

This went on for months. Ben accepted the loss of a daughter as tragic, but didn't seem to see it as a reason not to go on. Though he saw how hard it was for Maddy to do the same, and did what he could, ultimately he lost patience with her. They started to squabble over little things. After one particularly difficult argument, he threatened to leave her unless she got some help.

Finally forced to face the source of their long-unspoken break, Maddy returned to therapy, this time seeing a well-known psychiatrist who was known for treating people who have lost children. He worked with her intensively, and to some extent, he succeeded. In helping her to move forward, he managed to change her focus: she stopped self-medicating and drinking, she started exercising. She became more social. She filled up her days with appointments, lunches and activities. Her life looked a lot like it did before Elianna was born.

Book groups, exercise, and volunteer work kept her busy, but no matter where she went or how fast she moved, the cloud that hung over her head followed her. The fact was, she still cried when she'd see little girls dressed in pink outfits being pushed in strollers or when a Girl Scout would come to sell cookies at her door. Hardest of all were the Jewish holidays, especially Rosh Hashanah. Every New Year marked the passage of another trip around the sun. She felt that all she'd managed to do this whole miserable year was survive it. This year she struggled to put on a suit for synagogue. The last time she'd worn it was for the funeral. This year she didn't buy a new hat in honor of the new year, either. She couldn't. Instead, she pulled an old hat from its box in the cedar closet. Dressed and somewhat steeled to endure the familiar faces of friends and neighbors snapping from joy to sorrow upon seeing her, and feeling like a square peg in a round hole, she went to pray.

CHAPTER ELEVEN

3:12 P.M.

Maddy had always loved puzzles. It was reassuring that there was a solution, a final, correct arrangement in which all the pieces would fit. And validating that she could always figure it all out. But living a life after losing a child was like forever trying to finish a puzzle with no solution. There was a huge piece missing from her life, and no matter how she tried to fill the hole, eventually everything she threw into it disappeared in to the deep. Finally, she grew tired of trying.

Why?

She'd asked herself this question over and over, replaying each decision she made, certain it would have led to a different outcome. Even as she was drifting further and further away from her life of unrelenting hurt, the pain she felt when she thought about what might have been overwhelmed her.

She knew she was at the farthest point from help and closest to death—whereafter there is nothing—because pandemonium broke out in the emergency room, and the monitor that had been she could hear her own weak heartbeat started the shriek of a flat line.

In that instant, she was reminded that when Jews died, they were supposed to say the Shema—Judaism's central prayer. Martyrs were reputed to have recited it upon their tortured deaths, and it was a way to atone for any sins committed in life. It was also reputed to help repentant souls gain entrance into the World to Come. Though suicide was expressly prohibited, she hoped God would understand. She was anxious for its relief and release as she said the short prayer. "Hear O Israel, the Lord our God, the Lord is One."

As the words washed over her, it hit her. The why, the missing piece, was in the prayer! It wasn't actually in the prayer, but it was clear and so simple. It was right there all the time, tucked neatly inside the "One." "Hear O Israel, the Lord our God the Lord is One—AND ALL."

She immediately understood that everything is connected. She knew the why. "God is one" didn't mean there was one distant, distinct Being who watched over the earth and her inhabitants. It also wasn't a polemic against the trinity of Christianity. No, it meant God, maybe better called "Divinity," is in all life.

She understood: God was in the paramedics and the doctors, he was in "Adamsdad"—the online friend who'd lost his son and who helped her though many difficult days. God was in her family, friends and everyone she'd ever known. Who'd ever lived. God was in the radiant perfection of a rainbow and in the fierce power of a tornado. And God was even in the love and loss of Elianna. There was a taste of the transcendent in all of it.

She heard a single voice shout out, and all hands withdrew from her as the room fell silent. The shock that followed hit her like a baseball bat in the chest. Her body jumped off the table. The room was still quiet, but Maddy could hear the monitor emitting soft, distinct beeps.

How to find the way back? Filled with an overwhelming stillness and calm, she knew that even in a world with unimaginable loss, God was always a piece of the puzzle. Everything, good and bad, hidden and revealed, was a gift in and of itself: a reason to live. Life was tied to all life, but ultimately it was only our own we live. How to live, she thought, when she could feel the current pulling her body from this world? It had been like floating on a breeze, from cloud memory to cloud memory, until she'd reached the edge of life itself. Coming back to the world where everything was one, yet all answers were not for her to know, was much harder than floating: it was more like swimming. To what could she anchor herself? She tried to remember. She was now grounded in an understanding that helped

weigh her down, the current maybe losing some of its powerful pull. She
tried hard to meet the hands that had been offering themselves to her for
hours—and years. She hoped that she had enough left within herself to
reach them.

She remembered having such a feeling of purpose before. When
was it? Her mind alit on a particular Day of Atonement.

Fall 2003

Yom Kippur. The Jewish Day of Atonement. A fast day
and arguably the holiest day of the year. The one day when
everybody, regardless of their level of religious commitment the
remaining three hundred sixty-four days, would come to the
synagogue. It was common knowledge that rabbis spent their
summers preparing their remarks. Maddy knew how carefully
Rabbi Modine would pick his words. He wanted to say
something that reached each person in a way they felt
compelled to strive to become their best selves—especially
those who would come only this time of year.

This year was no different from any other. Rabbi
Modine was giving his big sermon. Maddy sat in her seat next
to Ben. Stephen and Brandon were in a teen service and
Elianna, a well-behaved, kind three-year-old, was in the
babysitting room. The rabbi stood at the podium and looked
around. The room grew immediately quiet. He held the sides of
his lectern and spoke quietly into the microphone.

"Friends. I ask you, what is wisdom? Is it more than
knowledge? How does one acquire it? Is it only for a select
few? Maybe. But it may be easier and available to each of us. I'll
give you a riddle. Let's see if you can guess the answer."

Maddy was rapt, as was everyone sitting within reach of his words.

"What is greater than God, more evil than the devil; rich people need it, poor people have it and if you eat it you'll die? Before I tell you the answer, you should know that one particular group of people solved this riddle quickly and correctly."

Maddy tried to figure it out. *Greater than God?* She couldn't think of anything. Nor could she think of anything more evil than the Devil. *What could it be?*

"The group that 'got it' right away? Children under five. The answer to the riddle? "Nothing."

People nodded as they realized how simple the answer was.

He continued, "Yes, the answer is simple—so simple children could see it easily. But why then, is wisdom so elusive for us adults? To answer this question, I want to tell you a story about King Solomon. He was king over all Israel, and was known for being very wise. We all remember the story of the two women claiming a baby was theirs. One day King Solomon was sitting in his chamber dispensing justice when a poor widow entered his court. This ragged and tattered woman was holding an empty wooden bowl and weeping bitterly. King Solomon asked her what had happened.

'As I was returning home with the flour I had just bought to bake bread for the Sabbath, a great gust of wind blew up, snatched at my bowl, and scattered the flour all over the road. I am weeping because I have no more money to buy new flour with which to make bread for my Sabbath meal.'

Now, Solomon wore a special ring on his right forefinger. With it, he had dominion over the winds and the spirits. After hearing her plea, Solomon kissed the blue stone in the center of his ring and summoned the first of the four winds of heaven. There was a noise like the beating of mighty wings, and the West Wind entered the chamber through the open windows. Its head was covered with green hair and the feathers of its wings were moist with sea spray. The West Wind prostrated itself before the Lord of the Ring. When Solomon asked the wind to give an account, the wind responded, 'While flying over the Isle of Cyprus I saw naked men digging in the heat of the day to extract the green metal out of the rocks. I saw them smelting the ore and drawing the copper from it to clothe the roof of the Temple which you, Sire, are building on Mount Zion. I covered them with a cool breeze to ease their efforts. But as for this woman, I neither saw her nor touched her property.'

"Solomon listened to the West Wind's account and, with a gesture, dismissed it from his presence. Again kissing the blue stone in his ring, he summoned the East Wind. There was a noise like the beating of mighty wings, and the East Wind entered the audience hall through the open windows. Its head was covered with red hair and its wings were yellow from the sands of the desert. It prostrated itself before Solomon and addressed the king, 'I came from the hot deserts and rested awhile over the mountains of Lebanon. There I observed men laboring in the deep forests cutting down cedar trees a thousand years' old. The laborers were fashioning the great beams from the trees to support the roof of the Temple, which you are building on Mount Zion. As for this woman, I neither saw her nor laid hand on her property.' With a motion of his hand, Solomon dismissed the East Wind, then kissed the blue stone on his ring and summoned the third of the winds, the

North Wind. There was a noise like the beating of mighty wings, and the North Wind blew in through the open windows. Its head was crowned with white hair and its huge wings were white like the winter snows. It prostrated itself before the king, turned to Solomon and said, 'I flew over the marble quarries of Lydia and blew cooling air into the faces of the men who were quarrying the stone from the mountains. I saw them cut the marble into blocks and polish them and prepare them to serve as cornerstones for the Temple, which you, Solomon, are raising on Mount Zion. As for this woman, I neither saw her nor touched her property.' Solomon thereupon dismissed the North Wind, and kissing once more the blue stone in his ring, summoned the fourth of the winds, the South Wind. There was a noise like the beating of mighty wings, and the South Wind flew into the hall through the windows. Brown hair grew on its head and its wings were red like the coral in the southern seas. The South Wind alighted in front of the Lord of the Ring and bowed low before him. All this time, Solomon's son, Absalom, was watching and learning from his father. But he was so enraged by the crime, he jumped up and addressed the wind, 'Since your brother winds are innocent of the crime against this poor widow, you must be the culprit. Admit your guilt!'

'Indeed it is true. I am guilty of the crime,' replied the South Wind. At these words, Absalom, filled with righteous anger, implored his father to raise the scepter to smite the South Wind, but his father restrained him and bade the South Wind speak.

'My lord the king,' began the South Wind, 'I was flying high above the shore of Arabia, and the seas below me were calm and clear, when suddenly I heard loud cries of distress. Looking down, I espied a ship from Egypt sailing toward the coast of Arabia with some three hundred men, women and children aboard. They were peasants and their families, driven from their land by famine and drought to seek fresh pastures in the oases of Arabia. I saw that their vessel had sprung a leak and was about to sink. The sailors tried to steer it toward the shore, but the water was already washing over it, and the ship was still some distance from dry land. It looked as if all those aboard would perish within very sight of land. I was greatly moved by their plight, so I descended and spread myself upon the surface of the water and blew with might and main against the waves, and against the sails of the sinking ship so that it raced toward the shore, enabling its passengers to land, to safety. At that very moment, the tip of my wing happened to touch the widow's bowl of flour, overturning it.'

When the South Wind had finished its tale, a deep silence descended on the hall, and no word was spoken. Then Solomon dismissed the South Wind from his presence and commanded his treasurer to give the widow one hundred gold pieces and sent the woman away in peace."

CHAPTER TWELVE

3:13 P.M.

Now the story made sense. Maddy understood that, though she'd lost a child, her loss was only a part of the whole story, the totality of which she could never understand. She didn't need to know why things happen. She couldn't ever know. And with no "why," she thought, there can be no "why me?" There was no question that she was broken—destroyed really—by her loss. Any mother would be. But to what end? What might her life bring? To what purpose was she born? In what way is she to help make the world whole?

With these questions, she knew she had to live. But she was exhausted. Trying with all her might to pull her eyes open or move any part of her thick, numb body, she knew she had a long way to go. She tried to focus on the voices in the room around her, to move closer to them, but her mind kept drifting. And she was powerless to resist. She knew that the stories of her life would be different now that she understood that, if not how, and certainly not why, everything is connected.

Fall 2002

"Hap-py Birth-day to you!" the energetic and excited group of girls was singing almost in unison to their friend Allison. Though Allison had blown out the candles, and the group was finished cheering her on, the room was still noisy. No matter how his mother jiggled him or rocked him, or tried to feed him or pacify him, a baby wouldn't stop crying.

Maddy liked this young mother. Her name was Sara and her three-year-old daughter Brittany and Elianna were in preschool together. Sara was a particularly nervous young mother who, at the moment, was having trouble with her infant son. His hysterics had reached a crescendo, causing the other mothers to look around the room, grateful that the noise wasn't coming from one of their own.

Maddy knew she could help. She approached Sara. "Hi, there! Any chance that I can hold that cute baby boy? You know I haven't seen him in so long, he's changed so much. Besides, Ill bet you could really use a break—he's got to be getting heavy."

"Thanks Maddy, really, but he's going through that phase where he doesn't like anyone to hold him except me."

Maddy laughed, "He couldn't get more upset than he is now! It doesn't bother me. Why don't you go get yourself a drink, and I'll just hold him till you get back." Maddy took the shrieking child, and somewhat reluctantly, Sara left them. Maddy held him close, willing calm and quiet into him, holding his tiny hands, smelling his head—she always loved that warm, sweet smell—and she rocked him and sang to him softly. As he settled in against her, he stopped crying.

When Sara returned, a little to Maddy's embarrassment, Alex was asleep on Maddy's shoulder. Maddy had tapped into something and had merely transferred it to the baby, but it was powerful. *Peace,* Maddy thought. Maddy felt the power of the calm, and she felt the connection to the baby, just as she'd felt a connection to so many things over her life. It was usually an insight, a unique perspective or thoughtful way of handling things, and was something that, whenever it happened, left Maddy wondering if it was something she possessed, something she was, or if maybe something outside of her was guiding, protecting, and assisting her.

CHAPTER THIRTEEN

3:14 P.M.

As Maddy thought of this story, she realized it was the first time since Elianna died that she remembered her, even peripherally, without feeling despair. The things they had done together were beautiful, even going to birthday parties of Elianna's friends—and no one could ever accuse Maddy of taking any of it for granted—not the parties, dance recitals, gymnastic classes and play dates. Not the baths, the books, the songs, not even the fevered hours. As she remembered her daughter, she was able to picture a happy, blue-eyed child with curly brown hair, laughing, running, and singing. It was like she had a video collection of Elianna's life stored in her mind. She could remember the sound of Elianna's voice, the wrinkle in her nose when she laughed, and the way she would turn her head away when she tried to tell a white lie. And Maddy remembered the way it always made, and hopefully would always make, her feel. Maddy knew that she could go on with only the memories.

If she could go on at all.

She tried to close the gap between her deadened body and the life she knew was waiting for her.

Fall 1999

"So, will you do it?"

Her friend Donna, a woman with whom she'd been friendly from Stephen's nursery school days, was asking her if she would chant Torah when her oldest daughter Emily became a Bat Mitzvah. Maddy was honored. Also a little intimidated. The chanting of the Torah portion is based on a complex system of vocalizations, or "tropes." The words are written on the scrolls as they were in antiquity—with neither vowels nor vocalization notes. Maddy knew that chanting from the Torah was a skill that required a tremendous amount of concentration and ability. Maddy also remembered learning that, according to Jewish law, there can be no mistakes of pronunciation, the reading must be heard by the congregation perfectly.

Temple Zion was well known for having many congregants who knew how to chant Torah. Maddy was not one of them.

"Look, Donna, I am really flattered to be asked to be a part of Emily's service, but I have to tell you, I don't even know the tropes!"

Donna nodded and laughed at Maddy.

"No problem! Neither do I! That's why I signed both of us up for trope lessons with the cantor."

Maddy had no excuse. The music director of their synagogue was going to teach them what to do.

"Well, then, I guess if we take the class together, we'll learn how. Okay. Then it would be my honor."

She wasn't sure why the honor felt so onerous. They started class the following week. The classroom was full of friends and acquaintances that Maddy had made in her many years at the temple. Cantor Lovash was a good-natured and kind man who welcomed each of them and congratulated them on their desire to accept the difficult challenge of such an important religious learning.

He proceeded to teach them the first trope, and after he sang it several times, the class was asked to repeat it after him. Maddy thought that if she sang quietly enough, he wouldn't be able to tell that she couldn't sing. But when he asked each of them to sing to him *one at a time*, Maddy realized what she'd gotten herself into. Sing?! What in the world was she thinking when she agreed to accept the honor of chanting a Torah portion? *I don't sing! I can't sing!!* She looked down the row; three more people and then she'd have to face the music, literally.

It was her turn to repeat the first trope, and she just panicked. She looked the cantor right in the eye and said, "I'm sorry, can I please just pass?"

Apparently he perceived this to be some great slight to the history of liturgical music. Normally, Cantor Lovash was an easy-going man. He was somebody who truly viewed his work as holy and he treated people as if they were holy vessels. Normally. But this request somehow insulted him, personally and professionally. Whatever it was, he got very red in his face, pointed at the door and said, sternly, "Maddy, you can either sing or get out!"

She quickly ran through her situation. One: she was a member of the board of directors, so consequently she knew that word of this incident would get out. Two: she was there with a friend with whom she'd already made promises to learn and participate. It would be wrong to leave her. Three: it had been years and years since she'd sung out loud, and maybe she needed to think about that. Seeing no other option, she took a deep breath, shut her eyes tight, and sang the notes.

She opened one eye and looked around. Then, almost from surprise, she opened the other. No one had gotten up and left. No one was laughing. No one was crying. No windows were broken. When she looked at the cantor, he smiled, said "good," and went on to the next person. *That's it?*

Maddy continued to practice, and almost three months later, on a Saturday morning, she stood before her congregation and chanted the ancient words from an ancient scroll in an ancient tune. It was a transformational moment for her. Powerfully connected to her past, to her God and to her people, she was again one with the humanity from which she had been severed in fourth grade chorus.

This moment was so different from the time back in Mrs. Fink's music class. Then, she'd become self-conscious and had lost her voice because she let Mrs. Fink define her. Now, she was defining herself. For Maddy it took thirty years to reclaim her voice, and with one simple act she was no longer a woman apart. She was filled with intense gratitude, to her friend Donna for bestowing the honor and clearing a path for her to learn, and to the cantor for pushing her through the wall she herself had built so many years before and helping her overcome more than she ever dreamed she could.

CHAPTER FOURTEEN

3:15 P.M.

Over the last few hours, Maddy had relived her lifetime of physical and emotional pain. It had brought her to the farthest point from the very life back to which she now struggled to return. Remembering the times when she felt connected to the source of the things that happened to her grounded her. One and all.

As Maddy tried to work her way back through the void, she could hear voices and noises. But they were muffled and Maddy couldn't make out the words. She felt a little, but she knew she was still very far away.

Spring 1998

"All I get is a card?" Ben was only half joking. It seemed that for his fortieth he should get something more substantial, especially from his wife.

"Open it, silly." She'd worked a long time on the details, and the card was the culmination of weeks of planning.

Ben carefully opened the envelope and removed the note. "Clue #1—I have a long, hard shaft, and hang out near balls." He looked at Maddy as he thought for a minute, his mind fleshing out the possibilities and examining the words for meaning beyond the obvious double-entendre. He nodded knowingly and headed into the garage to his golf bag. Taped to the driver was an envelope, on which was printed "Clue #2." Inside the envelope there was a note: "There are drivers and then there are drivers." This puzzled him, momentarily, but soon he figured out what it had to mean. He went to his car. When he looked in the driver side window, he saw a note tied with a bow, hanging from the steering wheel. He got in the car, clearly intrigued by the game. He untied the note and tore it open. "Clue #3: More room in here than in an elephant's!" He ran around to the back of the car and opened the trunk, as he believed that he had been instructed to, his curiosity visible on his face; his tongue was peeking out just over his top lip, a sure sign that Ben was thinking hard. "What, Maddy, are we going to play at the Mayfair Club?"

When he looked into the open trunk, he saw "His" and "Hers" travel bags. Sitting on top of the "His" bag were two wrapped rectangular packages and another card, this one a paper luggage tag, on which Maddy had written: "Clue 4: We are all passengers."

He put the clubs in the trunk next to Maddy's and went to the passenger seat with the gifts and the card. He got in the car, tore open the wrapping paper, and saw that he had two books all about where to golf, eat and hike on Hilton Head Island, the resort area off the coast of South Carolina. The card had an itinerary and two plane tickets—they were going to fly to Hilton Head for four days—no kids.

"Oh my God, are you serious?" He was thrilled. It had been years since they'd been away for even a night all alone together. Though the boys were nine and six and weren't babies anymore, they rarely left them, preferring to include them on their vacations. The card also had a few handmade coupons for back rubs and more. Ben told Maddy he was impressed with the effort that she'd put into making him what was now looking very much like an a-o-k fortieth.

They arrived at the beachfront condo and did what all couples who haven't been alone together for a long time do— in fact, it had started hours earlier with them holding hands on the plane, then standing arm-in-arm at the baggage carousel. By the time they were in the cab, they were making out like they were in high school. Maddy was amazed he could still make each her feel like that, even after so many years.

They talked for a while about the disturbing news they'd gotten the night before when Ben had called Ricky, Ben's former college housemate, Maddy's former heartthrob and all-around too-cool guy. While everyone in the house experimented with drugs to some extent, Ricky was the one who took it the most seriously. He tripped on acid and did coke and Quaaludes in far greater quantities than everyone else in the house *combined*. And like so many guys who tripped a lot, the real world got tougher and tougher for him to deal with. Each time he tripped, he came back a little more crispy, until finally, he completely burnt out. It was hard to hear from Ricky's wife that he'd had a sort of nervous breakdown, that he'd relapsed into heavy drug use, and that she wasn't sure that she or their new son would need him around once he got out of the institution and through rehab.

Maddy secretly thanked God that her relationship with Ricky hadn't worked out, and that she hadn't let her kind, intelligent and successful Ben go to someone else. They both felt grateful to be together, and knowing that their sons—or anyone or anything else—wouldn't bother them was an aphrodisiac. Unhurried, gentle sex was followed by time on the beach and some early evening exploring.

The beach was beautiful, the air was warm, the water was clear and inviting. Satisfied that the dune area was as they remembered it from a college camping trip, they returned to the condo to shower. When they got to the bedroom, something caught Maddy's eye and turned her stomach at the same time. There were dried bloodstains on the bed, and she most definitely didn't have her period. It was disgusting, and the thought that they had just been in that bed, and too involved to notice it before, made Maddy sick. She recalled every paranoid TV news item on what could actually be found on hotel room beds, walls and carpets. She was nearly hysterical. She called down to the manager and tried not to scream.

"Do you know what we found in our room? Do you? There are bloodstains on the bed! This is totally disgusting and completely unacceptable! You need to send someone to come here and change our bed. Immediately!!"

The manager promised to have it taken care of by the time they returned from dinner. They left for dinner, both feeling pretty upset, though Maddy more so than Ben. When they returned to their room, a little better for the complimentary wine sent by the hotel, the first thing they did was check to see that the bed had been changed. It was clearly freshly made up. So, feeling relief and maybe the effects of wine, they did what all couples who don't get away much do—again.

When they woke the next morning, the sun was shining and the day promised a perfect round of golf, beach, and food. Maddy got out of bed, made coffee in the little kitchenette, and sat on the balcony, where Ben joined her. There they sat watching and hearing the ocean, the birds and the trees blowing in the mild breeze.

When they went in to shower and prepare for the day, they passed by the bed, and Maddy stopped dead in her tracks when she saw *dried blood on the sheets*. She didn't know what to think, but was certain it wasn't there the night before.

"Ben?" He didn't appear immediately, so she yelled his name louder, "Ben!"

He came running in and saw what she saw on the bed.

"It doesn't make any sense, Maddy."

They tried to line up the placement of the stains with their body parts, like forensic scientist Henry Lee trying to determine the angle of entry of a bullet hole. Suddenly Ben burst out laughing. He pointed to a bloody scab on his knee.

"Hey honey—I think this is the reason right here. It must keep opening up!" He looked at Maddy, who was visibly relieved.

"Um. You wanna call the manager and explain it to him?"

"Shut up and kiss me!" Maddy, who was more relieved than embarrassed rushed over and hugged Ben who kissed her hard as they fell back onto the bed.

CHAPTER FIFTEEN

3:16 P.M.

Back through time and space. It made Maddy's stomach lurch like it had in her childhood dreams where she would fly. Perhaps they weren't dreams at all, thought Maddy. It felt so much like what she was doing now.

She remembered how the hair on her arms and neck had stood straight on end, and her skin tingled when, flipping through a prayer book during a Sabbath service, she discovered that Jews believed that the spirit leaves the body at night. In the first prayer in the daily prayer book, a prayer that is supposed to be said upon waking, Man gives thanks to God for compassionately returning his whole soul back to him. Maddy was absolutely certain that there was more to her childhood flying dreams than she'd ever realized.

A few days later, she heard the same concept again. She was jogging on her treadmill, watching a morning "news" show, when she saw an interview with a New Age spiritual master touting his new book. He believed that the feeling of falling and hitting the mattress, which many people experience and attribute to dreaming, was actually the soul reentering the body after a midnight walk. Maddy couldn't dismiss that idea any more than she could believe it. Deep down, she felt that it <u>could</u> be. She could always recall the feeling that she'd had in those early recurring dreams: she felt protected and guided, like she had been with angels.

If Maddy was flying, then she wanted her soul to reenter her body, so she could wake up. She needed respite from the long, exhausting journey. But there was still a great distance to go. She would not give up. Ever again.

Winter 1992

"Maddy, if I didn't know you better, I'd say you were a witch!"

Maddy couldn't believe it either, but she, Carrie, Carrie's sisters Barbara and Irene, all their boys and all four husbands had seen it with their own eyes. They were eating in a slope-side restaurant, and as they always did when they went skiing, they were having a ball. Now that Stephen and Brandon were eleven and fourteen, they were old enough to ski with their friends on family ski trips. The whole group would meet up at the end of the day for dinner.

As it happened, their large, laughing group was brought to a room in the back, where there was only one other table with people sitting at it. An angular man in his forties sat straight in his chair. A woman, probably his wife, and two pale children with large eyes sat with him. To any observer, Maddy's table, though not loud, was clearly having the better time. The man at the other table called the waitress over, and based on their conversation, which involved many gestures and head shakes, they got up and moved to another room in the restaurant. As he left, he said in a stage whisper, loud enough for everyone at the table to hear, "Who thought it would be so noisy here?"

Ben, not usually one to acknowledge such rude comments by responding, couldn't help feeling incensed. Who was he anyway, the noise police? They were on vacation, not in church. In a voice loud enough to be heard, but directed at no one in particular, he said, "Well Jeez, if he wanted a quiet meal, he should have eaten home!" With that the other group left the room. Ben turned to Barbara, who, before Ben could say another word, said, "I know! What a jerk!"

Irene added, "Yeah, who needs guys like that around when we're trying to have a good time?"

"He should only be well." Maddy smiled and quietly recited the curse, careful to accent the "only." She'd learned it from a friend's mother, a sharp-tongued Holocaust survivor, who explained that it wasn't as nice as it sounded at first blush. It said that being "well" was a limit. And a way to say it's not ours to judge. If she were superstitious, she'd say that it invoked the "Evil Eye," the darker spirit who meted out justice to those who thought the rules didn't apply to them. Taking their cue from Maddy, they let it go.

Not a half-hour later, the kids, who'd all gone to the arcade to play until the food was served, came running in to report that a man had passed out in his chair in the other room. The two doctors at the table got up and went to attend to him. When they came back, Irene's husband Joe was laughing.

"Maddy, I'll give you three guesses who passed out."

Maddy needed only one. She knew who, if not why.

CHAPTER SIXTEEN

3:17 P.M.

Life and death are separated by a line so fine that no science can precisely explain it. When life slips from a human, there is a defining moment where death takes a final and irreversible hold. Madeleine tried hard to loosen death's icy grip. She could hear the machines whirring and beeping, but she was still unable to land firmly in the world that created them. The best she could do was to try, and to hope she would keep her life from slipping away.

Winter 1992 (continued)

"I can't believe that I'm going to take our kids to Florida to see your parents!" Maddy was sitting at the computer about to buy three tickets to West Palm Beach, where they would stay with Saul and Miriam for a whole week. Ben would remain at home to work while Maddy took the boys to see their grandparents, who let her know just how much they missed their young grandsons every time they called. Since they weren't yet school-aged, the boys could travel relatively easily and on no particular schedule. She clicked on the "buy now" icon and it was done.

Maddy packed plenty of snacks and games for their flight, hoping the boys would be busy and unable to fuss much. She was so proud of them when the flight attendants and even some passengers, some in suits that said they were all business, went out of their way to tell her that they were impressed with how well-behaved her boys were. She was glad she'd prepared well, but she also felt like even without Ben, she wasn't alone.

As they came off the plane, her in-laws were standing there almost indistinguishable from all the other Floridian grandparents, except that her father-in-law had *two* cameras around his neck. He was snapping pictures of the kids with one, then the other. Maddy went over to Miriam, hugging her and kissing her cheek, "Good to see you, Mom."

Miriam smiled, "As you can see, it's our pleasure, Maddy."

Sam pulled two tremendous candy necklaces from his camera bag.

"For you kiddos! Come give poppy a hug!"

Maddy was pleased to see how happy her visit had already made her in-laws. She turned to Miriam, "It looks like we brought some good weather! Maybe I'll even get a tan!"

Saul piped in, his thick European-Israeli accent so heavy it sounded fake.

"The weather report is calling for nothing but sun for the whole week." He coughed hard, then continued, "You really lucked out!"

Saul didn't know how true that was to Maddy. Though his condo was magnificent, it would close in on her if they were all stuck inside it for too long.

He drove home in his usual fashion. Maddy knew what she was in for, and so had pre-medicated with a stiff drink on the plane. When he started weaving in his lane on the highway, accelerating and rapidly decelerating, and later missing the requisite stop at a red light, she managed to stay calm. To herself she swore she'd get a rental car next time—if he let her live that long.

On top of his usual driving miseries, he was further distracted by bouts of hacking coughs.

"Saul, do you have a cold?"

Saul looked at her in the rear view mirror, which caused him to veer into the next lane, where the owner of a new black Porsche honked and gestured.

"No, I don't have a cold, just this cough. The doctors have checked it out. And it's not pneumonia. I had a chest X-Ray a few months ago, and again last week, and everything is negative. It must be an allergy or something."

"Oh," Maddy nodded, but she was thinking that it was just like him to diagnose himself, and hoped that he didn't have anything that he could spread to the boys.

The days turned out to be sunny and warm. They spent hours all together on the beach, walking up and down the shore looking for shells, playing in the surf and building in the sand. Saul had added a pair of binoculars to his neckwear collection. He was standing at the shore and scouring the horizon for tankers, cruise ships and sailboats. All the time Maddy watched her kids carefully. Even though both boys could swim, she was concerned about leaving Saul with the kids by the water. Saul couldn't swim. At least at the shore, she reasoned, her boys would stay on the sand, and barring a tidal wave, they'd be in no deeper than their knees.

Maddy had no problem until the afternoon Saul decided to take the boys fishing from the pier across the street from their building. Maddy feared the boys could easily fall into the water, one pushing the other by accident, or poking the other into the Atlantic with an unwieldy fishing pole.

"I want to come too, Saul. It's been years since I have gone fishing."

She tried not to sound patronizing or worried. Saul was a dinosaur, a leftover from the time when men, especially doctors like himself, were afforded tremendous respect and deference. Anyone not paying proper homage to the "Saulosaurus Rex," as Ben and Maddy fondly named him, would pay the price.

They all went over to the dock. Things went well for a while, but then the boys started to act up. They were running around and Maddy was certain that one of them would end up in the water.

"Saul, we should really go. The reservation for dinner is early tonight, and we need to get the kids back to the unit and showered so they'll be ready to go!"

"You go. I'll bring the boys up in a little bit."

"No, Saul, I need the boys to come back with me."

"What's the matter with you? Do you think that I am too *old* to take care of them myself? Go! And leave us alone!"

Maddy was dumbstruck. His response, screaming really, was punctuated only by his sharp coughs. When he could continue, he did.

"We're staying. And we will be back in plenty of time to make your stinking dinner reservation!"

No way could Maddy leave her children with this man: not only could he not swim, he seemed to have fallen off the deep end himself. She took a child in each hand and proceeded to lead them from the dock.

"No Saul, they are my children, and I need them to come back with me right now."

Her tone was sharp. She hoped it sounded final.

It wasn't. He was still screaming at her when she crossed the street. Spit was flying from his lips and foam was collecting at the corners of his mouth. The words he yelled at her, whether true or not, belied a slew of hateful feelings Maddy never knew he had. It hurt when he shouted that he liked his other, now ex-daughter-in-law Marci better than he liked her.

Maddy knew this wasn't true. Saul was at odds with Marci from the start, her self-centeredness challenging him from the day Jake brought her home from medical school. The clincher, though, was that when Jake and Marci got married, she refused to take Jake's family name. Regardless of her reasons, which were very much a part of the movement many women were embracing at the time, he'd disliked her ever since for what he considered to be a most violent act of rejection.

And now, to be in Florida with him yelling at her that he preferred Marci to her! It blew her mind. She'd never seen or heard him like this before. She knew he was hot-tempered, but Maddy had never, in all the years she'd known him, heard him yell at his family. Too stunned to speak, she walked into the building quickly and quietly with a boy on each arm.

When she got up to the condominium, she put her kids in the bathtub and called her mother from inside the bathroom, speaking softly so that her in-laws wouldn't hear her. After Maddy explained everything, Katherine said that Saul didn't sound right in his head. She then went on to tell Maddy about someone she knew who started to act crazy like this, and it turned out that he had a brain tumor. Maddy was both frightened and a little hopeful, thinking there was really something wrong with him. She didn't want him to be sick, but if he were it would explain the horrible things he said. Maddy avoided Saul as best she could in a two-bedroom condo until the next morning, when, several days early, she and the boys flew home.

Once she got home, she replayed the incident over and over in her mind, as well as out loud to Ben, who couldn't seem to take a side. No matter how she figured it though, she didn't do anything wrong. It was up to her father-in-law to apologize. She waited for his call for three days, but the phone didn't ring. The more she thought about it, the more she felt certain that, at sixty-nine years of age, he wouldn't apologize, and the fence between them would never be mended. She also knew that people didn't live forever, and what if what Katherine said was true? Whatever the explanation for his behavior, she knew that she'd probably survive him in any event. So, believing that life was too short and that no one knew what tomorrow would bring, she called Saul and apologized to him. In the end, they buried the hatchet. Maddy didn't feel better, exactly; it had been really hard to say she was sorry for something she knew she didn't do. At least her heart wouldn't jump every time the phone rang.

Less than six weeks later, they found a tumor in Saul's liver that was causing the endless coughing. After many days of testing, they discovered that the cancer had spread to his bones and his brain. It was a precipitous decline. Less than a month after the discovery of the tumor, Saul, the dinosaur from a time gone by, became extinct.

At the funeral, listening to eulogies describing a man whom Maddy knew loved his family deeply, Maddy was filled with sadness and tremendous relief that she hadn't waited for Saul to come to her. At the time, it wasn't easy for her to approach him, but as Maddy stood with Jake, his wife, and Ben over the coffin one last time, she knew that she had done the right thing.

It was clear to all who knew him that Ben loved his father deeply, but he'd never expressed that feeling when his father was alive, and still couldn't now that he was gone. From the time Saul was diagnosed, Ben had been in denial: though he'd seen so much as a physician, and knew what outcomes were probable, he couldn't imagine that any of it applied to his father.

Jake pulled pictures of Saul's four grandchildren out of his suit coat pocket and tucked them in the breast pocket of Saul's suit.

"Dad, where you're going, you won't have a camera, but here are a few shots of the grandkids for you to show all the people in heaven."

CHAPTER SEVENTEEN

3:18 P.M.

Heaven. In Jewish theology, someone who takes his own life is barred from entering. Even in its modern interpretation, Maddy could not achieve heaven. Modern thinkers tended to see heaven as eternal life through the memory of those left behind. The spirit of someone lived on in the memories that others carried of them for generations to come. Maddy had believed that her life, so broken on earth, was hell. But now she realized that hell would be eternity knowing the whole point of God, to live with purpose, and to be unable to share it with anyone.

She felt and heard the hands and machines working on her. "Don't give up on me!" She screamed, but her voice couldn't reach them, she was still too far away from them to be heard.

Summer 1989

As Stephen grew, it became apparent to Maddy that there was more to having given him her grandfather's name than hoping he'd be imbued with Sam's kindness and honesty. Stephen was only two and a half years' old, yet there were already more than a few similarities between him and the great-grandfather he never knew. Maddy felt that it was not mere coincidence: she often felt her grandfather was making good on his promise to watch over Stephen.

As it had been with Sam, food was Stephen's passion. One morning he led Maddy by her hand to the pantry, where he would pick out his cereal for breakfast.

"I want this one," he said, pointing to a box of Chex. Maddy obediently pulled the box from the shelf and started to go to the table.

"No! More! I want this...and this...and this." He pointed to three other boxes. Maddy, being the non-breakfast eater that she was, couldn't imagine eating any one of these, let alone mixing all the cereals together and eating the product, but she knew exactly when she'd seen it done before. When she was a young girl and stayed with her grandparents overnight, Grandpa Berkowitz would mix Grape Nuts, Wheaties and Raisin Bran into a big bowl. Though Stephen had never seen it done, he seemed to know exactly what to do.

Maddy smiled while she created the concoction for her son. As she looked up at the sky through the kitchen window, she felt her grandfather smiling back at her. For the rest of that day, and every time Stephen made his breakfast mix, Maddy would marvel at the apparent connection to her grandfather, who had come through, of all unlikely places, a cereal bowl.

And just like the man he never knew, Stephen could talk to anyone: he seemed to understand a world that didn't spin too fast for him. He would converse easily with adults, including one incident where Stephen, unfamiliar with restroom etiquette, struck up a conversation with a man standing at the urinal next to him.

Stephen wanted to help. When Stephen had turned two, Maddy brought him to the ophthalmologist. Though she wasn't wiping his nose prints off the television, she felt it was important to make an appointment when he was very young, because Maddy herself was so nearsighted from such an early age. They sat in the exam room, and when their friend Dr. Dan came in, he greeted the boy.

"Hello there, Stephen! Are you and your mom going to have an exam today?"

Stephen looked up at him and answered, "Yes we are, and I want to go first."

"Do you want pictures or letters on the screen?"

Stephen knew his letters, and he sat up straighter when he said, "I know my letters!" He proceeded to read the chart all the way down to the copyright symbol, at which point Dan turned to Maddy and said, "This little boy must have inherited your husbands eyes, his eyesight is perfect." He turned to Stephen and said, "It's your mom's turn now, right?" Stephen switched seats with Maddy, who settled into the exam chair and took off her glasses. The white square of light at the end of the room turned to a blurry blob.

"Can you read that?" Dan asked, but knew that with her prescription glasses sitting on her lap, she couldn't possibly see it.

"Not at all, Dan."

Stephen hopped off his chair and ran to his mother's side, cupped his hand to her ear and whispered to his mother, "E."

CHAPTER EIGHTEEN

3:20 PM

Maddy was aware of a faint warmth emanating from her torso radiating to her arms and legs. Parts of her body were no longer ice cold. As she worked her way back through her life, she wondered if her satisfying memories were in some way responsible for the sensation. It seemed so. The emergency room noises didn't sound like they were coming from quite as far away. Keep going, *she thought.* Yet her body was still more cold than warm, and she knew that she couldn't keep swimming much longer.

Spring 1986

Maddy was three centimeters dilated at the beginning of the ninth month. The doctor made the mistake of telling her that, based on what he could see—even though it was her first pregnancy—she'd probably deliver early. Expecting each contraction to be the onset of labor, Maddy would time them. For weeks, nothing had come of any of them. Her hospital bag sat ready by the door. Not only was Maddy not early, the baby didn't come on her due date either. It didn't help that the baby was due on her birthday, or that she still hadn't delivered by Mother's Day, four days later.

Ten days after the baby was due, Maddy hadn't delivered. Also pregnant with her first child, and just sixteen weeks behind Maddy in gestation, Jake's new wife Anne was a very sympathetic ear. They'd shared stories of morning sickness, weight gains and cravings. When they spoke earlier in the day, Maddy had started to cry, telling Anne that at the rate she was going, Anne was going to have her baby first!

As she rose from the couch and turned toward her bedroom, she was nearly cut in half by a searing pain across her belly. This was unlike the other contractions she'd experienced, and timed, for the last almost two months. When another contraction shot through her, every pore in her body exploded sweat, even the backs of her hands.

This was only the start of labor and delivery, and Maddy wasn't sure she could handle the pain. Remembering the advice of a friend, she wondered if in fact she would be best off if she had anesthesia. There wasn't a lot of time to think it though. "Ben? I think I'm in labor." She had another contraction: not only did her whole body break out in sweat anew, but she could actually feel the adrenaline racing through her body.

Ben called her doctor, who said he'd meet them at the hospital. They put Maddy's bag that had been sitting by the door for weeks into the car and drove into Boston.

The check-in, while routine for the admitting nurse, was more charged for the soon-to-be-parents. Maddy was adamant as she addressed the woman, "Listen, I'm already pretty dilated and I'm ten days late. I absolutely don't want to miss the window of opportunity for an epidural, okay?"

The nurse looked over her reading glasses at her and said, "Honey, first we need to check to see that you're really in labor, then, when we know exactly where you are, we can talk about anesthesia."

This was exactly *not* what Maddy needed to hear. At the same time she was digesting the nurse's words, she had a contraction, the strongest yet.

At that moment, she seemed to separate from herself, and part of her got right in the nurse's face, *did I actually grab her sleeve?*, and whispered, "I am ten days past my due date. I am sweating out of every pore in by body. Even my hair is sweating. I can not miss my small window of opportunity for an epidural just because you took too long to figure out that I was in labor in the first place." Then as an afterthought she added, "I am not leaving here without a baby! Do you understand?" The contraction released, and Maddy sat back.

The nurse understood. She put Maddy in a wheelchair and had an orderly take her a separate waiting room, while Ben attended to the rest of the paperwork. Once in the labor room, a maternity nurse strapped a monitor to Maddy's belly, which had grown hard as a bowling ball, and confirmed she was in labor. They measured her inside and out and determined that the best way to get her labor to progress would be for her to walk. She walked the maternity labor and delivery floor for what felt like miles until her pains were so strong she had to sit on the floor in the hallway until they passed. Finally it was agreed it was time to call in the anesthesiologist. Maddy had already endured more pain than she'd bargained for and was anxious for relief. A bleary-eyed anesthesia resident, sheet creases etched into the side of his face, shuffled into her room. He started to introduce himself, but Maddy interrupted, "Yeah. Nice to meet you too. What do I have to do to stop this pain?"

He told her he needed to inject anesthesia into her spine. Without batting an eyelash, Maddy turned over onto her side, pulled her hospital gown wide open, and exposed herself from the nape of her neck to the backs of her knees. The resident turned to Ben and laughed. "She's not shy, is she?"

Maddy could remember the time that she'd broken her jaw. She didn't want an injection, and she'd been mortally embarrassed to have to bare her bottom to the doctor. How things had changed.

The injection ran down her spine in an icy wave, then she was numb. The anesthesiologist told her that she was supposed to be numb from the base of her spine to her belly button, and she was. But she was sure that even if she was in agony later, he wasn't going to wake up again and come to her room, leaving her to endure the worst of the pain unmedicated. So when he tested the extent of her numbness by lightly stroking a needle along her thigh and asking if she could feel it, even though she couldn't, she said that she could. He poked again, this time below her navel. She told him that she could feel it there too. He was puzzled, but he had no choice but to inject her again and make her a little more numb.

When he left, Maddy was numb to her teeth. She was very pleased with her deception. The relief from the pain was so complete, both Maddy and Ben fell asleep. The nurse woke her up a few hours later to tell her that she was ten centimeters dilated and it was time to push. Ben held one leg and the delivery nurse the other. After three pushes, the doctor told Maddy that the baby's head was just visible, and he asked her if she wanted to feel it. Maddy was thrilled. She'd been carrying around this baby for almost forty-two weeks, and she could actually touch it?

"Are you serious? Of course I do!" She reached down over her belly to a place she hadn't seen in six months, and she felt something hairy. She rubbed it, hoping her baby could know it was his mother.

"He has a full head of hair!"

The doctor moved her hand onto a round ball protruding from a wet and numb area. "No Maddy, that's you—he's over here."

The room exploded in laughter.

CHAPTER NINETEEN

3:21 P.M.

Did she just cough? Something happened, because the noise level in the emergency room just surged perceptibly. She sensed the people around her were frenzied, activity was palpable—if not discernible. Whatever it was, she needed it to keep happening. The silly, joyous memory had brought her this close. If laughter was what was pushing her closer to those trying to save her, then she would have to push herself toward another happier day.

Fall 1985

She closed her front door behind Kevin feeling satisfied, almost vindicated. Kevin had "come out" to her on the phone that morning, and that evening, concerned that she'd be upset, drove two hours each way just to see that she was doing okay. He thought she might need some support, or have questions for him. He also wanted her to see with her own eyes that he was still Kevin.

As they spoke, he assured her that though he was gay, he was very much the same person he'd always been. He explained that he still got up every day and brushed his teeth, that he put his pants on one leg at a time, that he got colds, and that he had the same triumphs and trials that he'd always had. His concern for others was what made him different, not his being gay. He was special—and always would be.

Maddy had a few questions, but it was all so new, she didn't know really where to start. She asked him if anyone—a deviant babysitter or family friend or, God forbid, family member—had abused him. She was greatly relieved to learn no one had.

She asked him when he knew. He told her he didn't know for sure until after college, but he'd always felt different, even in elementary school. His watershed moment came when he watched a porno film in his fraternity, not excited by the action until there was a scene with two guys. All of a sudden, he said, every bell and whistle went off. He was unwilling to try to understand those feelings then, simply becoming more active with more girls, hoping someone could make him feel like he had felt during that film. Finally, he realized no woman would make him feel that way.

She wondered how he knew. He told her that, after college, after breaking up with a wonderful girl, he started to think harder about what had happened that movie night in school. He called a gay and lesbian hot line, telling them that he thought he might be gay, but that he wasn't sure, and asking them how he could know. They told him to visit local gay bars and to talk to the people there. If he was gay, he'd feel a certain camaraderie immediately.

He went to a bar and met a few people who seemed to like him, and whom he liked too. They asked him his name, and he told them he was Kevin. He went back to the bar many times over the next few weeks. His new friends were people with whom he felt a certain kinship. When they tried to get to know him better, they asked him his last name. He told them he was "just Kevin." Thereafter, he'd go to the bar and people would greet him with, "Hey! Just Kevin!" A few months later, he knew who he was for sure, and his friends learned his last name, and many other details of a life that had many of the pitfalls of those struggling with sexual identity.

Maddy insisted he stay for dinner, not wanting him to drive into the night on an empty stomach. Over dinner, he told her about the "friendly" community of people who were gay or tolerant of gays. She asked him if she knew anyone that he knew who was "out." Some people surprised her. One didn't. Robby Myers, her first boyfriend, who was also her first kiss— the one that made her feel like she was kissing her aunt—was also gay. Kevin had run into him at a gay softball game, and they'd since become friends. Finally, the weirdness of the kiss that had happened so many years ago made sense. Understanding that Robby was gay, and knowing that he may not have even known it at the time, righted the whole unsettling first-kiss disappointment Maddy had carried for over a decade.

CHAPTER TWENTY

3:22 P.M.

Maddy wanted to know what was going to happen to her. She was lost, unable to determine how far she had come and, more importantly, how far she had to go. She became aware that the mechanical beeps had become irregular. Something wasn't right.

Summer 1983

"We should go. I'll postpone my start date to September and we'll drive to save money. We can leave right after graduation and make a summer-long vacation out of it."

"You're right, Maddy." Ben was holding the silver and white invitation to the wedding of one of Ben's medical school classmates. The wedding was to take place in Phoenix, Arizona, the bride's hometown. Maddy and Ben each had very little money, but they knew they had time, which was soon going to be more valuable than money once they stopped schooling and started working, Ben in his medical residency and Maddy in accounting at Price Waterhouse. In order to make the trip affordable they would be camping in national and state parks. Their goal was to see as many state and national parks as they could afford to see.

Katherine vehemently objected to Maddy taking this trip.

"You can't go. And that's final!"

"Mom, I wasn't asking permission, I was telling you what we're planning to do this summer."

"Well, I won't have you living under my roof if you go."

Maddy shrugged. She knew that living home was only a temporary arrangement, and nothing she couldn't live without. She'd moved back home after college to save money, but no amount of cash was worth being held hostage and prevented from living her life.

She would request a transfer to the Boston office to bring her closer to Ben when she got back. She also knew that she'd saved more than enough money since starting work to rent an apartment if she had to.

Katherine was relentless.

"You aren't a married couple!! You can't travel like you are! What will people think!?"

What will people think? Maddy thought it was sad that her mother was most concerned for some imaginary status she held on account of the successes of her children, that what Maddy thought was not important. It made Maddy feel unimportant. She remembered how her parents would call her room at Rome when they were just "checking in," but when they needed to speak with her, like when her dad had his second bypass operation, they called her at Ben's.

"Mom, we're going. I'm not on the parental payroll anymore so I can't see what more you have to say about it."

Maddy was thrilled to have the opportunity to see the United States—she'd only ever been to Washington DC, New York and Florida. She and Ben planned to make a gigantic loop: heading south to St. Louis, then driving west out the southern route straight to Colorado, then Arizona, Las Vegas and Lake Powell. They'd continue to the coast, staying in L.A., San Diego, Carmel, then taking the Million Dollar Highway up to San Francisco. They planned to see Hearst's Castle, Yellowstone, Jackson Hole, Wyoming, Chicago, and then home. The trip was over nine thousand miles, nearly doubling the mileage on her little two-door Toyota.

Maddy was planning and packing, something her mother could not abide.

"If you go Maddy, don't come back here. You are setting a bad example for your sister, who is only sixteen years' old."

Maddy wanted to tell them that their precious baby was having sex with the nice boy Robin had introduced to them at the last school play, but she held her tongue.

"Fine, I won't come back."

She knew their hold on her was broken as she turned around and left.

She and Ben drove straight through for a whole day, finally making their first stop, St. Louis. She called her parents—collect—from under the arch. They anxiously accepted the call, and thanked her for keeping in touch. Maddy thought her mother sounded maybe a little bit sorry.

Kansas was corn and beans and wheat, set in fields so vast Maddy could not see their end. The roads that sliced through them were so flat and straight that Maddy and Ben played backgammon in the space between the bucket seats, balancing the board on the shift and emergency brake, rolling dice and moving discs as they rolled through vast and beautiful country. They spent the first night in a state park. The fee for the campsite was five dollars. Since they only had three hundred dollars for the whole summer, they needed to be careful. Maddy stored each receipt for gas purchases, campsites and grocery store bills in a little notebook where, true to her accountant training, she also recorded a running total of their expenses.

They went through the West taking pictures and camping, and marveling at the vast beauty and diversity of their country. They got to Phoenix the day before the wedding. The groom had brought their good clothes out West for them, since they couldn't fit them in Maddy's car, which was packed tightly with a tent, two sleeping bags, two small bags of camping clothes, a propane stove, a few pots and utensils, a boom box and tapes, and a cooler. Besides, even if they did fit, they'd be wrinkled and pretty smelly by the time they got to Phoenix.

The wedding reception was to be held at a deluxe resort and spa, where they were greeted by a valet in a black suit and patent leather shoes, who took their dusty car to the garage, and a bellhop with a small red cap and gold ropes hanging from his shoulders took their duffle bags and backpacks to their room. The large room was luxurious by any standard, but they had been sleeping in a tent and had just driven across the desert, where the temperature rarely dipped below one hundred degrees. For Ben and Maddy it was a real-life oasis. They lounged by the pool—which Maddy was glad to find wasn't a mirage like the ones she'd seen off the side of the road for the last two days—and they enjoyed the prenuptial dinner, the best food they'd had in weeks.

The next morning, they rose, showered and dressed for the wedding. They ate breakfast with other out-of-town guests, and in a flurry of excitement, headed to the temple for the ceremony.

Once seated, Maddy looked around. She saw the groom wring his hands and wipe his forehead with the perfect triangle of handkerchief he'd pulled from his tuxedo pocket. As the music started, he walked down the aisle and turned to see his bride. Maddy and Ben held hands knowing that they, too, would one day be married. After the processional, the rabbi walked to his lectern to begin officiating. Maddy couldn't believe her eyes. It was Rabbi Gold—the rabbi from Beth Tikvah in Newfield—her very first rabbi! She remembered that he'd gone out West to take over his father's congregation, but she never imagined she'd come across him on her trip. When the service ended, she waited in the receiving line. When it was her turn to greet the clergy, Maddy smiled and started to say something like, "Do you know who I am?", when he took her by both hands, and, with great love and pleasure shining from his eyes, said, "Madeleine Berger, you've grown into quite a lovely young woman!"

He hugged her, and, stepping back to look at her, radiated warmth and joy. She realized how much she'd missed him. She asked about his family and he was pleased to tell her that every one of his five children was grown and living either near him in Scottsdale or in Israel. He called his wife, Tess, over, and as if they'd been away from Newfield for days and not years, Tess proceeded to ask her about Jack, Katherine, Kevin and Robin *by name*. Maddy shook her head and thought, *what a woman. What a small world. What a coincidence.*

When Maddy introduced Ben to the rabbi and his wife, the rabbi took great delight in meeting another Gold.

"We have the same last name? We must be related!"

Ben and Maddy both felt like they'd found long-lost family, and neither wanted to leave, but they were supposed to be at the reception after all, and after a few more rounds of hugs, they left. Maddy looked back over her shoulder as she left. She'd see him again.

CHAPTER TWENTY ONE

3:23 P.M.

What was it about a coincidence that made Maddy want to look back over her shoulder as if, if she did it fast enough, she could catch a glimpse of the Source Of It All, revealed and completed at that magnificent, joyous moment of synchronicity. Maddy did see Rabbi Gold again, years later. She had taken a trip to the west coast with Ben and the kids, and they'd looked him up. As excited as he was to see her the first time, seeing her children the ages she and her own siblings were when he moved from Newfield was even more of a thrill. Hearing about her transformation from 'Convenient,' assimilated Jew to Conservative educated and dedicated Jew, Rabbi Gold was proud of her, and told her so.

Maddy now needed the help of those she'd once fought to elude as she worked her way back to life. Before, she had alit on islands of pain, but now she rejoiced in oases of hope and light, places where a good deed, a coincidence or a belief that she was doing the right thing affirmed the oneness of it all. The same life. That would never be the same. She hoped she would be able to meet the hands of those that reached out to save her.

Fall 1982

Less than a week after Maddy charged Robin with the task of finding a dress for the wedding, she heard from her sister.

"Maddy? I got it! It's perfect! It is not too expensive, it will fit any shape, and, best of all it doesn't look like a "bridesmaid's dress!" It is the kind of dress your friends can wear to other parties."

Maddy was thrilled that Robin and her bridesmaids were as excited about her wedding as she was. All of them, that is, except Marci. Jake's wife was only included to preclude her from being the only family member not in the wedding in the first place, so her lack of enthusiasm was particularly bothersome to Maddy. Marci generally disliked anything that wasn't about her, and made her disinterest known, albeit in subtle ways.

Like insisting that Maddy send her a picture of the dress that Robin had selected. Everyone else just sent measurements. Less than a week later, Marci called and asked Maddy if she could wear anything else. Maddy acquiesced, and for years afterward she was piqued by the pictures in her wedding album showing her friends and family all arranged like chessman and Marci, like a checker, incongruous and defiant in the lineup.

Jake and Marci had moved from Miami to Manhattan. Unlike their days in Miami, there were no more drugs—the risks now far outweighed the benefits. Jake was finishing a fellowship and Marci had joined a private practice, and with two incomes, they often took advantage of the theater, food and fashion available to them in the "city that never sleeps." In addition to collecting clothes, music and theater ticket stubs, and names of maître d's, Jake and Marci had attracted to their chic uptown apartment a colorful cast of characters that Ben and Maddy grew to know well. A psychiatrist, an anorexic artist, a high-powered entertainment attorney, were all part of a large, surrogate family that welcomed Ben and Maddy like long-lost cousins.

Of the whole motley crew, Anne was Maddy's favorite. Book and street-smart, she had parlayed a love of music in college into being a world-traveling agent to top name musicians. She was also one of the few in the group who had never used drugs, claiming life was intoxicating enough. It seemed so to Maddy, as Anne was the one who was forever finding and arranging their activities. The only one who regularly resisted any group decisions was Marci. Maddy watched people bend over backwards and forwards to accommodate Marci, who seemed increasingly more difficult to please. Maddy often wondered if it was worth the effort.

Anne and Maddy worked in two very different fields, but both were agents. One afternoon, Maddy was visiting Jake and Marci, when Anne, who'd come by after work for a pre-dinner cocktail, pulled her appointment/date book out of her bag to get a phone number. At first, Maddy had thought it was hers: they had chosen the same system,, cover, color and size. It was up to the user to create useful referencing systems to increase the book's effectiveness, so Maddy asked if she could see how Anne's was arranged. Anne told her to look to her heart's content, and, flipping through the address book, Maddy couldn't believe what she saw: three phone numbers for Mick Jagger—New York, Paris, and Montserrat. There were two phone numbers for Cher, several for David Bowie, and many other numbers and addresses for rock stars whose names were well-known to Maddy.

Maddy turned to Anne, and pointing to an entry, asked, "Hey, if I dial this number, Mick Jagger will answer?"

Anne laughed, "Only if he's home."

Touché.

Driving back home after a particularly difficult visit— they'd ended up doing nothing because three of them wanted to go to a movie, but Marci only wanted to go dancing—

Maddy looked out the car window at the reddish Manhattan night sky and complained that Jake deserved better. She wished that Jake would find a new wife, someone more like Anne.

It was a surprise to everyone but Maddy when, just four months later, Marci and Jake separated and quickly divorced, and when six months after that, Maddy was asked to be the matron of honor at Jake and Anne's wedding. Maddy was all too happy to accept.

CHAPTER TWENTY TWO

3:24 P.M.

Maddy was pulled all at once from her feelings of validation in seeing Anne as the right woman for Jake by a loud siren. The emergency room was a cacophony of noises. A machine alarm was going off, voices were shouting. Maddy tried to hear what they were saying, but one piercing note came through to her loud and clear. The heart monitor, which had been beeping regularly like a metronome since she'd started swimming back to the room, was just wailing one continuous cry.

Summer 1982

It was a curious route that brought her to her headhunting, or "executive recruiting," as they were supposed to call it. She'd started out after college, putting her degree in accounting to work as one of the first women auditing for a "Big Eight" accounting firm. It was a stodgy and staid environment: they had just repealed their longstanding policy that required employees to wear hats when they went outdoors, and no one could wear sneakers into the office, even though affordable parking in the unpaved lot was at the far corner of the city. The old-time attitudes extended to include a serious work ethic that bordered on inhumanity. Employees, especially junior staff, were expected to work a hundred or more hours a week and to be available for, and agreeable to, more, if necessary. And it was often necessary.

Once she became a certified public accountant, she left that rigorous and thankless arena to become accounting manager for a busy real estate developer in Boston. The company was growing rapidly, as was the whole real estate industry. The fact was, though she was working very hard, she realized it was still a man's world wherein she would be able to go only so far before she hit her head on the glass ceiling. The signs were subtle, but not lost on Maddy, who finally got tired of the rampant undertones of misogyny.

One afternoon while in a meeting, her boss, the controller, asked her, "Maddy, could you please tell us how many man-hours it would take you to set up the subsidiaries on the new system?"

Maddy answered before she could stop herself, "It would take about eighty man hours, but a competent woman could probably do it in about sixty."

The room, filled with suits and ties, stared at her like she'd just shot someone. She left them a few weeks later to be the controller of a smaller, more chic real estate company. This time, though, the principal was a man who loved and respected women—he'd been named one of *Boston Magazine's* "Ten Most Eligible Bachelors." The office was younger, edgier and more energetic than her old office, and she put in many hours just trying to get the company's finances organized. Like most successful entrepreneurial ventures, they'd grown so quickly that their reporting systems were non-existent. Maddy's goal was to bring the company to a point where it had balanced bank accounts, valid ledger balances, and an accurate monthly statement of expenses.

The chief financial officer was a hawkish guy who'd also come out of public accounting. It was obvious that he didn't care if he burned Maddy out in the mountainous amounts of catch-up work that needed to be done as a result of the company's rapid growth, but Maddy was used to it, and so was able to bear the endless hours of paperwork and reconciliations, until ultimately, he succeeded in wearing her out, which Maddy suspected was part of the plan all along.

The final straw was when she came to him with questions about a tax return that he'd prepared. His answers only confirmed her gut feelings that some of the deals he'd reported weren't exactly as she'd remembered them. She said that she couldn't in good conscience sign the returns, to which her boss suggested that she leave—effective immediately. She said that she did not want to leave them high and dry, and that she'd give a proper two weeks notice. He said that the potential for sabotage or subterfuge was too great to keep her around for two weeks, so, were she to quit, she would be escorted out immediately. She'd grown accustomed to hearing him blow smoke at potential competition or vendors, and she knew that he was just trying to frighten her with his tough-guy attitude.

She returned to her desk, but the unsigned return sitting in front of her made it hard to concentrate on anything else. She decided to take an early lunch, but instead of getting food, she went to a local recruiting firm to see what else she could do.

She met with a handsome young man, dressed in a sharp blue suit, punctuated with expensive shoes and watch. She told him how she hoped there was some kind of job where the object of the game wouldn't be to use her up, but would instead allow her to make a difference. He asked her if she'd ever considered recruiting. She could search for jobs for accountants and people in the field, which she knew really well. He told her that it was a fun and lively business environment, and that she'd have the challenge of making a two-sided sale. Furthermore, her knowledge, gained in auditing, accounting and finance in a variety of industries and businesses, would all come into play. He reminded her that she'd never be considered overhead, she'd be contributing directly to the top line, and almost parenthetically, he added that the potential for income was great.

Maddy didn't know what to tell him. This would be a complete career change, and she'd worked so hard to become a CPA, she hadn't thought about leaving accounting altogether. Then she remembered the argument of the morning, and the shady land deal that precipitated it. She also remembered the check for over five hundred thousand dollars that she'd cut to an employee as compensation for "finding" the property that the company had just gotten permission to develop. It was a man her age who was on the "sales" side of the business. He would regularly come rolling in to work around lunchtime, hung over and reeking from dope. His job consisted of driving around the state in a Saab convertible looking for undeveloped acres. For this he made a fortune, while Maddy worked ninety-hour weeks for a tiny fraction of his salary. It just didn't seem fair.

Maddy didn't have to think about the new job offer for very long. Her gut said to do it. She accepted the recruiter's challenge at that meeting, and met with several other recruiters and the principle who escorted her to the door with an offer of employment. More money to start and unlimited potential; Maddy knew she'd done something impulsive, but also something really right. She returned to her office, where her boss was shocked to watch her pack up her few personal belongings and escort herself out.

She started as a headhunter the very next morning, and only hours in, she knew it was the job she was always supposed to have. Finding the right job for the applicant and the right applicant for the job was like solving a puzzle. And she was good at puzzles. She and another new hire named Phil were shown to their desks, which faced each other, in the middle of an open bullpen. She was introduced to all the other headhunters, over thirty fresh, young faces, all wearing nice suits and expensive shoes. Dan Sheehan, Mikey Meehan, Sean O'Donnell, Tommy McCarthy, Billy Sullivan, and Danny Cullen. As Maddy looked around the room she realized that, other than the boss and herself, everyone was Irish, and other than the secretaries, she was the only woman in the division. Somehow, though, she still felt like she fit right in.

Maddy and Phil were told to try to find candidates for a particular job. They were each given a well-worn card that listed the requirements of a different job, but it was clear that both jobs had been unfilled for a while. They were then told to sift through the registration cards that were filed in alphabetical order in a tall set of file drawers, try to match the skills and salary requirements, and come up with a few candidates they felt were suitable for that particular job.

Maddy found two candidates that looked good right away. After a while, Phil also came up with a few suggestions for his job. The pit boss, Michael O'Connell, "Mickey" to everyone in the office, then had each of them call their selected applicants, explain the job to them, and see if they were interested in interviewing. Mickey pointed out to Maddy that one of her applicants was a woman, and although there was absolutely no way an employer could specifically ask the recruiter to find a man or a woman, the industry and location Maddy was looking to put her in—a machine shop in one of the tougher neighborhoods in Boston—was the kind of place a man would be better off. He also was quick to point out that she was a bit undereducated for the specifications, and that she had been registered with them for a long time. To Maddy, though, it seemed like a perfect job for her candidate. She lived in Dorchester, not far from the factory; the job was just two stops away on the "T."

Maddy spoke with her applicant, who anxiously agreed to look at the job, and Maddy set up the interview. Late the next afternoon, she got a call from the company. They wanted to hire the woman, who'd already called Maddy to say that the interview had gone well, and that if they were to offer her a job, she'd take it. She told Maddy that she was most impressed with the health benefits and pension opportunities, as well as the continuing education reimbursement they offered to all employees. Maddy's heart was beating, and though everyone looked busy, all ears were trained on her as she called the woman and made her the offer, which, as she'd indicated before, , she accepted.

Within twenty-four hours, Maddy had made her first placement. Phil was on the phone when it happened, still trying to get a suitable candidate to interview for his job. He gave her a "thumbs up," and the whole office came over to her to congratulate her. Mickey showed her how to write up a placement slip, so the company would get billed and she would get paid. He showed her how to track her placements, the total was a factor in her end-of-year bonus, though he wouldn't say exactly how.

Two days later, she made another placement. And the next day she made another. . Poor Phil, still trying to get someone to go on an interview, gave her a weak "thumbs up", his encouraging smile belying his growing disappointment in the way things were unfolding in this new job. Within a year, Maddy had become one of the top producers in the office. She loved the job, for the challenges and for the guys she got to work with. They would all go out at the end of the day and drink to wash off the pressures and frustrations of recruiting before returning home to their families. One night, they were at their favorite bar and everyone slowly made their way home. It was just Tommy McCarthy, whose desk was behind hers, and Maddy left at the table when he asked her what her secret was—how it was that she was doing so well. She'd always liked Tommy, so though she was a little buzzed from trying to finish the pitcher the rest of the boys had left behind, she tried to give him a real answer. Maddy explained to him that she could see who belonged where. It was like a giant matching game: different pots and covers, and Maddy knew there was a cover for every pot. She told Tommy how, after doing an interview, she could see which pot went with which cover.

While a typical interview was supposed to last from fifteen minutes to a half-hour, Maddy's sessions would sometimes go on for over an hour. More than once one of her coworkers had come knocking on the door to the small interview room, making sure that everything was all right, since she'd been in there for quite a while. When she was done interviewing the candidate, she had a very good idea of what they were looking for, and rather than spend her time looking for what they stated they were looking for on their application—money, location, title—she went with her gut, which told her what they really needed.

Tim was listening, taken by how animated Maddy was in her description. He told her that she had more than talent, and while he couldn't say what it was, he could see it in everything she said. He also saw that while she was good at listening to the applicants, more importantly, the applicants listened to her. It was strange: she didn't really know them, but she'd have no problem coaching them. She'd tell them what to wear, or that their salary requirements were way out-of-line, or that their education was not adequate for certain types of jobs—the things you would only tell a close friend or relative. The applicants weren't mad either, they were grateful that someone was telling them "how it is."

By bonus day, Maddy had already taken home more in salary than she did the year before, working as an accountant. That, coupled with the incredible satisfaction she got doing the job, would have been more than enough to make her happy that she'd followed her gut. But when she was called into the boss's office, and he handed her a six-figure check, her first thought was that there was a typo—and politely told him so. But he assured her that she'd earned every penny, and encouraged her to keep up the good work.

On her way home, she deposited the check, skeptical that making this much money while having so much fun was actually legal.

CHAPTER TWENTY THREE

3:25 P.M.

Successes, coincidences, miracles. Wherever she let her mind land, she was aware of the fact that she'd known that everything fit together all along, even if she couldn't see how. She also realized that laughter and hope were the keys to staying grounded. Why hadn't she been able to understand that before? Perhaps she'd been running too fast. She must have missed it the first time through. She promised herself that if she lived, she'd go slower.

The dull prick of an injection, and an icy stream flowed from her arm through her entire body. It was like taking a drink of too-cold water on a hot day; the cold numbness seeping, cell by cell chilling every corner of her being, filling the parched empty spaces. But the cold left numbness like it was embalming fluid. Maddy feared this was really the end.

Spring 1982

Looking around, Maddy noticed that every employee of Price Waterhouse who was young and in shape was entered in the race. She hadn't been in the firm for three weeks after graduating college when they recruited her for the run. Since then, on many a night they'd meet up at the lobby of the home office long after-hours and train together. Maddy was there, rain or shine, in the heat—or more often, cold—of the Boston evenings. She loved to run. She would measure her paces by her breaths—two in, three out, two in, three out. Running was a form of meditation, and her breathing was the path to reaching a higher plane. She'd rarely be winded, but often by just breathing in-in-out-out-out, before she knew it they were stretching out and the training session over.

Then the big day—Patriot's Day—a very unpredictable time of year in Boston to run a marathon. This year, it was sunny and warm for April, but not too warm. Truly a perfect day for running, Maddy thought, as she looked for her coworkers in the sinewy, singlet-clad swarm of road-warriors.

Once the whole group of accountants was collected, as a final inspiration and well-wish, the managing partner personally gave each of them a nylon shell with the company logo on the back. She pinned her paper number to the front and back of it, and crowded up to the starting line with her coworkers. They looked like a bunch of yuppies on a tour, but there was no umbrella to follow. The gun went off, and they all started to run in place. After what seemed like many minutes, they started to move.

The race was long, and often her rhythmic breathing was all she had to keep her going—that and the crowds. The people who stood on the sidelines had no idea how much they did for her and all the runners. Some runners, about to give up, were clearly buoyed by some small child's handmade sign of encouragement, a thumbs up from a spectator in a wheel chair, or a primal scream to "Go!" from an enthusiastic stranger on the sidelines.

Maddy could actually fill up on the energy of these cheerleaders. It was like they were transferring their own energy to the runners who needed it, and no one finished a race solely on their own power. Definitely not Maddy. She finished, the last five miles having been propelled by a T-shirt she saw on a young spectator in Cleveland Circle: "Dana Farber Cancer Institute Marathon Challenge: I miss my son but as you run, you honor his memory."

Maddy thought, how tragic to lose a child to cancer. To anything, really. She had only lost a grandfather, and that was when she was still a young girl, but her friend Meg, from Queensfield, had an older brother who never came back from Vietnam, and Meg's mother was never quite right after that. She would walk around her house singing hymns in a too loud soprano voice with vibrato. She'd polish the silver, rubbing a spoon with a cloth so hard and so intently that Maddy feared an incendiary spark would result.

The T-shirt's message gave her a sense of purpose. She ran to honor a small child she never met, and wouldn't let up until she'd crossed the finish line in his honor. Before she knew it, she was passing under the digital clock where finishers could mark their times. Shivering from exhaustion, exertion, and elation, she knew she would pay the price for running so long, but it didn't matter: she had made a difference, and that made the pain pale in comparison.

CHAPTER TWENTY FOUR

3:26 P.M.

When her whole body went from cold and numb to burning fire all over, Maddy was certain it was the beginning of eternity in Hell. The siren wouldn't stop screaming; yet as her ears started to burn, its volume was fading.

Though she'd hoped and worked for more, she knew that, in the end, she was getting what she deserved. She'd taken her own life. It didn't matter that it was before she'd understood that life wasn't for taking, but for giving. It was for giving. She knew this now, but it was too late.

Summer 1981

"No, Maddy, you don't have to stay. There are nurses here who can make sure he's not alone, or too frightened."

The nurse was not convincing Maddy, who was crying into a Kleenex handed to her through the reception window. All she'd done was bring her kitten in for rabies shots. She and Ben had picked a kitten up from the Humane Society when they returned from their summer trip, neither thinking much about the fact that once they started working, the poor kitten would have no one to play with all day. Once they realized how lonely their only cat would be, they returned to the shelter to bring home her brother.

On her way out of the vet's office, she had been settling her bill at the desk when she overheard the woman standing next to her arguing with the other office assistant. The woman wanted to return some medicine, but they didn't want it back.

"I think I should be able to get a refund! This stuff was expensive! What difference does it make if I opened it? It's dog medicine, for Christ sake!"

The woman pushed the Ziploc bag back over the desk, her manner unmistakably firm.

"But this has been opened. We can't take it back, I'm sorry."

The receptionist pushed the bag back to the woman. Her manner also unmistakably firm.

"Fine. Just keep the damn medicine—and the box and the leash."

She tossed the contents of both hands across the desk and walked out.

Maddy looked down to see a gray and brown cocker spaniel sitting in a travel cage on the floor. She went back to writing out her check, but froze, pen in midair, when she realized what was happening. Maddy was afraid to ask.

"She didn't just leave this dog to be put down, did she?"

The nurse nodded and shrugged as she threw the pills in the trash. Maddy was incensed.

"Just like that? No kisses? She didn't want to hold him so he wouldn't be afraid?" She was crying now, wiping her eyes on the tissue that the assistant had given her.

"It will be okay. We'll take care of him. Really we will."

"I don't think I can leave now."

Once Maddy had decided that she'd stay she was filled with a sense of doing something incredibly right. But, even as he breathed his last, Maddy could feel the faithful old animal try to raise his head towards her, his milky eyes trying to see who was there for him, as if to thank her. As she held the shaking animal, petting him and telling him that it was okay, he drifted off to his eternal rest.

CHAPTER TWENTY FIVE

3:27 P.M.

She hoped with everything she had left that she would see the world again. It wasn't always a perfect place, but she wanted to take her place in it.

What had been only muffled sounds were now recognizable words, a sentence. "She's breathing and I just got a pulse!"

Maddy was getting closer, and wanted desperately to open her eyes and be looking up at the doctors, and not down at herself. She remembered her broken jaw and how she thought one would know if they were dead. In a way, back then she was right. If she could look up and see the world around her, she would be alive. If, when she opened her eyes, all she could see was herself, then she was dead.

Fall 1979

Though Maddy had a paper due the next morning, Edna said she needed the lights off so that she could sleep. Edna was a big girl—over six feet tall—and well over two hundred and fifty pounds. She ordered and ate several pizzas at a time, and to Maddy's disgust and peril, she bit her toenails and left them like landmines: when she dared to cross the room barefoot, little spikes would stab Maddy's feet, making her gag.

Just like Maddy had had no choice in getting her as a roommate her sophomore year at Rome, Maddy had no choice but to sit in the hall outside her room. She set up the typewriter, a pack of cigarettes she kept for the rare all-nighters,

Coca-Cola and Oreos, and cursing her lousy luck in roommates, she plowed through her paper. At about two thirty in the morning the door across from her opened and a thin, sleepy girl came out. She was an all-American girl in every way, except she had Asian features: dark, almond eyes, straight black hair, beautiful, even skin, and white straight teeth. Her parents emigrated from mainland China to the United States before she was born. When they gave birth to her, they gave her the prettiest name they'd heard in America: Maude. Maude grew up on the Florida coast, and had a great tan and a sweet southern drawl.

"Hey, Maddy, why'ya up so late?"

Maddy put the cigarette down, exhaled, and blowing up through her bangs said, "I have this stupid business calculus take-home test due in the morning, and White Westinghouse won't let me sit in the room with a light on."

Calculus was her best subject, she could intuit what the letters and numbers *meant* and how the formulas worked. She once had a dream that her professors gave the class a previously unsolvable problem—like Fermat's Theorem—and she was the only one to solve it. Math was number puzzles.

She never thought seriously of studying it, however, until the summer between sophomore and junior year. The company's accounting firm had sent a very handsome, well-groomed and finely dressed accountant to her father's office. Maddy decided right then and there that she would switch her major to accounting. Jack and Katherine were pleased, so Maddy didn't tell them that she made the choice solely so that she could work around guys in suits.

Maude took an Oreo out of the box, ate it and then ate another and another. Then she got up and she went to the bathroom across the hall. Before she went in she said, a little too brightly, "G'nite now."

Maddy's heart sank. She knew what Maude was doing. Maude was, by genetics, shorter and more squarely built than the girls she grew up around, who weren't Chinese at all. Maude hated that fact, and had in the last four months lost a lot of weight. *Too much*, Maddy thought. She was always going for a long run, and lately had taken to walking around the campus bundled in layers of sweats even though the Atlanta heat was stifling—as if the baggy clothes could hide her loss.

Maddy couldn't stand to watch. She didn't exactly decide to confront her—it was more like she decided not to *not* confront her. She didn't know what to say or do, but she knew that she had to follow Maude into the bathroom. She got up, quietly opened the bathroom door, and entered just as Maude was vomiting the Oreos she'd just eaten. Maddy swallowed hard. She could handle mostly anything—dissecting frogs, gory movies—but the sound of someone retching usually made her sick to her stomach. She forced herself to stand there, swallowing hard, as Maude flushed and opened the stall door.

"What?" Maude wiped her mouth with her sleeve. Maddy thought she sounded defensive. Defeated.

"You know what Maude."

Maddy was surprised that while she was shaking, her voice was steady.

"No I don't! Why don't you just mind your own business and go back to your stupid paper!"

She turned on her heels, and wheeled out of the bathroom.

Maddy stood there, unable to move, sad and speechless. She'd tried, and Maude rejected her. *What did I think she'd say?* She grabbed the door handle, pulled it open and stuck her head out of the bathroom just as she was closing the door to her room. She called to Maude "Hey! I like you a lot, and it hurts to see you do this to yourself. You need help Maude. Let me help you."

Maude turned to her, her eyes narrowed, angry and afraid. "I said leave me alone!" With that she slammed the door.

Maddy sat quietly back down on the floor outside her room and tried to focus. She'd been typing for a while when the door across the hall opened.

Her words came out like air being let out of a balloon.

"Maddy, I can't stop it! I know I have a problem! I can't make it stop! I don't know what to do!"

She threw her arms around Maddy, who, upon the weight of this revelation and the lack of weight of her friend's body, also started to cry.

"It's okay, Maude, it's okay."

Maddy stroked her hair like her father had when she was a little girl. "Shhhhh. You'll be okay! I swear Maude, you'll be fine." Maddy held her as she rocked in her arms until the waves of hysterical tears, then sobs, then gasps, subsided.

"I'll tell you what we're going to do." Maddy hoped what she was doing was the right thing. "I'll finish my paper, and turn it in first thing in the morning. I won't stay for class. I'll just drop my paper off, and come back here for you. We'll go to the dean's office together. Okay?"

Maude agreed, and with that, she returned, once again, to her room. She closed the door gently this time.

When the morning came, Maddy brought her paper to class, as she'd planned, but when she returned to her dorm, Maude wasn't there. She asked Edna, "Hey, have you seen Maude?"

She stopped gnawing at the last piece of chicken left in the giant bucket she'd mostly eaten the night before long enough to say, "Yeah, she came here about fifteen minutes ago, and left you this note."

Edna handed her a piece of lined paper, folded in four, now stained with grease from Edna's well-coated fingers. The hastily scribbled note said simply, "I went without you, but thanks for your help."

Signed at the bottom with a heart was the letter "M."

News filtered back to the girls in the dorm that Maude's parents had picked her up and brought her home that same day. The school year passed, and in May, when everyone was pairing up for housing requests for the next year, Maddy received a letter from Maude asking her if she'd like to room with her in September—off campus in an apartment. Maddy thought it would be great, especially since she didn't want to have to spend another year with someone like Edna, and since Ben was off to med school, she needed a roommate.

It was years later, at Maude's wedding, that she took Maddy aside and thanked her for what she'd done that night. The trauma of the moment had long passed, but the fact that Maude was there at all, let alone healthy and seemingly very happy, was testament that Maddy's decision to follow her into the bathroom so many years ago, without a plan but with the hope doing something to help, was the right one.

CHAPTER TWENTY SIX

3:28 P.M.

"Find me!" Maddy tried to scream it, but she knew better than to think those trying to save her life could hear her. She was desperate for them to know not to give up. That she hadn't given up. "Please save me! I'm tired of fighting and I want to come home."

It made her think of a story she'd heard years before about Morty, a deeply pious man who got word of a tremendous flood, and who believed that God would save him. When a rescue team knocked at his door, yelling, "Morty! Come out, there is going to be a tremendous flood!"

Morty refused to go with them. He yelled back, "No, I don't have to come with you, God will save me."

Reluctantly, they left. The waters rose, and Morty was forced to the upstairs bedroom, when a small motorboat came by.

"Morty, get in the boat, we're going to save you!"

"No, God, will save me." And with that he sat on the bed and waited. When the water came up to the top floor, he climbed onto the roof and sat on the chimney. Suddenly, a helicopter came by with a rope hanging down. Through a megaphone, barely audible over the howling wind, they screamed, "Morty, grab the rope! We can save you!"

"No! God will save me!"

The winds were whipping and the rain was torrentially pouring on and around this old, cold man. Finally, the waters came up over the chimney, and he drowned. He got to heaven and, at the gates, met God. "My God! I thought you were going to save me!!?"

"Morty, I sent a car, a boat and a plane! What more did you want me to do?"

Spring 1978

Maddy looked at the clock at the front of the classroom and realized that at that exact minute, while she grappled with the meaning of a South American writer's use of metaphor, her father was either alive or dead. That thought caused her throat to close up and her eyes to burn. She could feel it coming, and though she tried not to cry, the corners of her mouth started to twitch. Soon she couldn't see the paper as her eyes filled with tears. She put her head down on her desk, unable to continue with the exam.

Jack's first quadruple bypass was six years ago, and right now, Maddy figured, he was either on a heart lung machine, his heart artificially stopped as they performed four more bypasses, or he was dead. Her teacher, Gretchen Westford, was one of the younger, cooler teachers at Queensfield. She'd seen Maddy put her head down, and had come over to Maddy, tapped her on her shoulder, and asked her to step out into the hall.

"Madeleine, what's going on?"

Maybe it was her sympathetic tone, but Maddy started crying again. By that time she'd finished explaining all that was going on in her family, and through her mind, she was sure she'd not only failed her English exam, but that she'd made a fool of herself in the process.

Gretchen told her to wait in the hall. She returned a few minutes later, and she placed two items in Maddy's hand. One was a twenty-dollar bill. The other was a piece of paper with a phone number on it.

"There is a cab waiting outside for you. Go home. And call me when you know how your dad is." She pointed to the paper, "That's my number. As far as the exam goes, forget about it. I'll average your other grades. You shouldn't be here. Now go."

Maddy hugged Gretchen, and cried again, overwhelmed. She'd never before been the recipient of so much unsolicited generosity. Maddy had heard about random acts of kindness, but there was something to be said for these more thoughtful acts of goodness, too. The whole way home in the cab, Maddy prayed for her father while conjuring up ways to pay back her teacher's kindness. She couldn't think of anything that would come close.

CHAPTER TWENTY SEVEN

3:29 P.M.

Chaos. Cloud-like islands of memories on which she would alight. Knowing. And knowing nothing.

Chaos. Alarms blaring, machines beeping. Doctors and nurses yelling orders, trying desperately to revive the gray-haired woman on the table, who was desperately hoping they would succeed.

"Help me! I'm here! I'M HERE!!"

Spring 1978 (continued)

While she'd returned Gretchen's cab fare and written her a heartfelt thank you note, she'd never been able to return the favor to her directly. But she now remembered a time when she had passed the favor of a ride along. It was in a grocery store in Boston. It was very cold and had started to sleet. She was in the checkout line behind a tiny old woman, bundled in a worn cotton coat, a hand-knit scarf, and pilled, gray wool mittens. The woman asked her, "Did you drive here?"

Maddy told her that she had.

The woman then asked her, "Could you please give me a ride home?"

Maddy never gave rides to strangers, but this was a little old lady and it was snowing out. Maddy told her that she would. The woman then asked if Maddy could wait a minute while she went back to buy milk, sugar, and detergent—items too heavy for her to ever carry home. Maddy helped her pick up the few additional items and brought her home. She carried the items up the three flights of stairs to her apartment. She also left the woman her number in case she ever needed a ride. She never heard from her again.

CHAPTER TWENTY EIGHT

3:30 P.M.

When she thought back to the time she'd prayed for her father, who had put his heart into the hands of God and the doctors when she was just a teenager, Maddy believed that something had happened. It was like God had heard her prayer.

Now, as she lay near-lifeless in the emergency room, she prayed for herself, and she felt that others were also praying for her. She concentrated on the oneness and how everything that happened to her—and to everyone—was all related and was tied to that single idea. Maddy wanted to be a part of the oneness again. She wanted to live.

Spring 1978 (continued)

The girls were all seated in the white folding chairs in variations-on-a-theme of white gowns. The boys, all in suits, shifted in their seats, uncomfortable from the confinement and the heat.

"And this year's recipient of the Mary G. Martin Award for Excellence in Spanish is Madeleine Berger!" As Penelope Cullinaine Hautain had promised years before, Maddy ultimately did graduate with the grades she was capable of earning. And some honors as well. Maddy finished third in her class—summa cum laude.

Things had fallen into place for her at Queensfield after all. She thought back to the fall when she was made the captain of the cross-country team, and the meet that redeemed her painful loss to rival Sage-Worthington Academy and her personal nemesis, Jennifer Whitten. The incident had become legendary, and in spite of the fact that Dave promised not to tell, somehow the team found out all about it. Her teammates must have planned all year, and even though Dave had graduated and Maddy had—mostly—let it go, her teammates were not so magnanimous.

The meet was uneventful, until Jennifer's pained scream cut across the field slicing into the cheering from the field events. Someone had "accidentally" dropped a shot put on her foot, and it looked like she was not going to be able to run her race. Furthermore, on the bus ride home, Maddy heard about a prank that wouldn't bear fruit for a few days. Some of her teammates had managed to coat Bear's shotput with something from the chemistry lab, that would not only make everything it touched red and pimply, it would itch like crazy for weeks. As a captain, Maddy outwardly expressed disappointment in their antics, but she was secretly happy to see them suffer at the hands of dirty play.

While she was doing well in school, playing the "good student," Maddy was a different person out of school. She had met her current boyfriend the previous summer. She and Richard Duchamp had been dating all year, and there wasn't one thing about him that her parents liked. First of all, he was not Jewish. No less offensive to them was the fact that he was a high school drop out. He smoked cigarettes. He'd been in the navy, and sported a large anchor tattoo on his right shoulder blade. He lived in Newfield, the blue-collar town her parents had tried very hard to leave behind by moving to Westham.

Maddy loved Richard, mostly because he treated her like a princess, providing her with an endless source of treats and adventures. Mostly though, they'd get a little high, go hang out with some of his friends, and end up going back to his house, where they'd have sex in his parent's living room. That she'd never gotten pregnant was a miracle in itself, especially since they used no protection whatsoever.

Her parents tried everything they knew to break them up, but that only served to strengthen her resolve to be with him. Until her parents went all out and offered her a trip to Spain with the International Living Tour Group as a graduation present. She had an opportunity to spend eight weeks in Spain, living with a family, and traveling with a group of American kids, none of whom would be Richard Duchamp.

Maddy agreed to go, even though she knew it was a ploy to get her to break up with Richard and saw right through it. She planned to go, then return to him, much to the dismay of her parents.

But the trip wasn't what she'd planned. The family with whom she stayed lived in Oviedo, the capital city of the northern province, Asturias. Maddy was surprised to see that the Spaniards of the north weren't the dark and swarthy people that most Americans envision when they think of Spaniards. In reality, they are fair-skinned and blonde. And devoutly Catholic. The Cabral family was no exception. There were four children, two boys and two girls; the girls were sandwiched in the middle. The older girl was Maddy's age, and they shared a room. Maria was responsible for Maddy's entrée into the Spanish culture. Maria was dedicated to staying with Maddy and making sure she was okay, and Maddy immediately liked her. Every day was an adventure. But not the kind of adventure she'd had with Richard, which often bordered on hoodlum shenanigans. Here they would wake up early and go to buy bread from the bakery. Then they'd go to the Associacion por Jovenes—the youth center—and play with the other kids from the town. There was no drinking age so kids who wanted to drink did. Also, there was no problem with kids smoking cigarettes. Those who wanted to did. The funny thing was that though the kids could drink and smoke, they did so only occasionally and never to excess.

Adventure consisted of walking through the lush green hills that surrounded the city, clapping their hands and singing songs, or sitting in one of the hillside "barras" drinking Coca-Cola or wine or the local grain alcohol, "robeiru," with the locals.

The one thing that her real parents didn't anticipate was that how living with a Catholic family would affect Maddy. It didn't make her feel more Jewish, it made her think that people everywhere were all the same and wanted the same thing: peace, love and a little grace.

She was required to go to church. Even though she was Jewish, her Spanish family insisted that she accompany them to church every Sunday morning. Maddy was chilled by the cool air that pressed against her inside the church. The smell of musty books and furniture polish mixed in her nostrils. The huge crucifix, replete with dead, bleeding Jesus, hung—larger than life—over the robed ancient, who was the priest. The priest spoke in Latin and in Spanish. Strangely, Maddy understood more than she thought she would—and the message was always the same: *be good to others on this earth,*

One thing that was very different here was that kids of all ages played together. At home, kids even one grade apart were forbidden by unwritten law to be friends. Here six-year-olds were tagging along with the fifteen-year-olds. All kids were required to perform military service when they were eighteen, so no one seemed to be in a rush to grow up.

284

Maddy kept a journal of her summer adventure and, so no one could read it when she got home, she kept it in Spanish. She met a boy her age—Maria's boyfriend's best friend— though all they did was kiss. For the incredible worldliness of the people, they were sexually way behind all the Americans Maddy knew. *Probably*, she thought, *the result of living in a Catholic country.*

Six weeks flew by, and it was time for Maddy's tour group to travel the country. The Americans gathered in Madrid from all around Spain and embarked on a bus tour. When they got to Barcelona, they went to a beach resort that was primarily for tourists from England and Germany. Maddy marveled how the young tall blond German men there were sitting and drinking, laughing and singing. All the German men she knew were short, dark, barrel-chested men. It was like they were from different worlds.

The American teens met up with a group of young English rugby players who were also on tour. They were a team and a drinking group back in England, and they were wild. One Brit in particular caught Maddy's eye. He was handsome and muscular and sexy. They danced and drank, and when he invited her back to his hotel room, she thought to herself, *why not?*

The door closed behind them and they danced, kissed and slowly undressed each other. When she looked at him in the dim light of the room, she was shocked to see that he had a grossly deformed penis. But it didn't seem to bother him at all. In fact he seemed proud of it! She tried to be casual, but she couldn't stop staring. Then it hit her—he was uncircumcised! Greatly relieved, she had to see what sex was like. She wasn't disappointed. When she left, she knew she'd never see him again. She wrote about it in her journal, though, so she'd never forget.

What she did forget, though, was exactly what she saw in Richard. When she got home, he was so small, insular and unworldly. Sitting in a car, having sex and smoking weed were not half the fun they were before she went to Spain. She tried, just to spite her parents, to make it work, but about a week after she got home, she broke up with him.

For a while, he called her several times a day. She thought that she'd become involved with one of those psychos who'd haunt her for the rest of her life, but after a long heart-to-heart, he agreed to let her go. Her parents were smugly satisfied that their ploy worked, but Maddy knew they'd be smart enough not to show it.

CHAPTER TWENTY NINE

3:31 PM

While her parents had succeeded in getting Maddy to break up with Richard, it had always felt like they didn't trust her to make her own decisions. Now she understood that her mother was not a monster. Selfish, maybe. Married young, definitely. The anger Maddy felt toward her for trying to break up her relationship with Richard was washing away as Maddy understood that Katherine had done the best she could.

Maddy also understood that her father was not the man he'd started out being. His heart gave out a little at a time, each surgery or procedure and the concomitant medications took more of the vibrant, loving man who was her daddy with it. It was certain that one day his heart would just give out.

Buoyed by this knowledge, Maddy continued to swim, and every once in a while, she'd stop long enough to catch her breath on another island of understanding. So many things had happened to her by sheer luck or coincidence. Maddy realized, though, that there was no such thing as coincidence. Things seemed to always happen for a reason, even if she wasn't able to see what that reason was. She knew that she'd been "lucky" before, and as she struggled to remember more, she hoped that her luck hadn't run out.

Winter 1976

"Hello there Madeleine, schweetheart . I do believe that Victoria ish in the pool."

Even though it was just after eleven in the morning, Maddy knew that Mrs. Fairchild had already spent many hours watching television with a nice bottle of sherry beside her. Mrs. Fairchild added, "Would you like shumthing to drink, dear?"

"No thanks Mrs. F, I'll just go find her."

Victoria's house was a museum. Her father owned a company that manufactured luxury yachts, and he owned a piece of property in the most elite section of Westham, where he rarely slept. Consequently, Mrs. Fairchild was lonely, but wealthy. She was happy to reap the social and economic benefits of her absentee husband's success.

And the benefits were manifold. They lived in the Briarcliff Mansion, the largest house on the elite street. It was a tremendous four-story main house, with a four-car garage attached. The garage did house cars: a Ferrari, a Jaguar a Mercedes and a four-wheel -drive car for those times that none of the other cars could make it down the long and windy hill to the main road. Above the garage was a game room, replete with pool table, full bar, several pinball machines and a juke box. There was a maid's room with full bath, another guest bathroom, and best of all, behind the garage was an indoor pool.

Maddy went right to the pool.

"Hey girl, can I join you?" Maddy knew that the answer would be yes—she'd come over to swim laps with her—but she thought she'd ask just the same.

"Sure, there's a pipe waiting upstairs for you, if you need some chemical motivation."

The great thing about getting high before swimming was that when Maddy got out of the pool with red eyes, everyone believed that it was because of the chlorine. Maddy smoked a bit, put on her suit, and dove in next to Victoria. They swam for a while, got out, dried off, and went to hang out in the pool room upstairs. Maddy and Victoria played guitar, then went to the kitchen for a snack.

Elena, their housekeeper, never let Victoria near the fridge. She insisted on preparing everything for her and her friends.

"Very well, Elena, how about turkey sandwiches?"

"No problemo. I bring them to you, okay?"

"Sure, thanks." And with that they went to Victoria's bedroom. They called Chip. "Come over!"

"Can't. My sister won't give me a ride."

They talked for a while longer, when Chip came up with an idea for a get-together that was his wildest yet.

"Madeleine, I'm going to pick you up tonight after midnight. Since my sister will be sleeping, she won't miss her car one bit. We'll come to Victoria's. Everyone there will be out cold, so we can party and play in the garage until morning. I'll have you home before your old man's alarm goes off. What do you think?"

Maddy thought it sounded crazy.

"You're truly nuts, Chip. How am I going to get out of my house?"

As she tried to picture it, her bedroom window was a full story over the garage, and her bedroom windows were transoms; they ran across the top of the wall. But they did open. And if she climbed up on her desk, she could jump out of the window closest to the front landing, which was only a half-story down.

"So maybe I can get out, but there was no way I'll make it back in."

An out-of-the-box thinker, Chip told her, "You don't have to go in the same window. Leave the bathroom window open, you know, the one near the downstairs playroom? I'll boost you up into there, okay? Just remember to leave the toilet seat down, so you have something to step on when you climb back in."

It actually seemed like it would work. They agreed to meet at two-fifteen, and Maddy set her radio alarm, very softly, for two. When she heard it go off, she woke, slipped into her bathing suit, jeans and a sweat shirt, and having unlocked the window the night before, just pushed lightly on the frame, which opened easily. Sitting in the street at the end of the driveway, lights off, engine running, was Chip. He got out of the car, guided Maddy to the side landing as she jumped out the window, and then opened the car door for her, closing it very quietly behind her. She took a sip from the Heineken beer he had on the seat beside him, then settled in close to him, as the fifteen-year-old proceeded to drive to Victoria's house.

They hung out all night. Somewhere around four-thirty, the drunken, sleepy threesome did something that they'd, on some level, resisted for all the years they'd known each other. They started out wrestling, but when Chip pinned Maddy, he bent down and kissed her. The surprise on their faces made Victoria laugh out loud. Chip and Maddy both jumped up and wrestled Victoria to the ground and kissed her. They wrestled and kissed, and before things got too out of control, they all jumped in the pool. They swam and drank and laughed until dawn's light broke. They got back into the car for the unlicensed ride back. Maddy prayed that her parents were still asleep. Chip helped her climb in the basement window. She stepped on the toilet seat lid, which she'd remembered to put down the evening before, and quietly crept up to her room. No one was up yet. She got into her nightshirt and under her covers, throwing her jeans and sweatshirt down on the far side of the bed.

She fell asleep immediately, and woke a half-hour later, when her father started the shower. When he finished, she got up, showered, and got ready for school. Other than looking a little tired, she was the same as always, except she didn't feel the same.

On the way to school, she thought how lucky she was she didn't get caught. Then she started thinking about riding with an unlicensed driver, and a drinking, pot-smoking one at that. Not only was she lucky she didn't get caught, she thought, she was lucky to be alive.

CHAPTER THIRTY

3:32 PM

There were many times she had felt overwhelming gratitude or appreciation. In spite of the fact that there seemed to be a hand guiding her, until now she couldn't understand what part that hand had played in her daughter's death. Now she realized that the hand didn't make her daughter die. Her daughter died because a drunk driver hit their car. The hand was what tried to push her nearer to people who could help her. It was everyone who'd tried to comfort her after the tragedy, and all who had guided her before: her family, who had all done the best they could for her; Carrie, who had finally tired of the endless disappointments; Denise from Rome, and whatever cleared the way for her to cross the busy street on roller skates when she was a girl, escaping with only a broken jaw. It was her online friend "Adamsdad," and the rabbis. And now it was all the doctors and nurses. God was one and all: they were all related.

Spring 1974

While Queensfield was non-denominational, it was still predominantly Protestant. Maddy's parents insisted she stay connected to her roots, albeit from a healthy, assimilated distance. They made her attend religious school twice a week after school and on Sundays. By high school, the classes had attrited to a handful of students who were either actually interested in learning, or, like Maddy, being forced to make it look that way. Most students, and all of Maddy's friends, had dropped out after their Bar Mitzvah. Maddy felt little connection to the seven other students: an odd group of people with whom Maddy shared little but the label "Jewish."

She could have fought with her mother, but even though class was lonely and boring, she loved going to the sanctuary for their student services. There she felt like she was in the presence of something timeless and immeasurable that kept her coming back. Sitting in that room, she felt that there was more to life than what she could see. And that not seeing was okay.

She liked the feeling she had when she was in the sanctuary so much, she started to attend Friday night services. She would go alone and sit with a group of women who were mostly widows and single, middle-aged women. Maddy didn't like this sanctuary as much as the now not-so-new sanctuary back in Newfield. And she had disliked this rabbi starting when she moved to Westfield and to this synagogue, when she was twelve. Rabbi Gold felt like a man of God. This rabbi was a man of ladies, or at least that was his well-known reputation. Maddy always got the heebie-jeebies when she was near him.

Not that he knew who she was. On the day of her Bat Mitzvah service the rabbi put his hands on her head to bless her. As he got to her name, he had to look at a paper to be sure he had it right, even though she'd been in his Bat Mitzvah class for the last six months. In spite of him, she felt something special when she sat or stood in front of the ark, the cabinet in which the Torah scrolls were kept. Like the closet in Narnia, it might one day take her to the world where God lived and everyone there knew it.

She was moved each time the whole congregation would chant the Shema. The voices blending to one, the prayer proclaiming that God is One, felt like it was actually ascending towards Heaven, where, Maddy imagined the Aslan-like God would hear and respond.

CHAPTER THIRTY ONE

3:33 P.M.

Just thinking about the Shema reminded Maddy of her new understanding of the prayer, and she worked to make her way closer to the voices and hands that continued to work around her. She thought about "One." She kept repeating it, and it felt like a meditation, a mantra. Like her rhythmic breathing when she used to run, it gave her the strength to keep working toward the voices. She added the word for "one" in all the languages she'd ever studied. Uno, echad, une, ein, one. The word, in any language had in it the same message, and it filled her with hope.

Fall 1973

In second form, the class was a whole group of happy-go-lucky kids. By third form, Maddy's class started to separate into cliques. It was like watching cell division. The kids who were athletic pulled together, away from the kids who partied. The kids who were active in theater did the same, now quite separate from the science nerds. There were a few kids who fit in everywhere and nowhere. Maddy was one of them. It was stressful on the fringes, never sure if she was in or out. Maddy found a source of strength and encouragement in Monsieur Berard.

A native-born Parisian, Berard taught Maddy's Spanish class, and he was a character. Students loved that he would feed the squirrels that came to his window of his classroom, the only room in the attic of the old house. There'd be a *clack clack* of little claws on the window, and without missing a syllable in his lesson, Monsieur Berard would open the bottom drawer of his old wooden desk and take out a handful of peanuts. He'd go to the window, and when he opened it, a grey and white squirrel would climb down his arm on to his shoulder and take the peanut from his hand.

There was a whole family of squirrels, and they would regularly interrupt and entertain the class. Occasionally he'd let a student feed them. Maddy would get answers right, and as a reward, be permitted to leave her seat and open the window when the animals called.

But it wasn't the squirrels. Monsieur Berard knew how kids were, even though he and his wife never had any children of their own. He liked Maddy and saw the problems she was having as a peripheral character in many of the school's social dramas. He would let her spend study hall with him in his classroom, rather than make her endure the stresses of life in the larger group. Even though she wasn't singled out for their antics, Maddy hated to be a part of it. When she was in Monsieur Berard's attic, she was in a different world. He would tell her that she was as pretty as any girl and smarter than most everyone. That she was ahead of her time, and when her time came, it would be great. And she believed him. He understood that she was at that age when girls are the most insecure and he also knew that she listened to him. Based mostly on his say-so, she was filled with hope for her future. With his kind words and deeds he let her know that there were places bigger and better than Queensfield...and it was one of the primary reasons that she made it through.

CHAPTER THIRTY TWO

3:34 PM

Remembering all the kind things people had done for her and that she had done for people, she understood that they were all connected, if not how. It wasn't what happened to a person that allowed them to see God's handiwork, it was in how they responded and reacted to the bad things that God was revealed. Life was loving and losing—and in no particular order. The thought that her daughter's life—and death—were connected too, caused her to feel anger and despair fall away.

The fire that had been burning through her began to mellow to a soft warmth which was spreading to her arms and legs.

Winter 1969

"Come on Maddy! If you don't tie them tight enough, I won't be able to jump right!"

Maddy dug the little claw tool back into the laces of Tina Flynn's ice skates, and pulled hard on the laces. Tina was an awesome skater, and today was the first day that her dad would let them out onto the pond behind the house, now that he was certain that it was frozen solid.

"Is this right?" Maddy wanted to be done with this as much as Tina wanted to have her finish. Maddy was bundled up in snow pants, boots, a heavy wool sweater and turtleneck, jacket, scarf and hat. The mittens were by her side. She was starting to sweat.

They finally did get out to the pond, and it was fun just like all the other days they'd spent together. Except that tomorrow Maddy was moving from Newfield, and she knew that she wouldn't be able to play with her best friend every day anymore. She thought about all the fun they'd had learning about their impending womanhood together. Each hoping they'd she'd be the first to get her ears pierced, the first to get her period, the first to wear a bra, the first to kiss a boy. As the second of five children in a chaotic Catholic family, Tina was a good match for Maddy. They'd hide upstairs in the Flynn's attic, out in the woods behind their house or in the camper in the driveway. Maddy loved all of the Flynn's five cats and three dogs, except the one that was old and snappish. Tina's mother was the Girl Scout leader and a great cook. Maddy loved to be at their house. If they weren't cooking, or doing art projects— where they could be as messy as they wanted, then she and Tina were upstairs, putting on make-up in her room—make-up that she "borrowed" from her big sister's shelf in the bathroom. They practiced kissing mirrors and hugging pillows and fantasized about all the boys in their class.

They knew it was all going to end soon, but they didn't want to think about it. So they just skated around and around the small pond until it got dark and Maddy had to go home.

CHAPTER THIRTY THREE

3:35 P.M

Even though her world was still pitch black, she felt close to the doctors and nurses, as if she could just open her eyes and see them. But try as she might, she couldn't make her muscles move. Maddy could hear the doctors and nurses clearly, though she couldn't make out the words. Whatever they were saying, their voices lacked the panic she'd heard earlier. They were still working on her—she thought she could feel the slightest pressure on her right arm...

Fall 1967

Five-year-old Maddy was outside in her front yard in Newfield, spinning around and around and around until she was so dizzy she fell to the ground. There she lay on the grass, arms and legs spread out from her body, watching the clouds and trees whirl in circles over her head. She believed that God was moving everything around just for her, and that God's arms were holding her down on the grass.

CHAPTER THIRTY FOUR

3:36 P.M.

Maddy had grown up to unlearn all that she knew that day. When she was on her back in her front yard all those years ago, she knew what she'd only relearned at the end of life: that God's arms <u>were</u> holding her to the ground, and that He <u>did</u> blow the clouds over her head, and that she <u>should</u> delight in both.

Maddy tries to open her eyes, hoping she wouldn't be looking down at herself. She pulled hard at her heavy lids, and was almost blinded by the light of five harsh bulbs burning right through her eyes right into her brain. She rolled her eyes to one side, and saw Ben there. She rolled her eyes to the other side, and she saw a nurse.

She closed her eyes and dreamed of nothing at all.

AFTER

She woke up knowing that, even though the puzzle was too complicated to solve, she'd learn to live with the pieces she had. And as she put those pieces back together, it was like paper clips to a magnet, hardly an effort. She and her husband were going to be all right. Her friends showed unbelievable support and understanding. She knew that all the wounds to others could be healed in time.

Ten days passed like a minute.

During the ten days between Rosh Hashanah and Yom Kippur, she felt very connected—her understanding of how all is one put her very close to God. She remembered the trip she took to Israel when she was forty, and how she was so affected by the powerful energy she felt there. She knew that the power that shook her to her core was the power of God. Why else would a tiny speck of land in the middle of the desert be so hotly contested? It must be where God rests. While she felt that God's heart might be in Jerusalem, God's hands were everywhere.

It was Yom Kippur: the holiest day of the year. It was a Day of Atonement for sins committed over the past year, concretized by abstention from food. Some Jews abstained from all bodily pleasures including sex, bathing and wearing leather; any pleasures or symbols of material wealth were shunned. It was a day punctuated with prayers seeking forgiveness. Maddy and Ben went to synagogue together, hungry but not unhappy. The boys were not home. They had returned to college when Maddy came home from the hospital.

The rabbi spoke, "We are now at the part of the prayer service that discusses, in concrete terms, the central theme of the High Holidays, and our philosophy of life."

Maddy listened to him speak as she sat with the High Holy Day prayer book open in front of her.

He continued, "The prayer 'Unetanneh Tokef'—'We Will Observe'—is said to have been written by Rabbi Amnon of Mayence, who uttered these words in his last moments as he lay dying in martyrdom. They were his affirmation of faith in God. When we read this prayer, we can sense his understanding of a Day of Judgment on which God opens the book containing the record of the past year. The legend says that the book is in our own handwriting: we write it ourselves. One by one, as a shepherd counts his sheep, God reviews the deeds and determines the destiny of every living soul.

"We need to understand that man can influence his fate and change the course of his life through three simple acts: Repentance, Prayer and Charity. All that man strives for is futile. By having faith in God we acquire a piece of Divinity. Man's origin is dust, and he returns to dust. It is our faith in God that gives life meaning and purpose, hope and dignity. Faith is not about having all the answers—that is the purview of religion. Faith is our acceptance of a living God. Faith lifts us above despair, it makes us feel connected to the universe, and it teaches us to regard our reverses as a challenge to live better.

"Each of us becomes holy and truly free, as we are all fashioned in God's image. When we proclaim our faith in God, we are claiming that we have become a spark of the Divine. We become coworkers with God, and as such, have the capacity to transform the chaos and suffering around us into order and joy.

This is what I believe we call 'Heaven on Earth.' Please rise as we recite the Unetanneh Tokef."

Maddy stood up and, in unison with hundreds of other congregants, she read the following words:

"On New Year's Day, the decree is inscribed and on the Day of Atonement it is sealed, how many shall pass away and how many shall be born; who shall live and who shall die. Who shall attain the measure of man's days, and who shall not attain it. Who shall perish by fire and who by water. Who by sword and who by beast, who by hunger and who by thirst, who by stoning who shall have rest and who shall go wandering, who shall be tranquil and who shall be disturbed, who shall be at ease and who shall be afflicted, who shall become poor and who shall wax rich, who shall be brought low and who shall be exalted. But Repentance, Prayer and Charity avert the severe decree."

Maddy was awestruck. She was hearing in this ancient prayer exactly what she had so recently come to truly understand about God. "Who shall live and who shall die" is not a childish notion of an all-powerful God actually naming those who'd either survive or expire physically. The death and life refers to the vibrancy or vacancy of the human spirit. She realized that there were three ways to ensure a rich spiritual life: to ask forgiveness of those whom you've wronged, be more responsive to those in need, and always be mindful of the connectedness of all things.

Maddy knew that her life would begin again that day. Repentance started by asking the one you've harmed for forgiveness. She closed her eyes, and in a very soft voice speaking to God and herself, she said, "I'm sorry that I tried to end this gift of life, and I promise to always treasure it as the incredible opportunity to live and love that it is. I am grateful for the chance to continue my journey. I will love everything in this world with all of my heart, and will try much harder this year to be worthy of your love and support and to love and support those who need me."

When she opened her eyes, she felt different. Freer. With that non-scripted, spontaneous prayer, in God's eyes, and in her own, she'd been forgiven.

When she turned her attention back to the service, the congregation was preparing for the next prayer in the service: the Shema. She closed her eyes, and unlike the martyrs accepting death, she was very much a part of the living, proclaiming the unity of everything in the world. She covered her eyes and chanted the prayer, listening as her voice blended in with the others.

When she opened her eyes this time, she was overcome with a feeling of lightness. She was floating, not to the end of life, but to the beginning of a new life, carried on the "eagle's wings" mentioned so often in the book on her lap. Her heart, which ten days earlier had stopped beating, was lighter than it had been in years.

The service ended. As Maddy walked home, she followed the random pattern of shadows and sun that fell onto the road through the trees—b'shalom and shalem—whole and in peace.